SEEKERS

TOKLO'S STORY

WITHDRAWN

Seekers: Toklo's Story
Created by Erin Hunter
Written by Dan Jolley
Art by Bettina M. Kurkoski

Lettering - John Hunt
Production Artist - Michael Paolilli
Graphic Designer - Chelsea Windlinger

Editor - Lillian Diaz-Przybyl
Print Production Manager - Lucas Rivera
Managing Editor - Vy Nguyen
Senior Designer - Louis Csontos
Director of Sales and Manufacturing - Allyson De Simone
Associate Publisher - Marco F. Pavia
President and C.O.O. - John Parker
C.E.O. and Chief Creative Officer - Stu Levy

A **TOKYOPOP** Manga

TOKYOPOP and 🐸 are trademarks or registered trademarks of TOKYOPOP Inc.

TOKYOPOP Inc.
5900 Wilshire Blvd. Suite 2000
Los Angeles, CA 90036

E-mail: info@TOKYOPOP.com
Come visit us online at www.TOKYOPOP.com

For information address HarperCollins Children's Books, a division of HarperCollins Publishers,
10 East 53rd Street, New York, NY 10022.
www.harpercollinschildrens.com
ISBN 978-0-06-172380-3
Library of Congress catalog card number: 2009921415
10 11 12 13 14 LP/BV 10 9 8 7 6 5 4 3 2 1
❖
First Edition

SEEKERS
TOKLO'S STORY

CREATED BY
ERIN HUNTER

WRITTEN BY
DAN JOLLEY

ART BY
BETTINA M. KURKOSKI

HAMBURG // LONDON // LOS ANGELES // TOKYO

HARPER
An Imprint of HarperCollinsPublishers

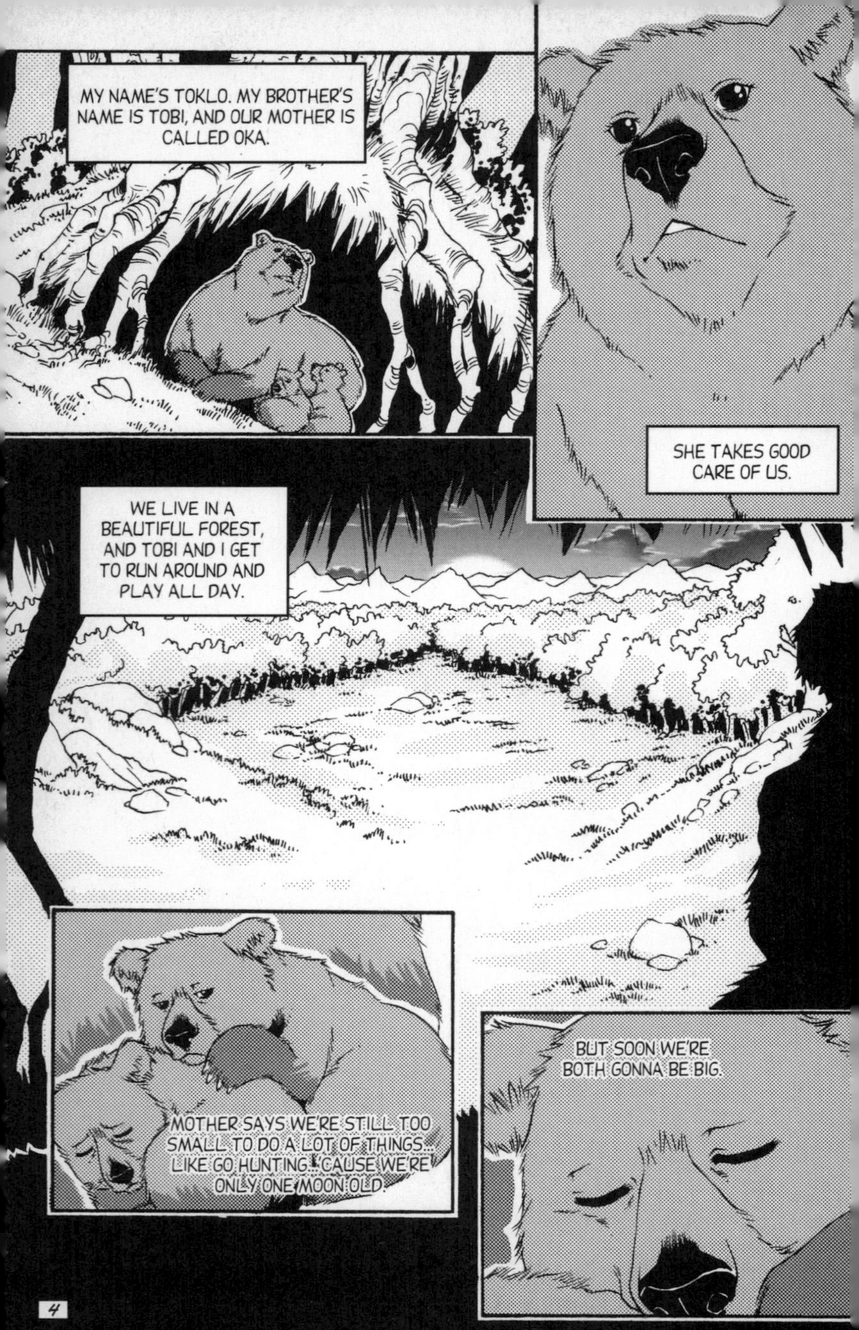

MY NAME'S TOKLO. MY BROTHER'S NAME IS TOBI, AND OUR MOTHER IS CALLED OKA.
SHE TAKES GOOD CARE OF US.
WE LIVE IN A BEAUTIFUL FOREST, AND TOBI AND I GET TO RUN AROUND AND PLAY ALL DAY.
MOTHER SAYS WE'RE STILL TOO SMALL TO DO A LOT OF THINGS... LIKE GO HUNTING, 'CAUSE WE'RE ONLY ONE MOON OLD.
BUT SOON WE'RE BOTH GONNA BE BIG.

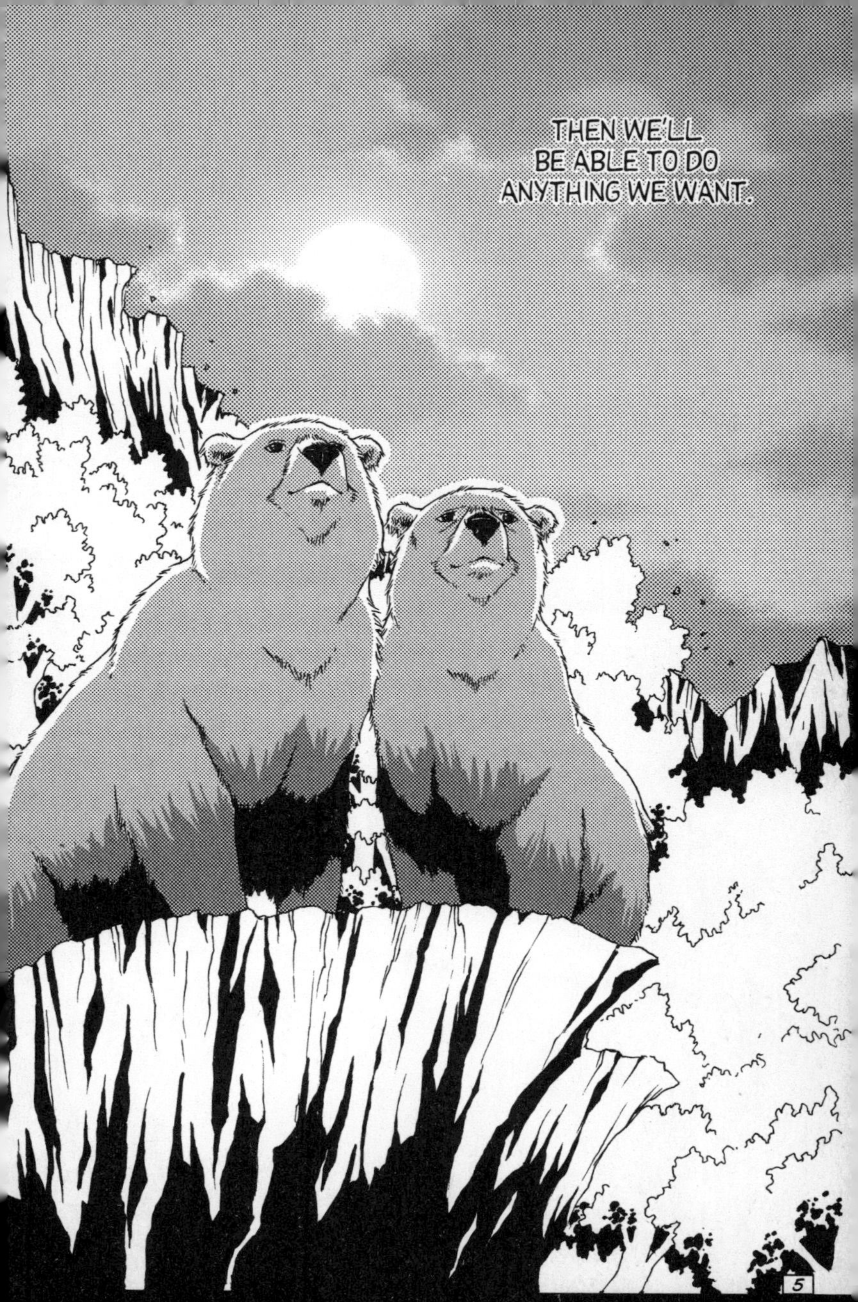
THEN WE'LL BE ABLE TO DO ANYTHING WE WANT.

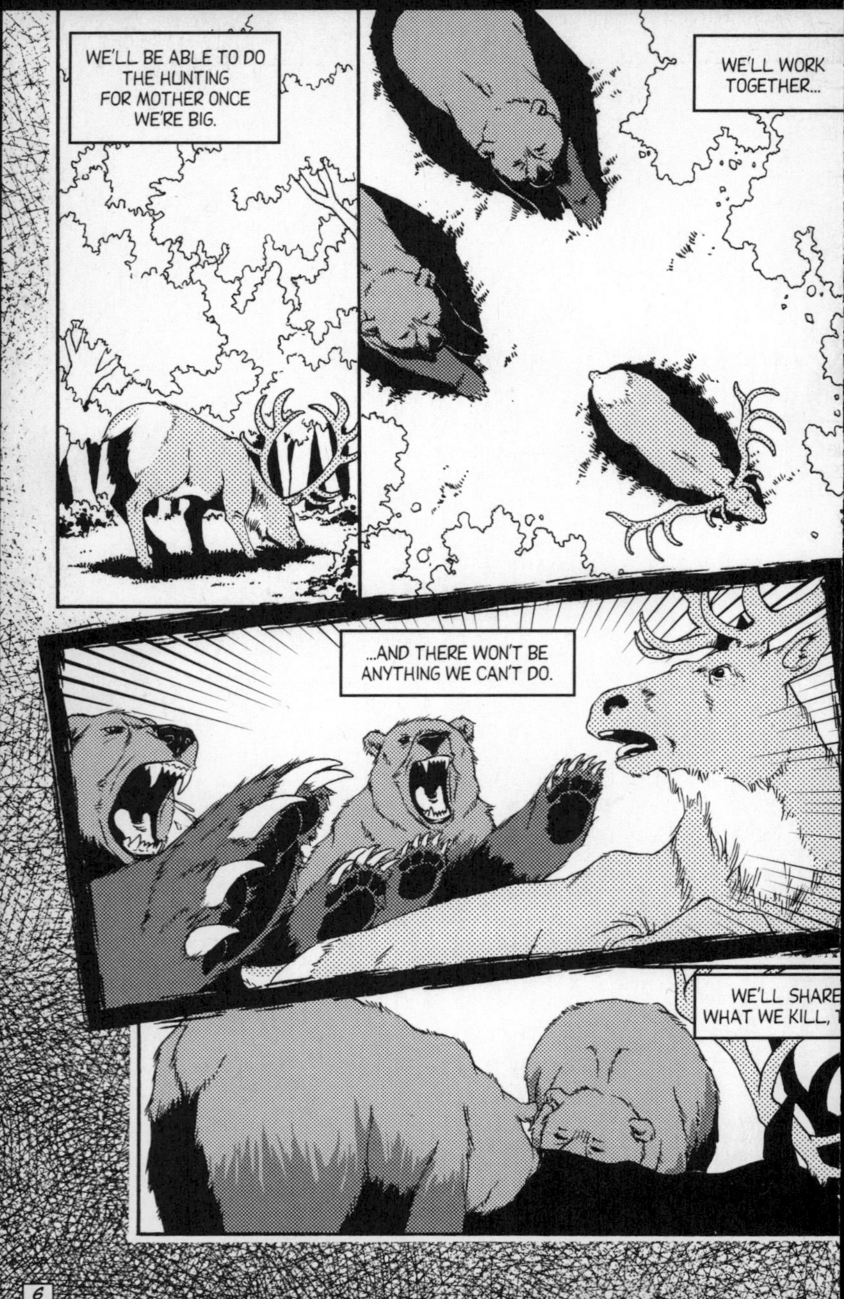
WE'LL BE ABLE TO DO THE HUNTING FOR MOTHER ONCE WE'RE BIG.
WE'LL WORK TOGETHER...
...AND THERE WON'T BE ANYTHING WE CAN'T DO.
WE'LL SHARE WHAT WE KILL,

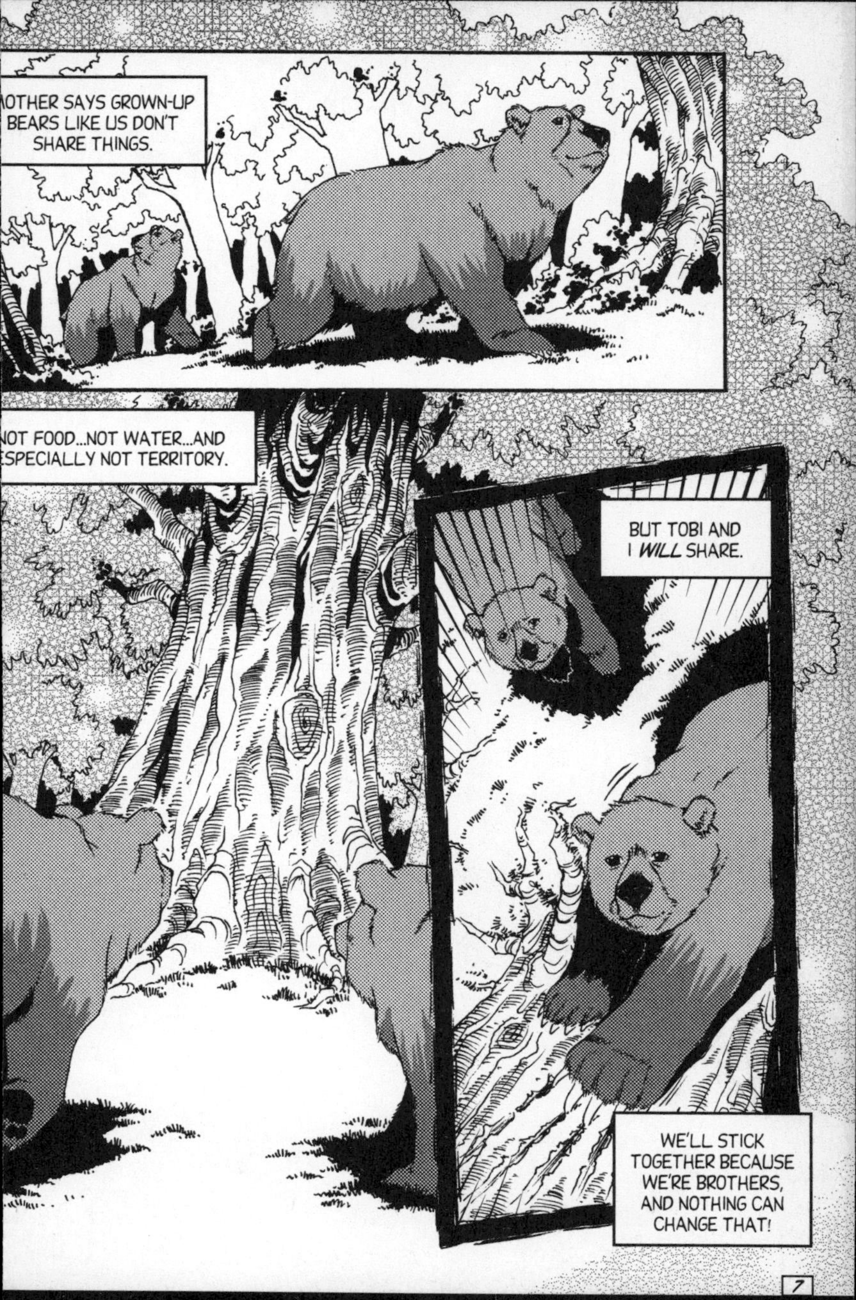
MOTHER SAYS GROWN-UP BEARS LIKE US DON'T SHARE THINGS.
NOT FOOD...NOT WATER...AND ESPECIALLY NOT TERRITORY.
BUT TOBI AND I *WILL* SHARE.
WE'LL STICK TOGETHER BECAUSE WE'RE BROTHERS, AND NOTHING CAN CHANGE THAT!

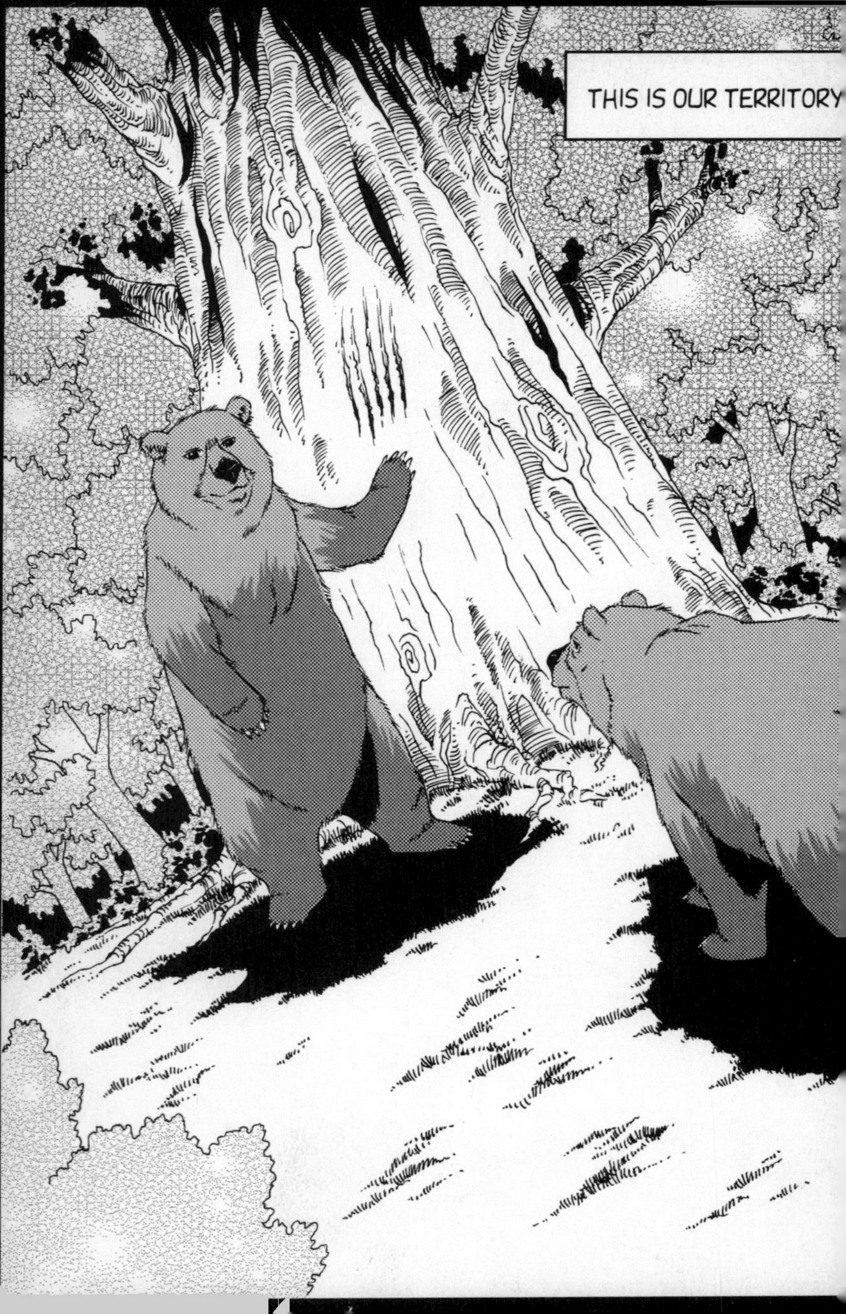
THIS IS OUR TERRITORY

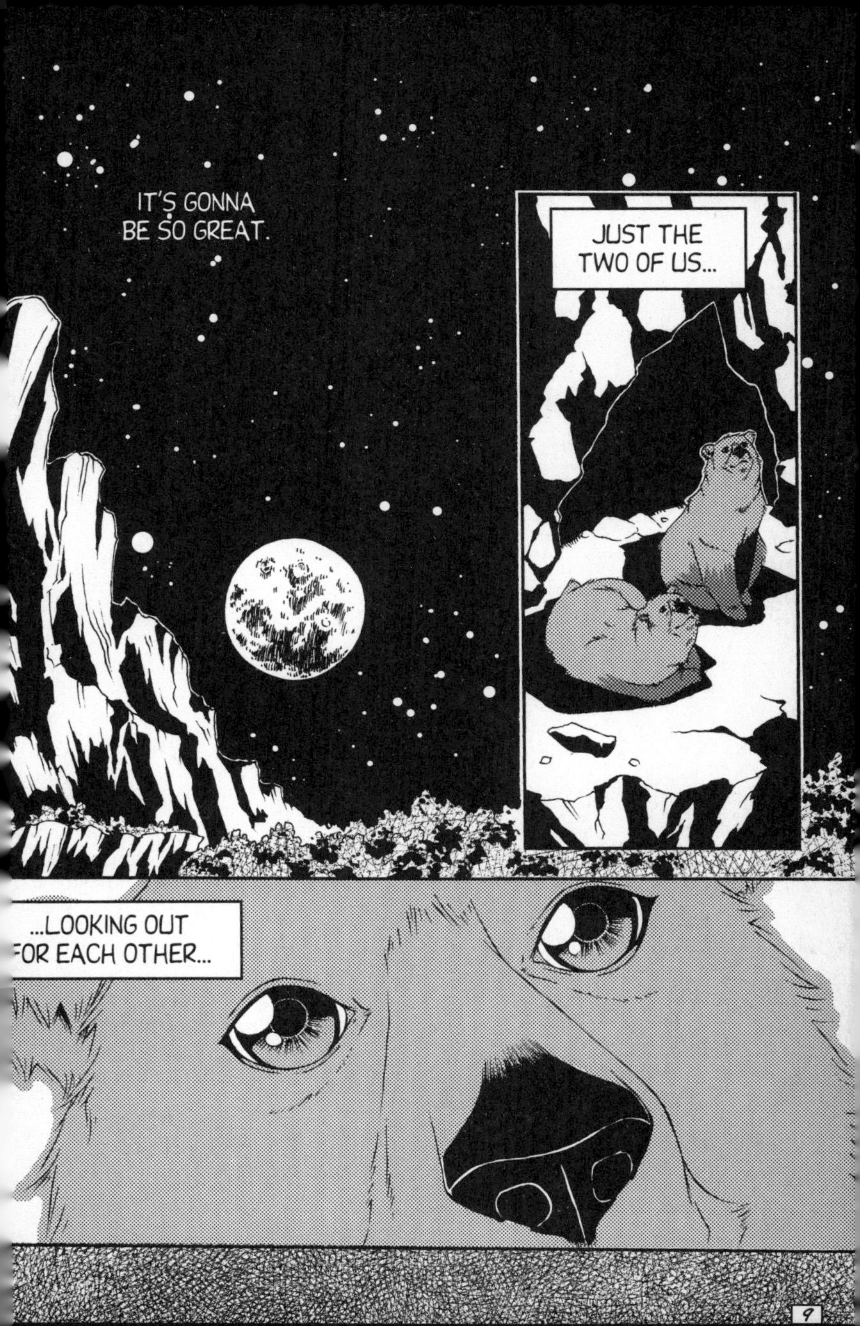
IT'S GONNA
BE SO GREAT.
JUST THE
TWO OF US...
...LOOKING OUT
FOR EACH OTHER...

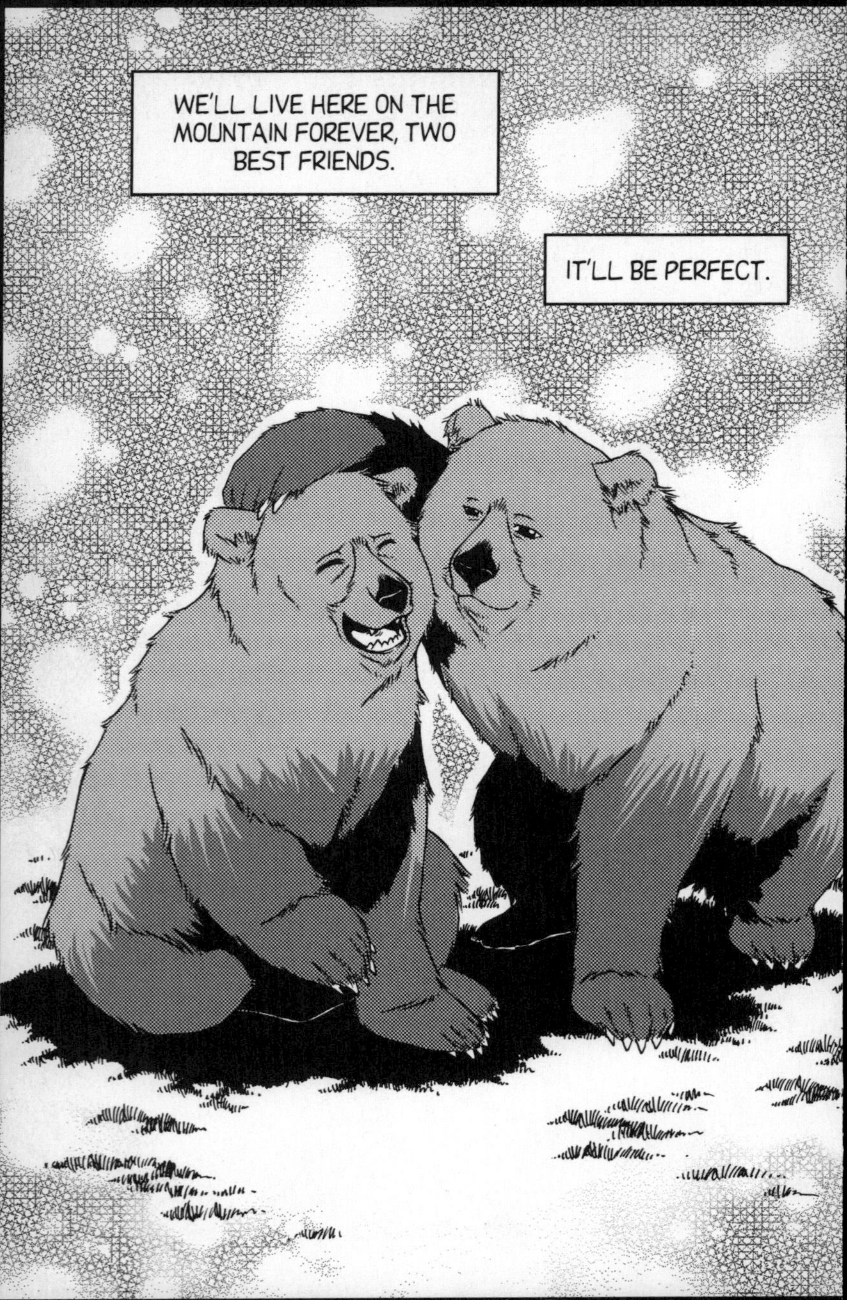
WE'LL LIVE HERE ON THE MOUNTAIN FOREVER, TWO BEST FRIENDS.
IT'LL BE PERFECT.

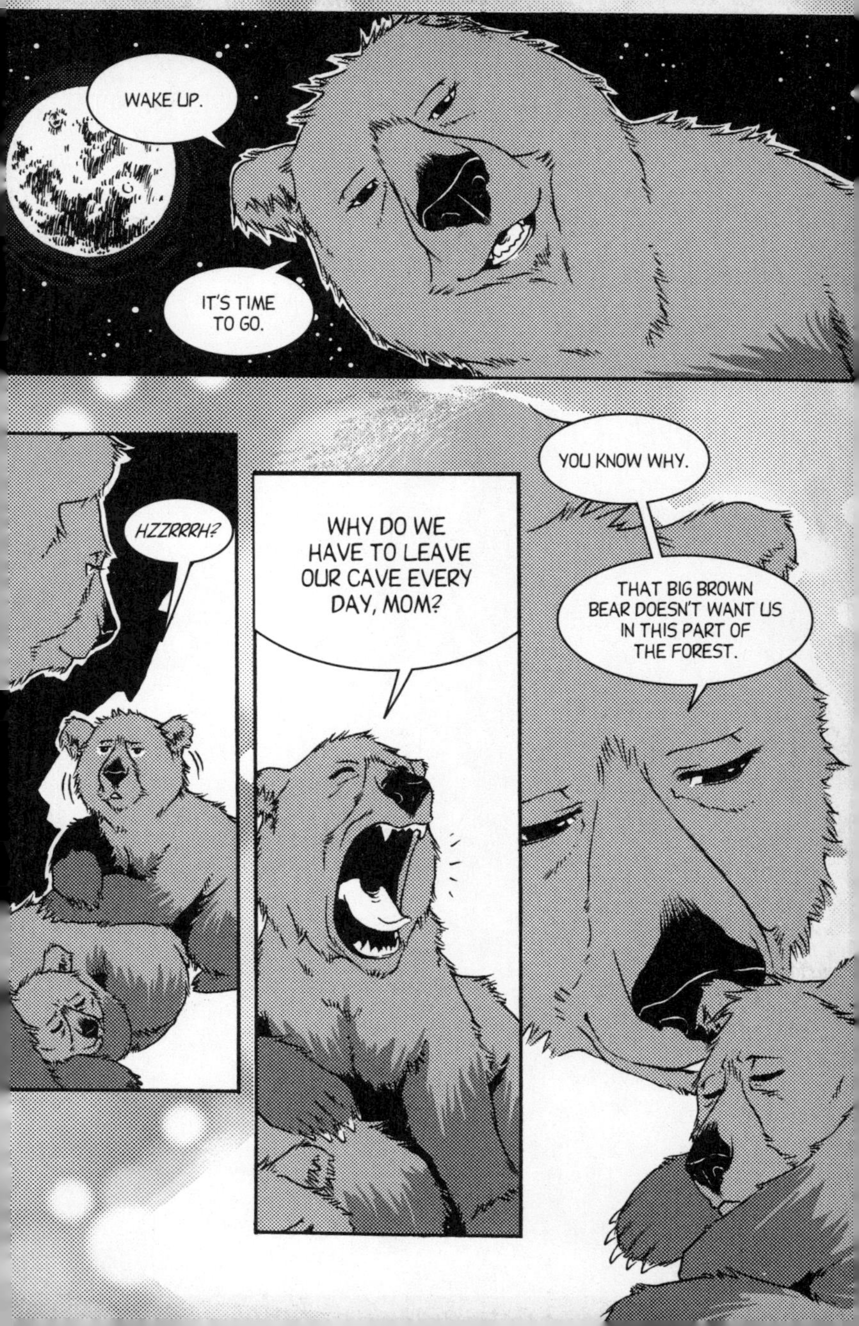
WAKE UP.
IT'S TIME TO GO.
HZZRRRH?
WHY DO WE HAVE TO LEAVE OUR CAVE EVERY DAY, MOM?
YOU KNOW WHY.
THAT BIG BROWN BEAR DOESN'T WANT US IN THIS PART OF THE FOREST.

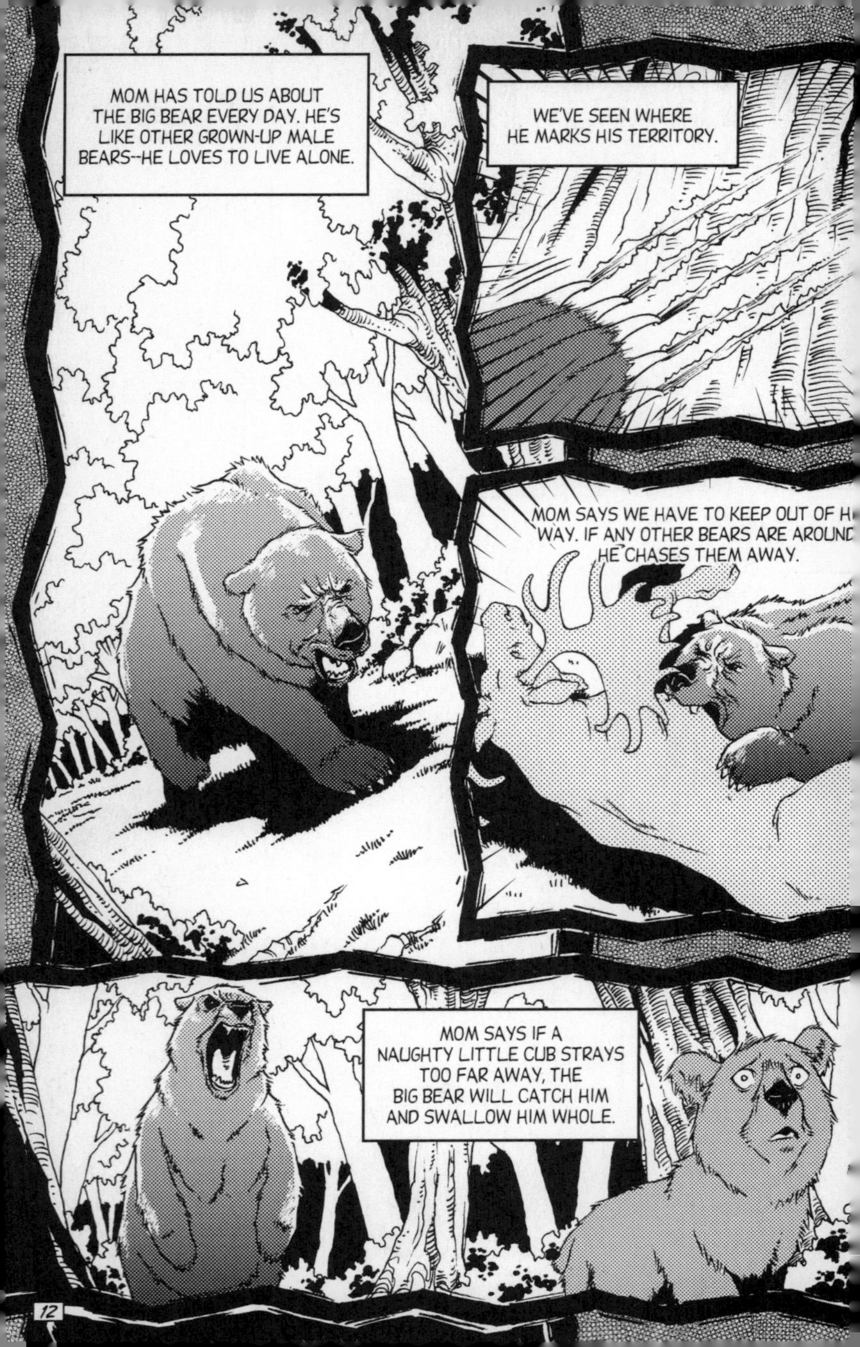
MOM HAS TOLD US ABOUT THE BIG BEAR EVERY DAY. HE'S LIKE OTHER GROWN-UP MALE BEARS--HE LOVES TO LIVE ALONE.
WE'VE SEEN WHERE HE MARKS HIS TERRITORY.
MOM SAYS WE HAVE TO KEEP OUT OF H WAY. IF ANY OTHER BEARS ARE AROUND HE CHASES THEM AWAY.
MOM SAYS IF A NAUGHTY LITTLE CUB STRAYS TOO FAR AWAY, THE BIG BEAR WILL CATCH HIM AND SWALLOW HIM WHOLE.

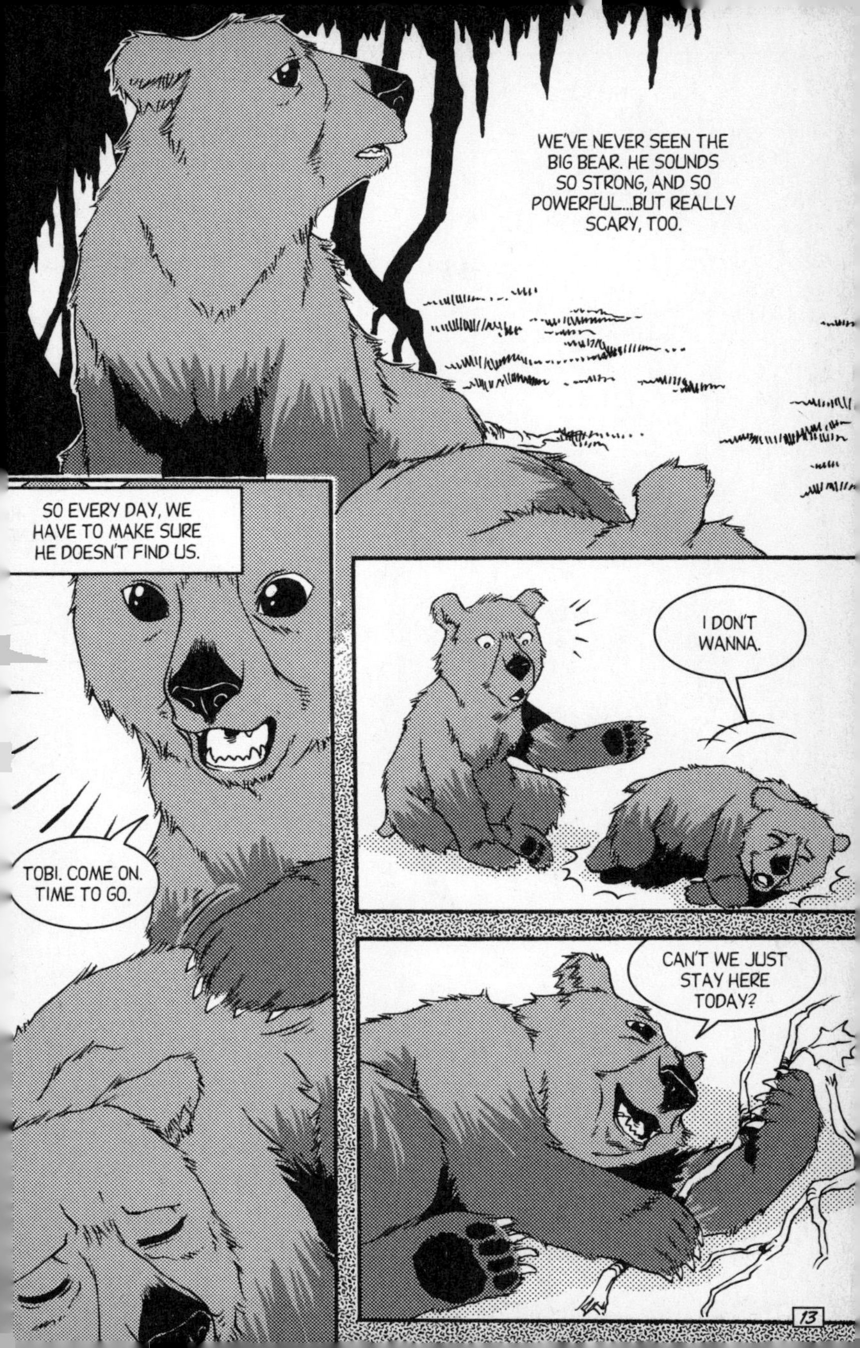
WE'VE NEVER SEEN THE BIG BEAR. HE SOUNDS SO STRONG, AND SO POWERFUL...BUT REALLY SCARY, TOO.
SO EVERY DAY, WE HAVE TO MAKE SURE HE DOESN'T FIND US.
TOBI. COME ON. TIME TO GO.
I DON'T WANNA.
CAN'T WE JUST STAY HERE TODAY?

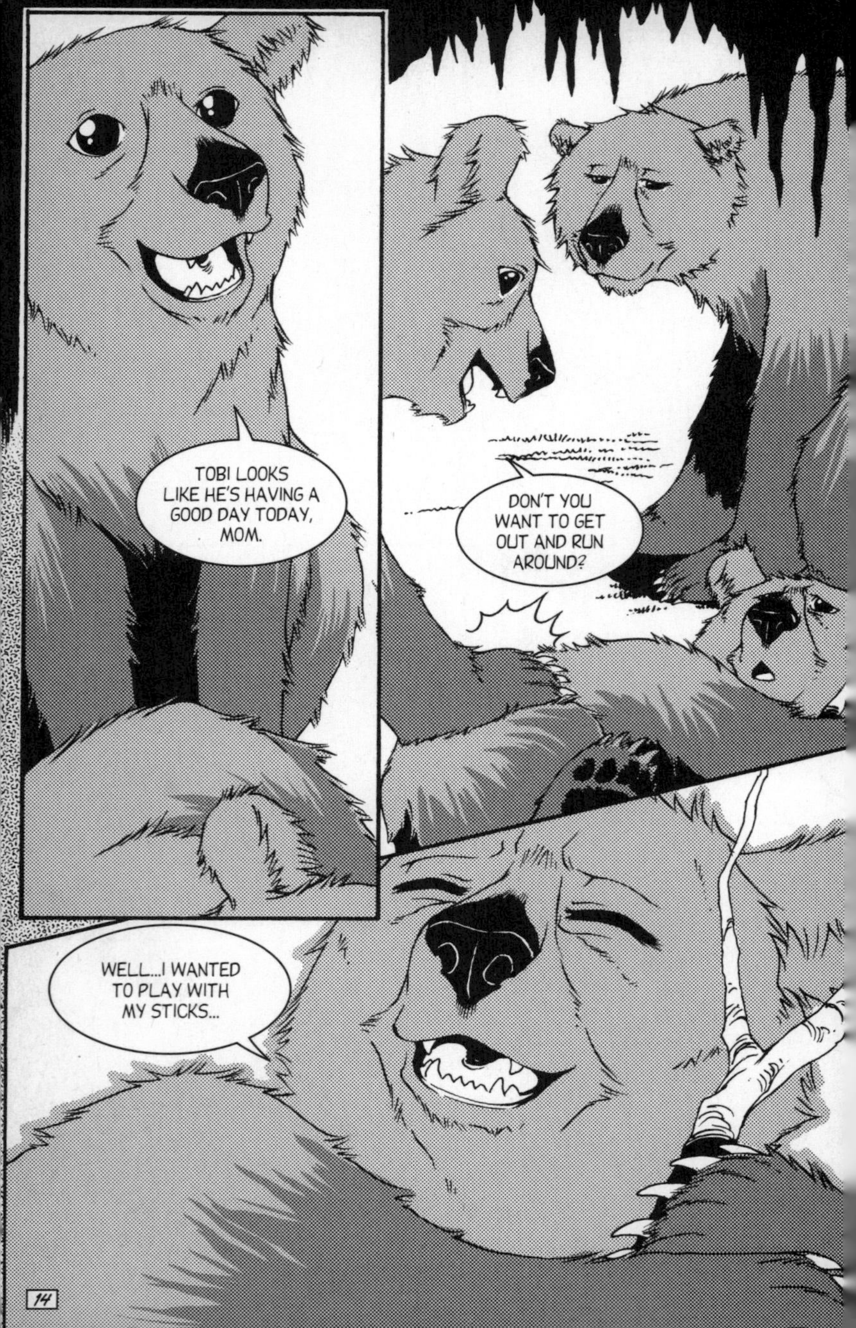
TOBI LOOKS LIKE HE'S HAVING A GOOD DAY TODAY, MOM.
DON'T YOU WANT TO GET OUT AND RUN AROUND?
WELL...I WANTED TO PLAY WITH MY STICKS...

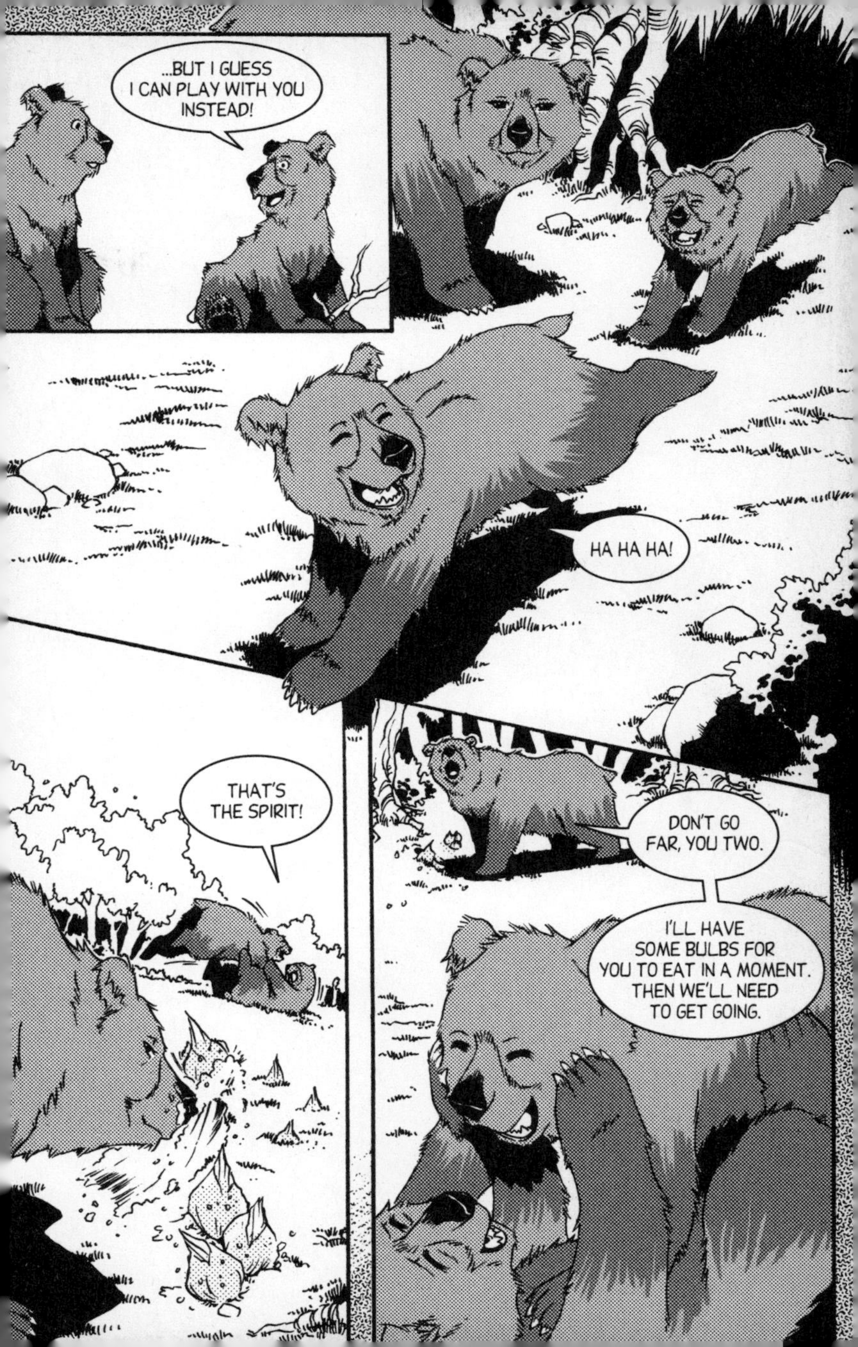
...BUT I GUESS I CAN PLAY WITH YOU INSTEAD!
HA HA HA!
THAT'S THE SPIRIT!
DON'T GO FAR, YOU TWO.
I'LL HAVE SOME BULBS FOR YOU TO EAT IN A MOMENT. THEN WE'LL NEED TO GET GOING.

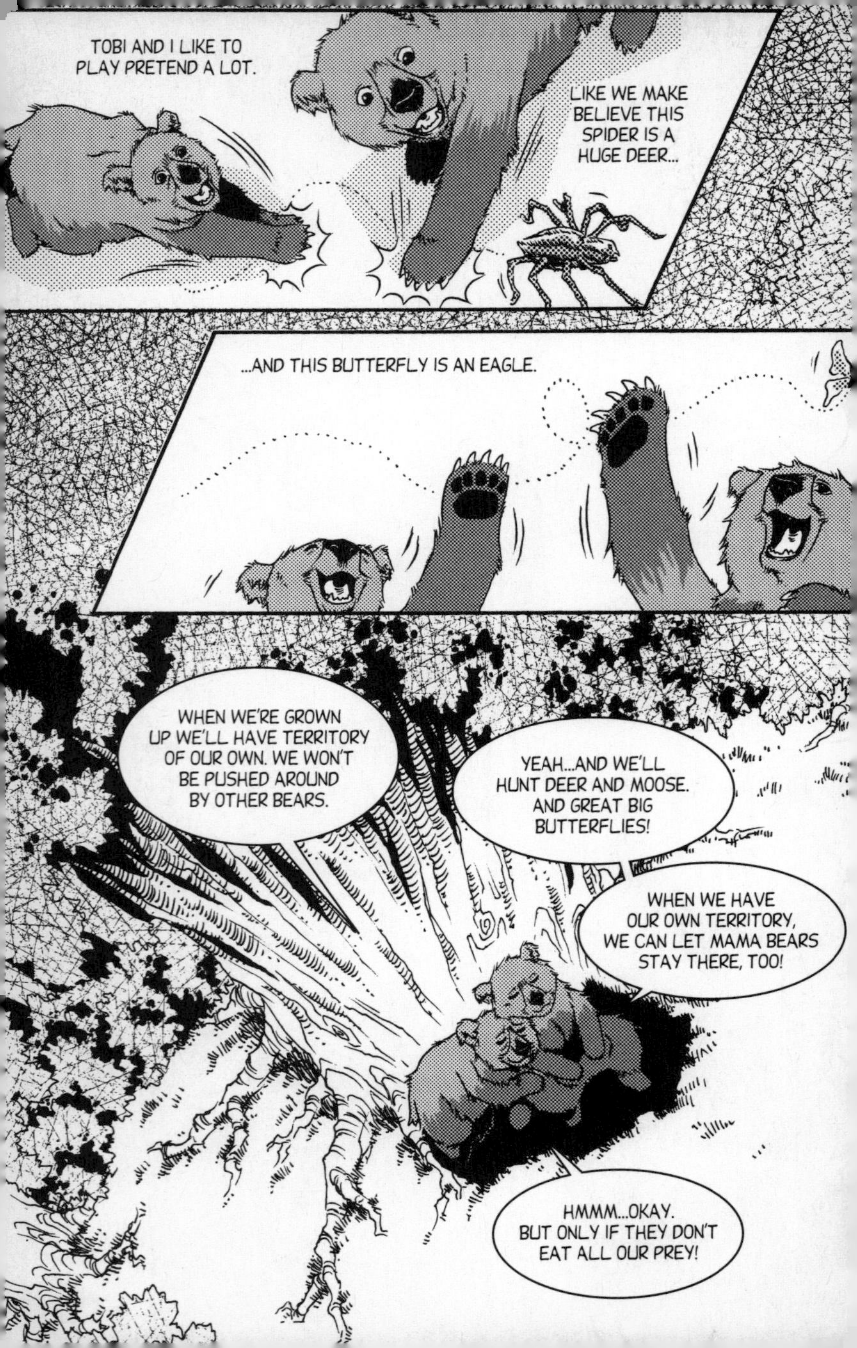
TOBI AND I LIKE TO PLAY PRETEND A LOT.
LIKE WE MAKE BELIEVE THIS SPIDER IS A HUGE DEER...
...AND THIS BUTTERFLY IS AN EAGLE.
WHEN WE'RE GROWN UP WE'LL HAVE TERRITORY OF OUR OWN. WE WON'T BE PUSHED AROUND BY OTHER BEARS.
YEAH...AND WE'LL HUNT DEER AND MOOSE. AND GREAT BIG BUTTERFLIES!
WHEN WE HAVE OUR OWN TERRITORY, WE CAN LET MAMA BEARS STAY THERE, TOO!
HMMM...OKAY. BUT ONLY IF THEY DON'T EAT ALL OUR PREY!

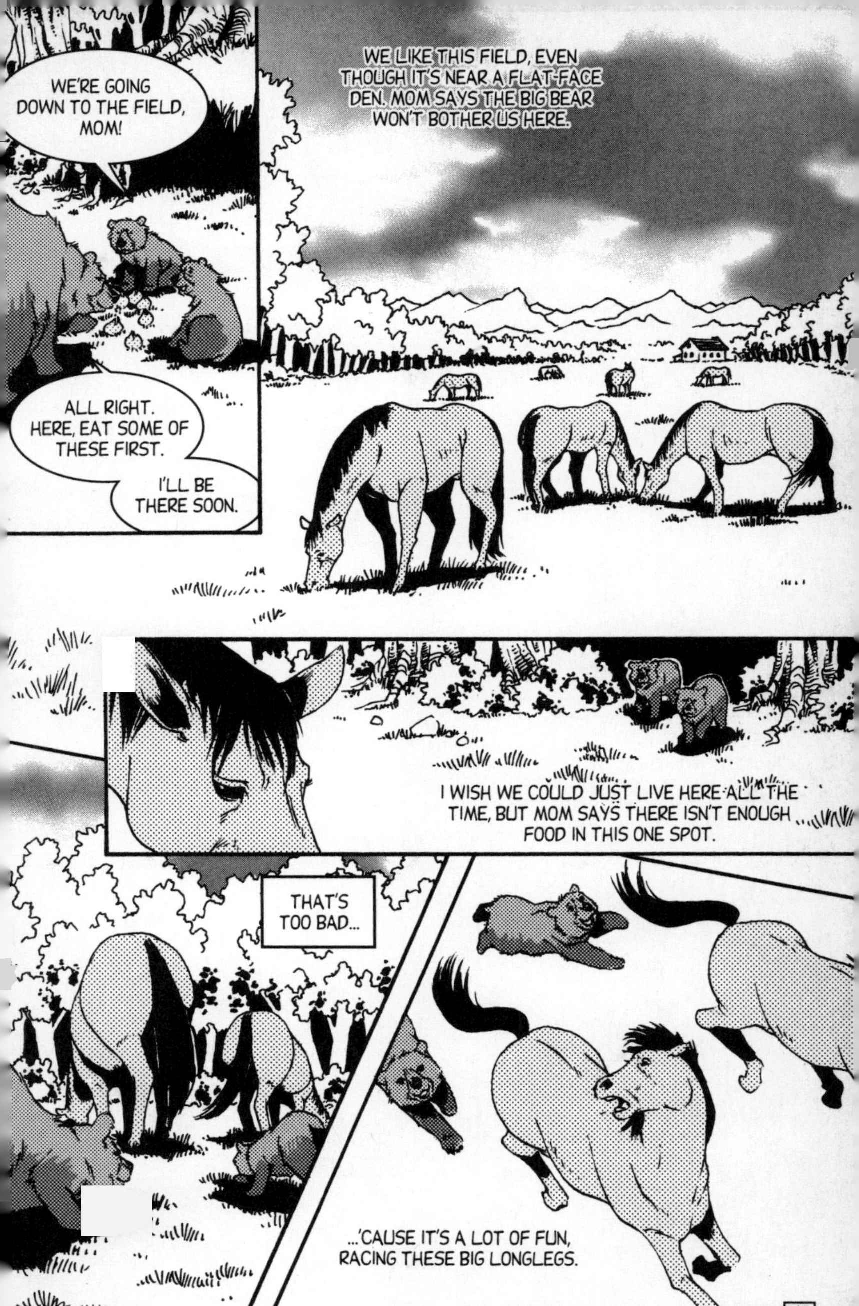
WE'RE GOING DOWN TO THE FIELD, MOM!
ALL RIGHT. HERE, EAT SOME OF THESE FIRST.
I'LL BE THERE SOON.
WE LIKE THIS FIELD, EVEN THOUGH IT'S NEAR A FLAT-FACE DEN. MOM SAYS THE BIG BEAR WON'T BOTHER US HERE.
I WISH WE COULD JUST LIVE HERE ALL THE TIME, BUT MOM SAYS THERE ISN'T ENOUGH FOOD IN THIS ONE SPOT.
THAT'S TOO BAD...
...'CAUSE IT'S A LOT OF FUN, RACING THESE BIG LONGLEGS.

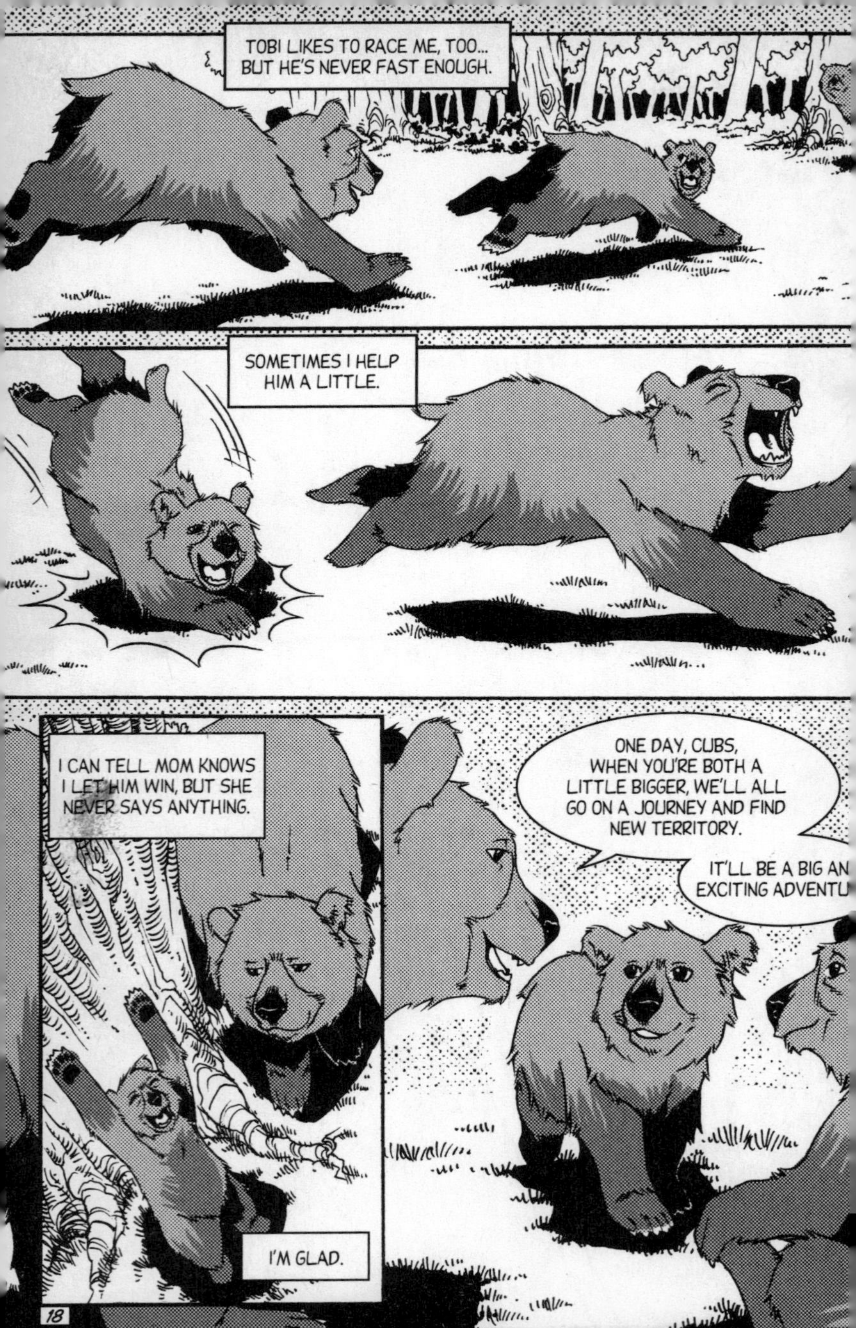
TOBI LIKES TO RACE ME, TOO... BUT HE'S NEVER FAST ENOUGH.
SOMETIMES I HELP HIM A LITTLE.
I CAN TELL MOM KNOWS I LET HIM WIN, BUT SHE NEVER SAYS ANYTHING.
I'M GLAD.
ONE DAY, CUBS, WHEN YOU'RE BOTH A LITTLE BIGGER, WE'LL ALL GO ON A JOURNEY AND FIND NEW TERRITORY.
IT'LL BE A BIG AN EXCITING ADVENTU

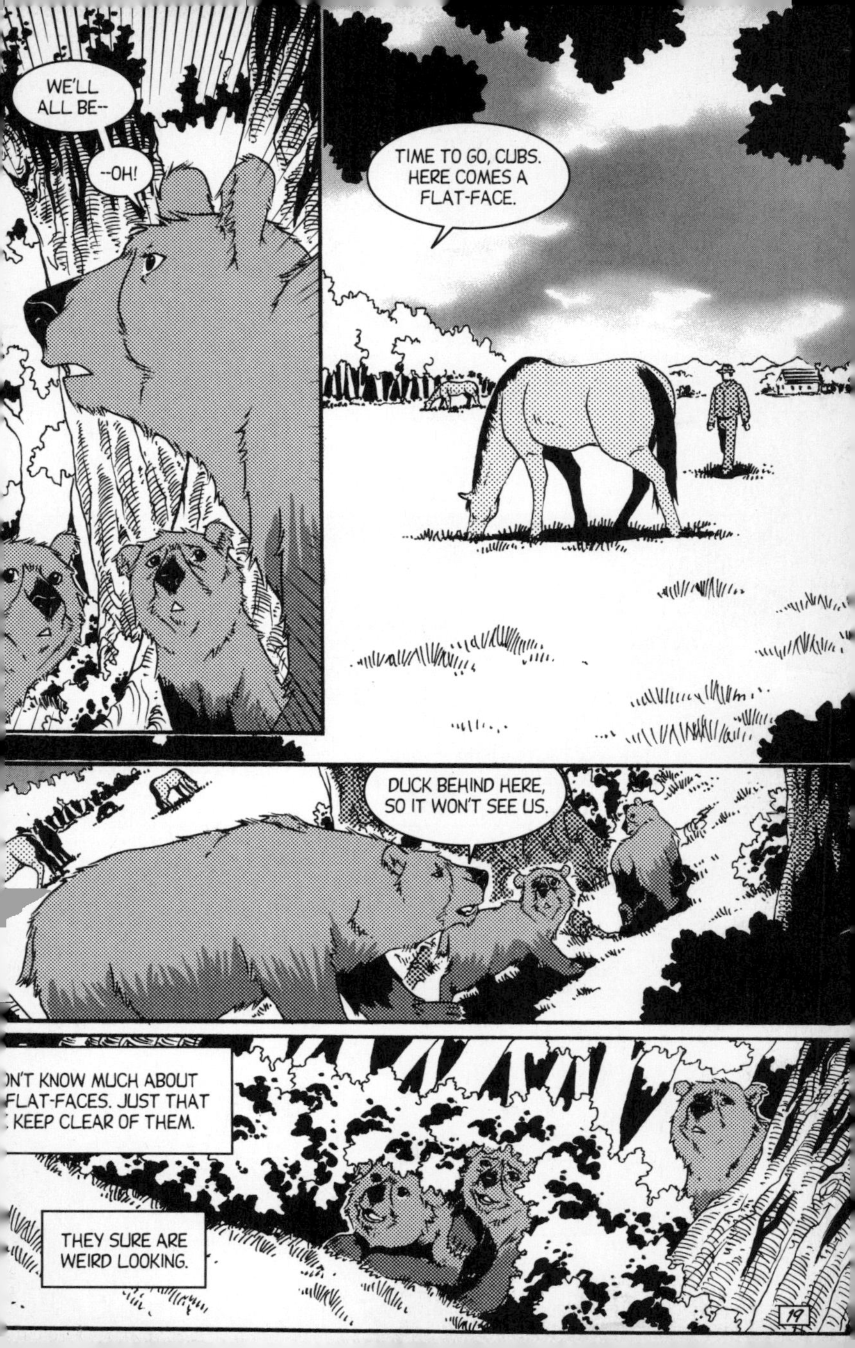
WE'LL ALL BE--
--OH!
TIME TO GO, CUBS. HERE COMES A FLAT-FACE.
DUCK BEHIND HERE, SO IT WON'T SEE US.
N'T KNOW MUCH ABOUT FLAT-FACES. JUST THAT KEEP CLEAR OF THEM.
THEY SURE ARE WEIRD LOOKING.

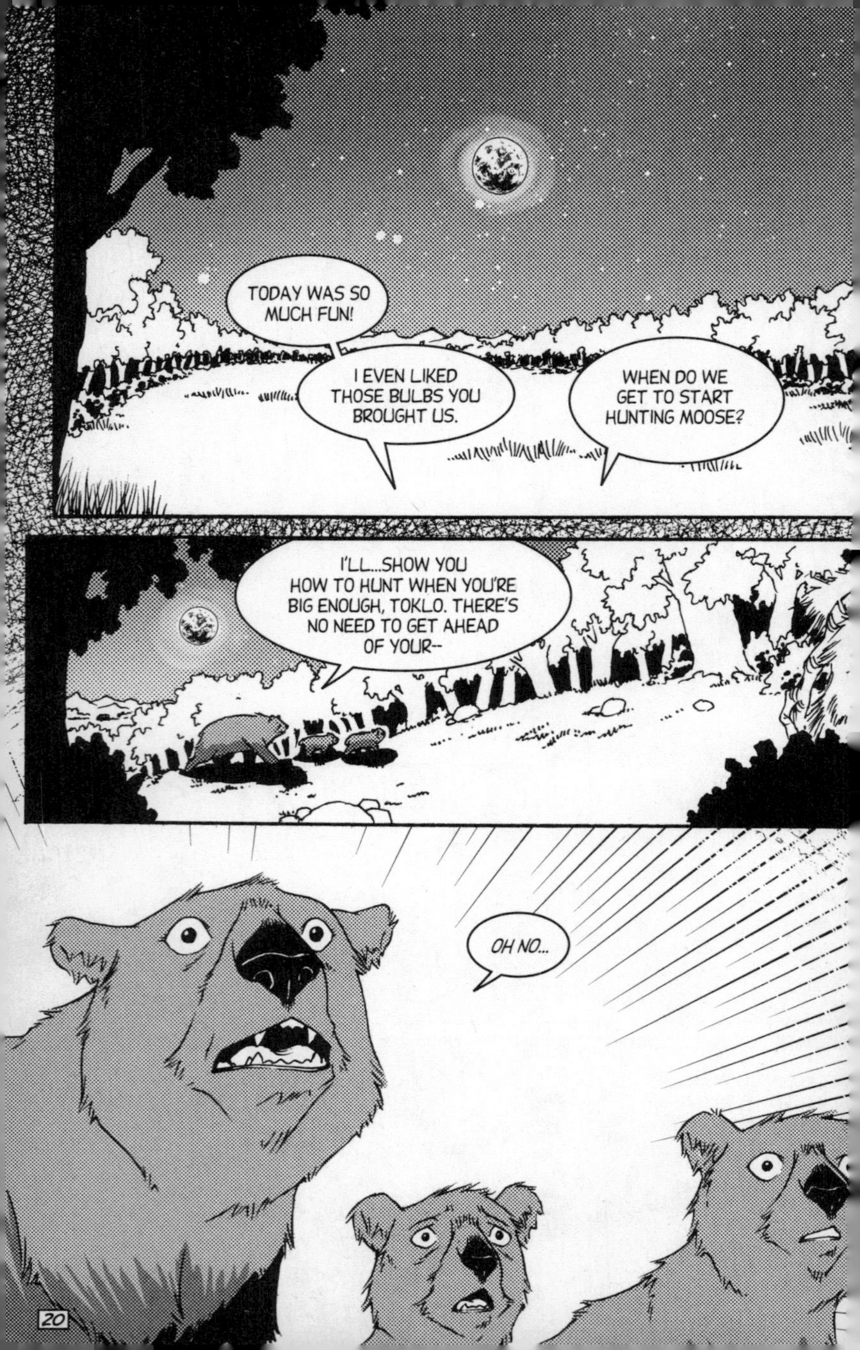
TODAY WAS SO MUCH FUN!
I EVEN LIKED THOSE BULBS YOU BROUGHT US.
WHEN DO WE GET TO START HUNTING MOOSE?
I'LL...SHOW YOU HOW TO HUNT WHEN YOU'RE BIG ENOUGH, TOKLO. THERE'S NO NEED TO GET AHEAD OF YOUR--
OH NO...

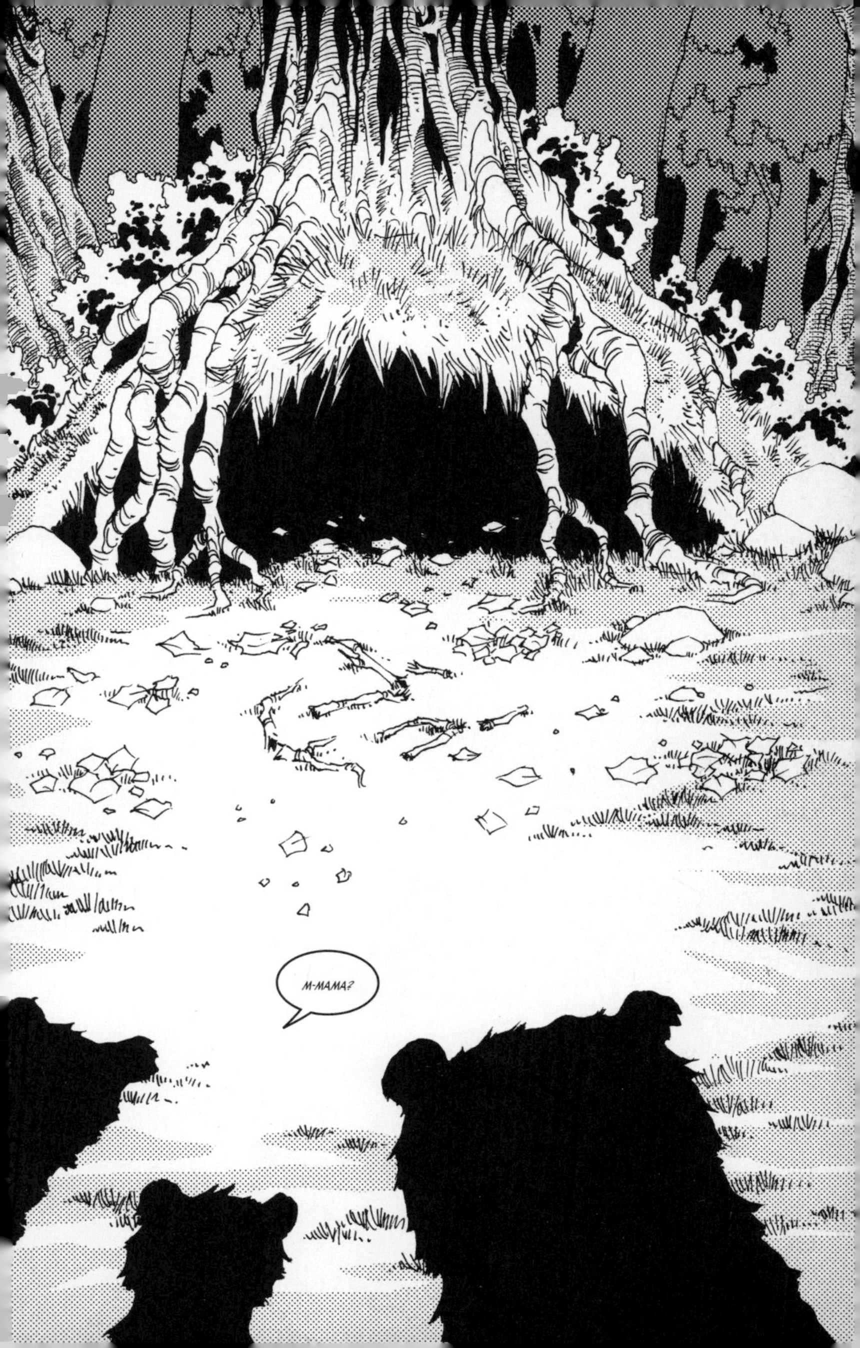
M-MAMA?

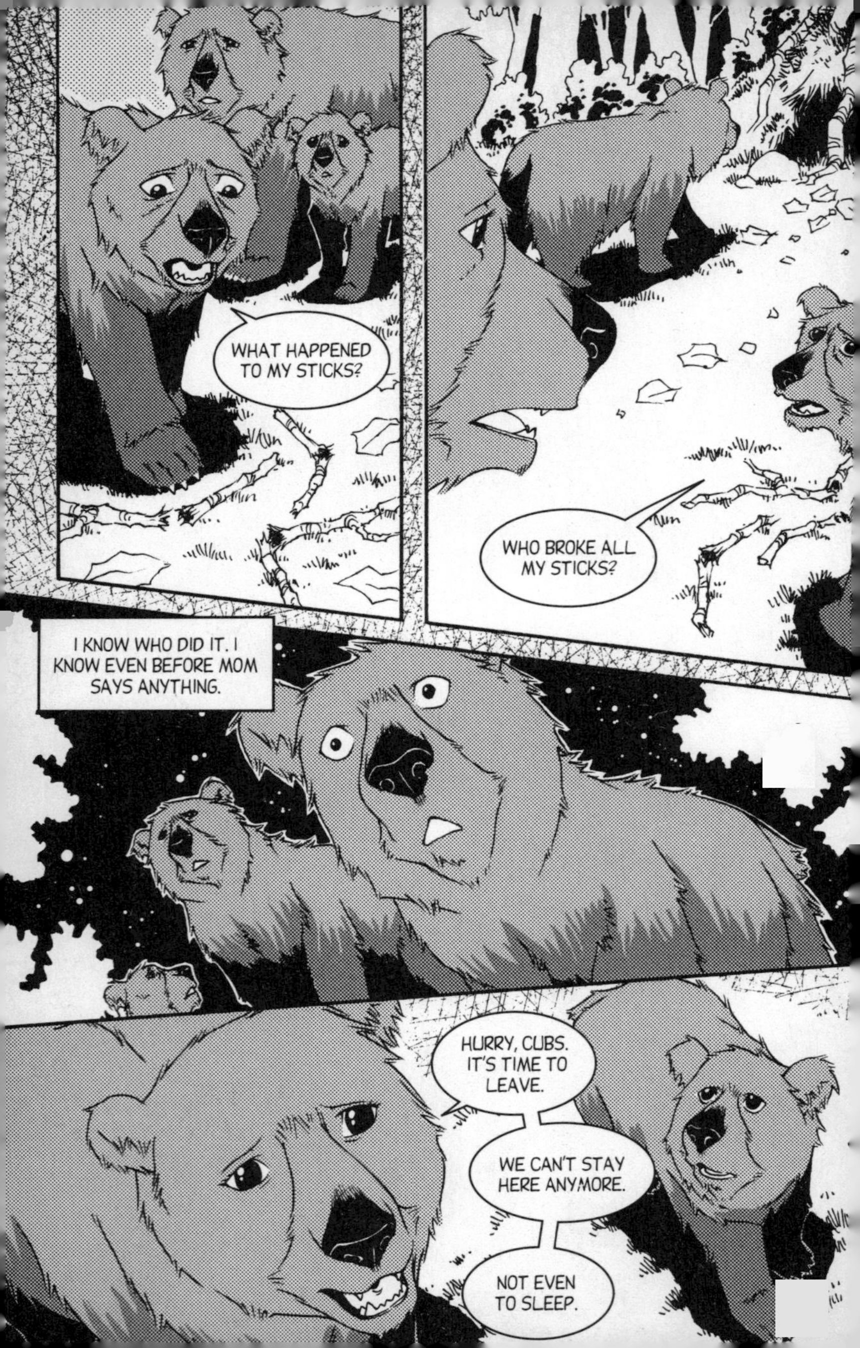
WHAT HAPPENED TO MY STICKS?
WHO BROKE ALL MY STICKS?
I KNOW WHO DID IT. I KNOW EVEN BEFORE MOM SAYS ANYTHING.
HURRY, CUBS. IT'S TIME TO LEAVE.
WE CAN'T STAY HERE ANYMORE.
NOT EVEN TO SLEEP.

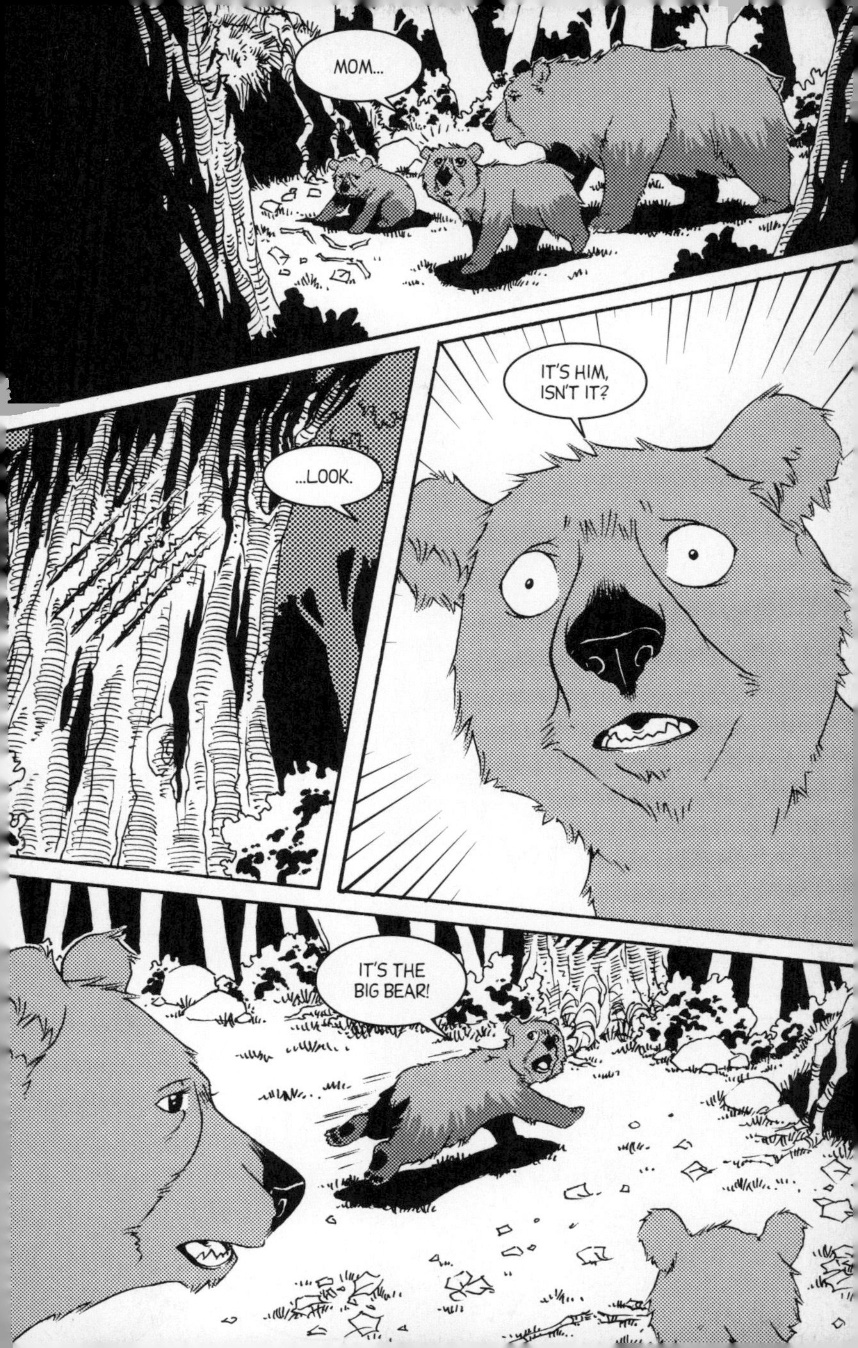
MOM...
...LOOK.
IT'S HIM, ISN'T IT?
IT'S THE BIG BEAR!

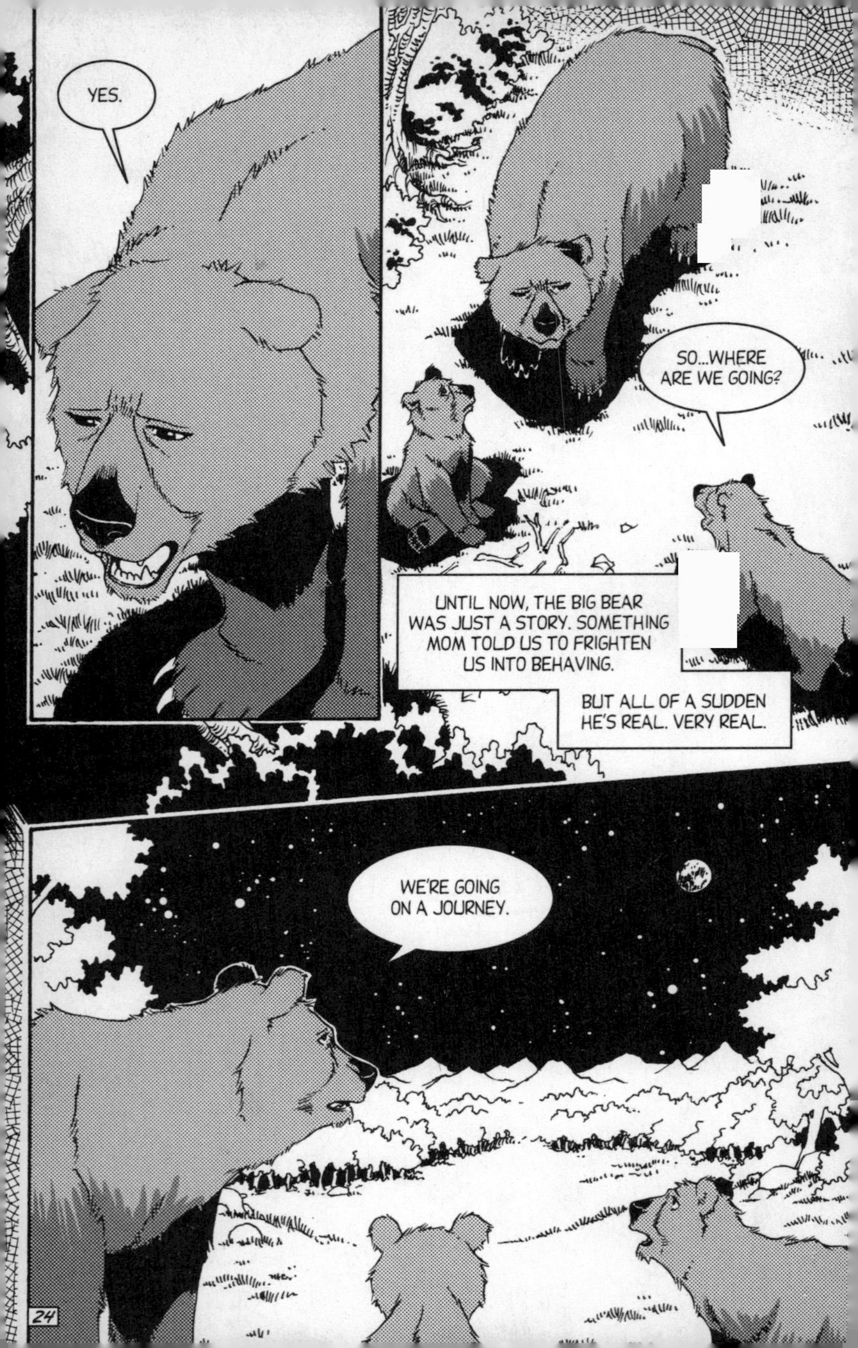
YES.
SO...WHERE ARE WE GOING?
UNTIL NOW, THE BIG BEAR WAS JUST A STORY. SOMETHING MOM TOLD US TO FRIGHTEN US INTO BEHAVING.
BUT ALL OF A SUDDEN HE'S REAL. VERY REAL.
WE'RE GOING ON A JOURNEY.

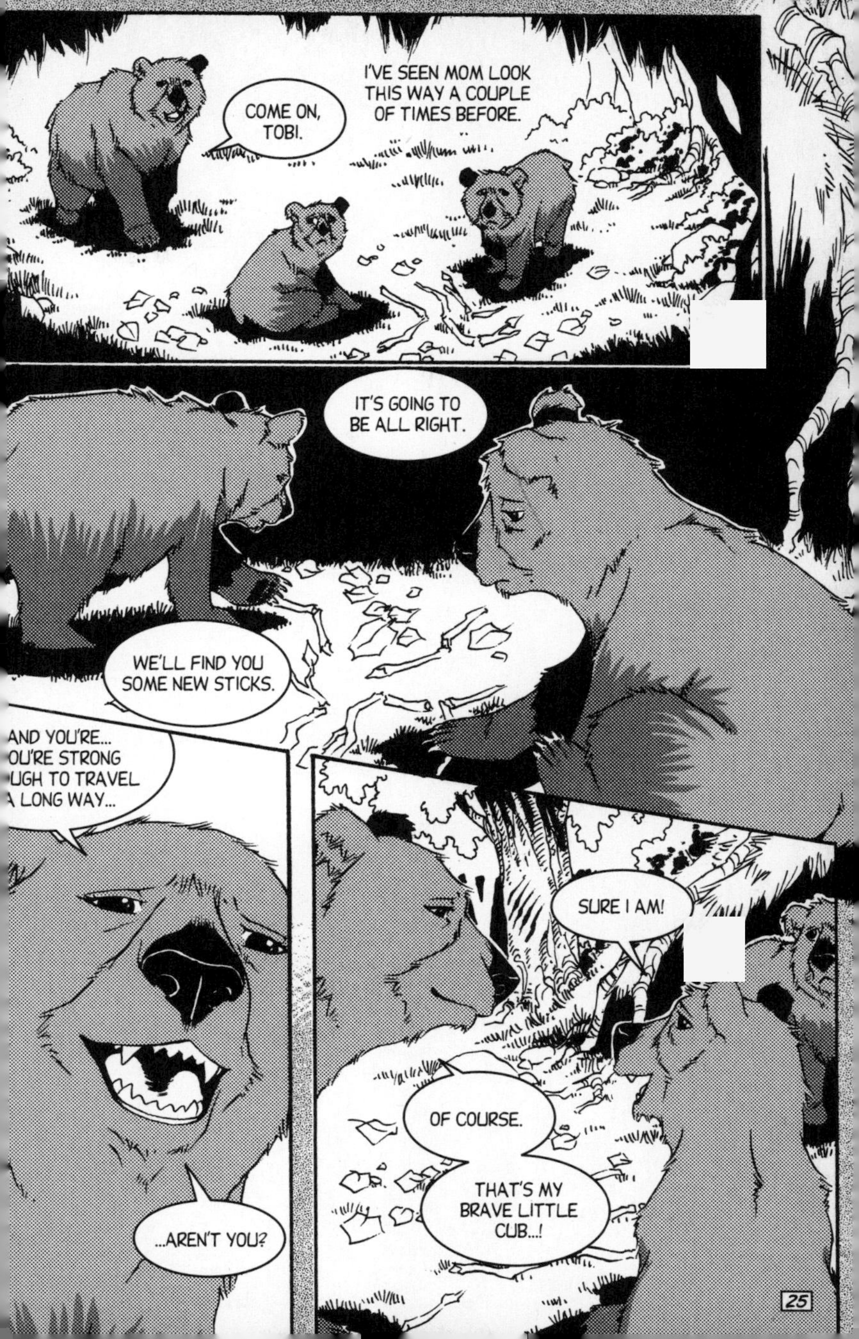
COME ON, TOBI.
I'VE SEEN MOM LOOK THIS WAY A COUPLE OF TIMES BEFORE.
IT'S GOING TO BE ALL RIGHT.
WE'LL FIND YOU SOME NEW STICKS.
AND YOU'RE... OU'RE STRONG UGH TO TRAVEL A LONG WAY...
...AREN'T YOU?
SURE I AM!
OF COURSE.
THAT'S MY BRAVE LITTLE CUB...!

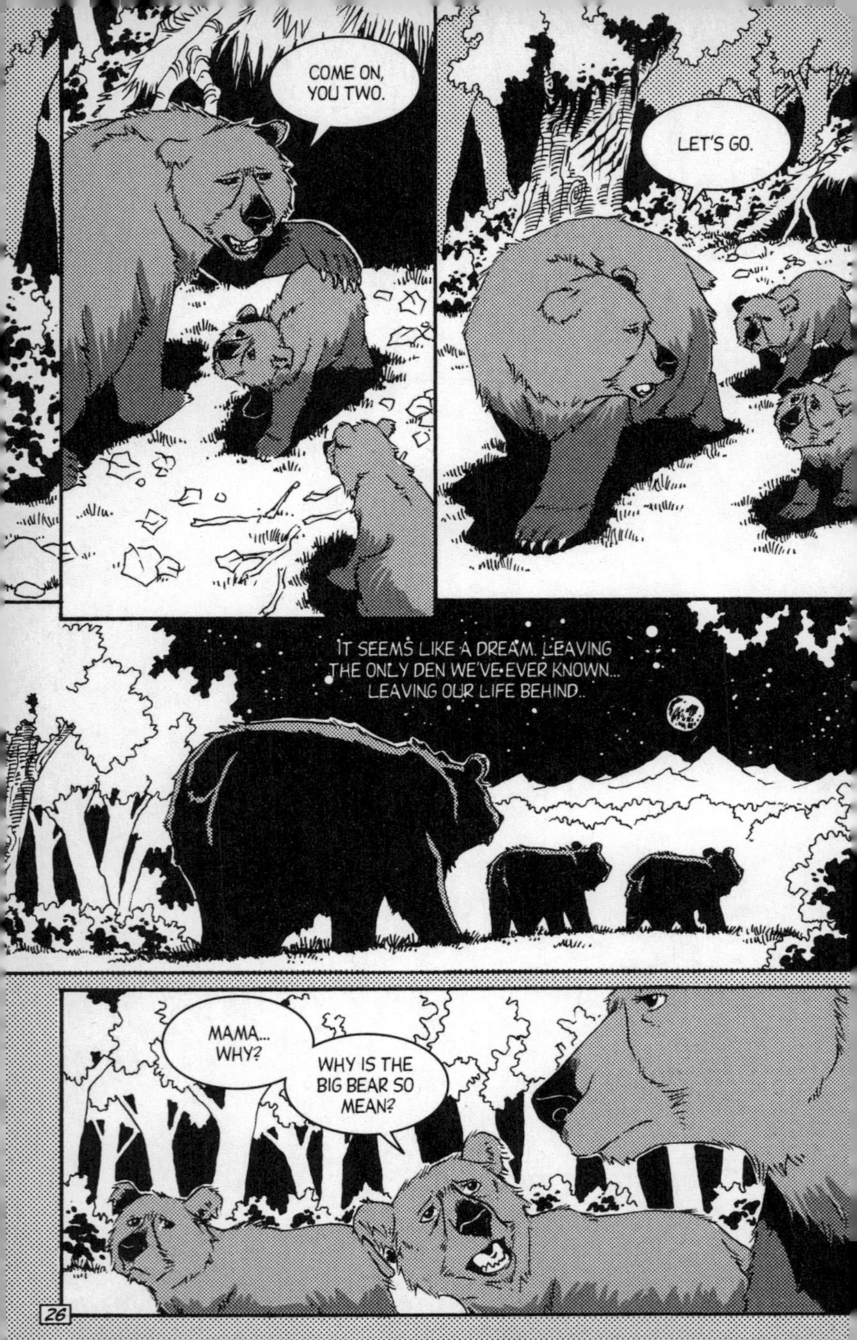
COME ON, YOU TWO.
LET'S GO.
IT SEEMS LIKE A DREAM. LEAVING THE ONLY DEN WE'VE EVER KNOWN... LEAVING OUR LIFE BEHIND..
MAMA... WHY?
WHY IS THE BIG BEAR SO MEAN?

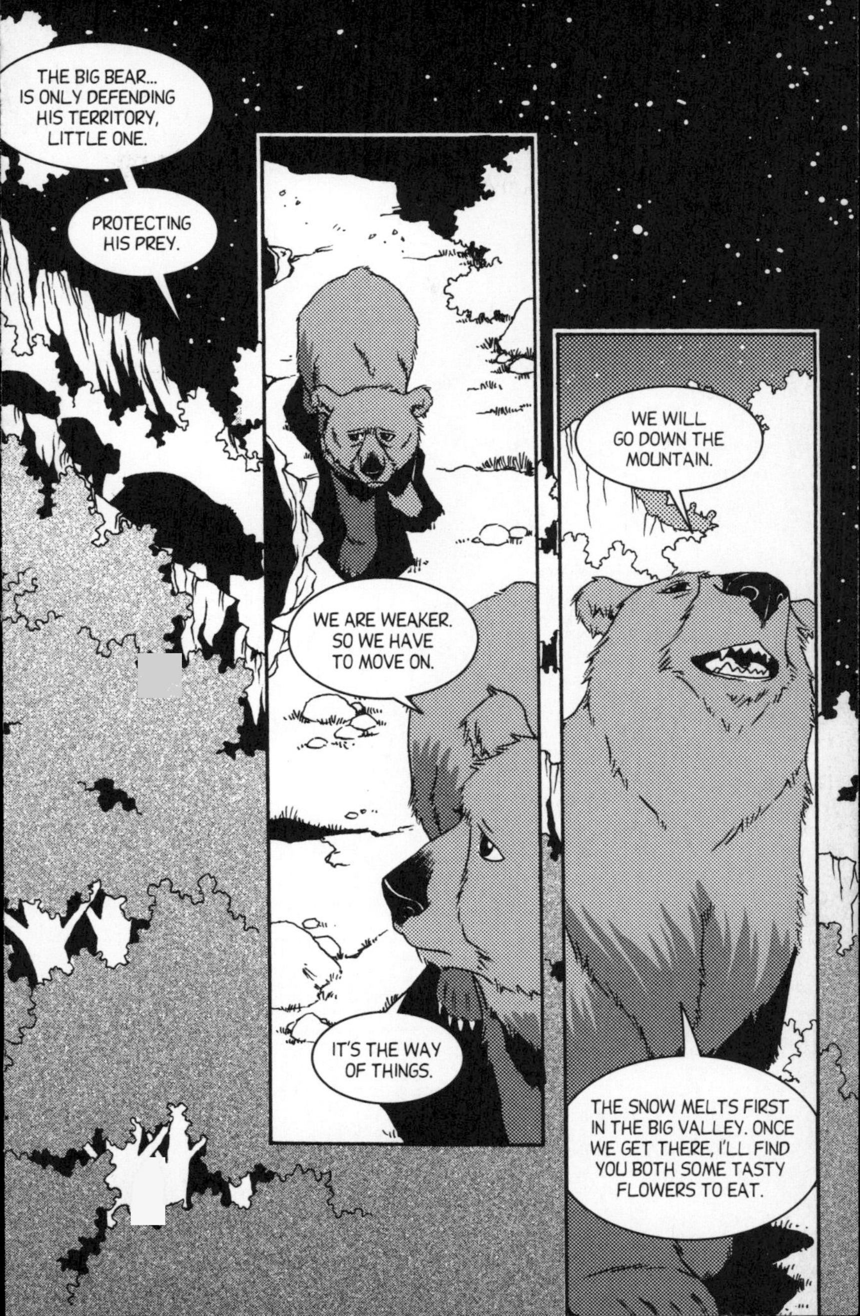
THE BIG BEAR... IS ONLY DEFENDING HIS TERRITORY, LITTLE ONE.
PROTECTING HIS PREY.
WE ARE WEAKER. SO WE HAVE TO MOVE ON.
IT'S THE WAY OF THINGS.
WE WILL GO DOWN THE MOUNTAIN.
THE SNOW MELTS FIRST IN THE BIG VALLEY. ONCE WE GET THERE, I'LL FIND YOU BOTH SOME TASTY FLOWERS TO EAT.

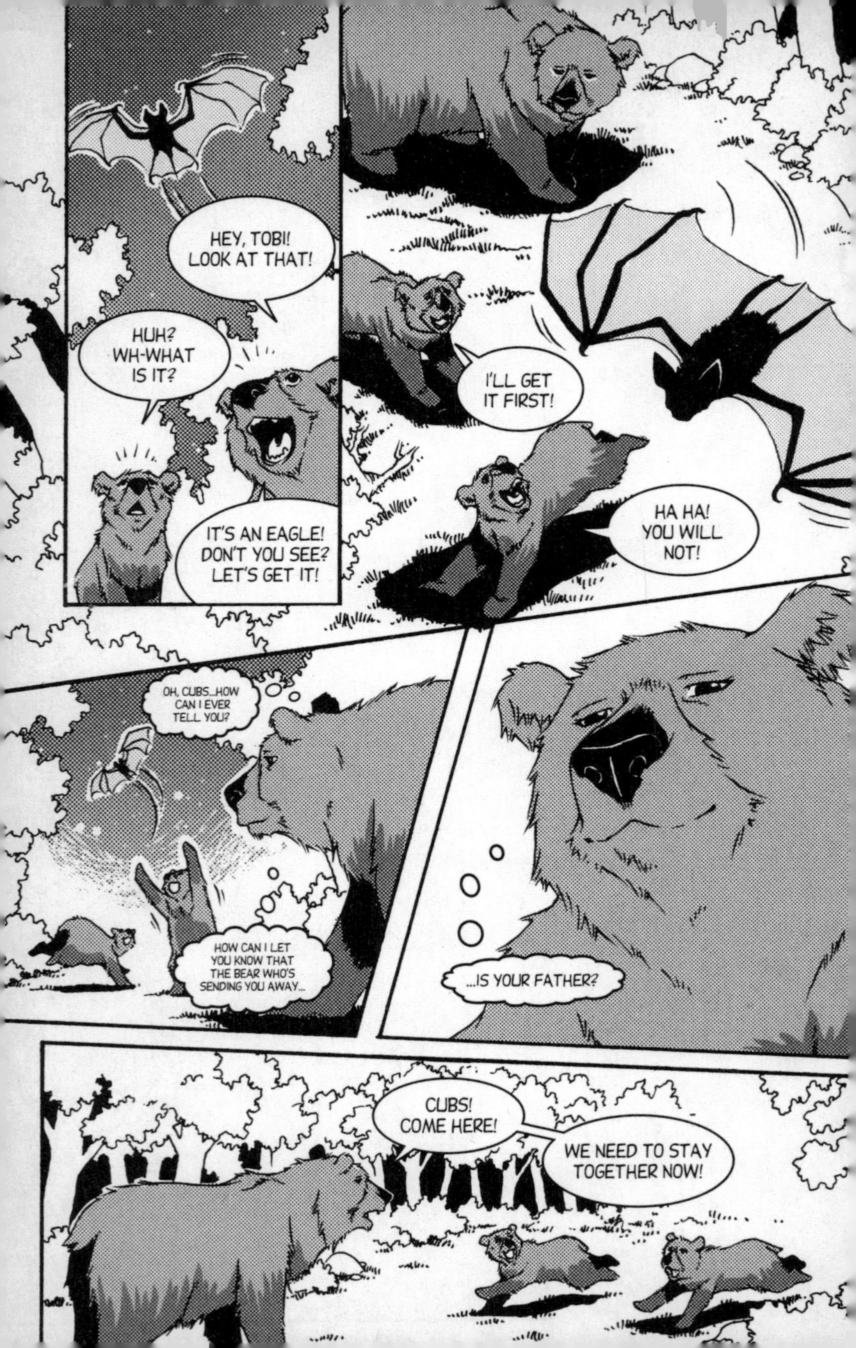
HEY, TOBI! LOOK AT THAT!
HUH? WH-WHAT IS IT?
IT'S AN EAGLE! DON'T YOU SEE? LET'S GET IT!
I'LL GET IT FIRST!
HA HA! YOU WILL NOT!
OH, CUBS...HOW CAN I EVER TELL YOU?
HOW CAN I LET YOU KNOW THAT THE BEAR WHO'S SENDING YOU AWAY...
...IS YOUR FATHER?
CUBS! COME HERE!
WE NEED TO STAY TOGETHER NOW!

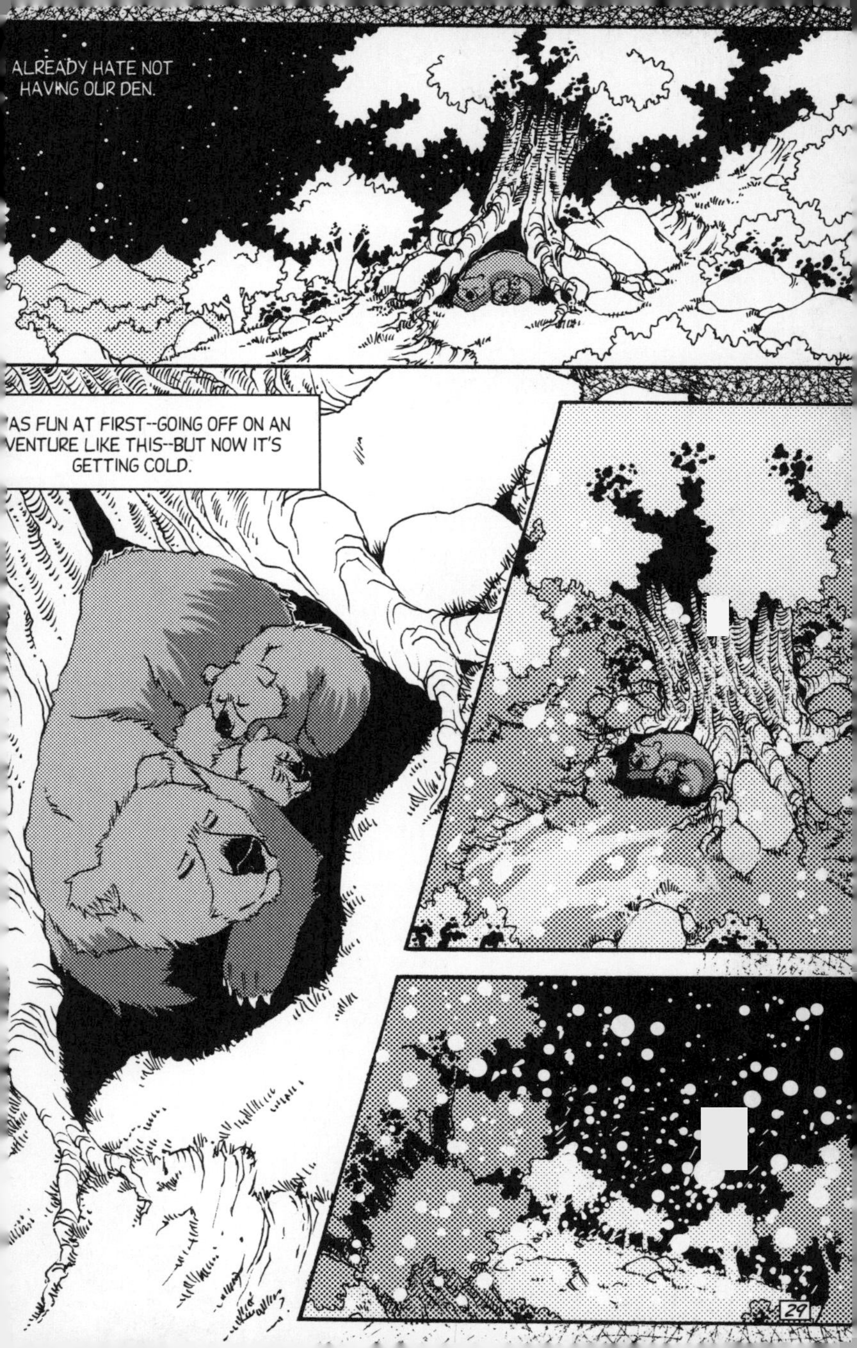
ALREADY HATE NOT HAVING OUR DEN.
'AS FUN AT FIRST--GOING OFF ON AN VENTURE LIKE THIS--BUT NOW IT'S GETTING COLD.
29

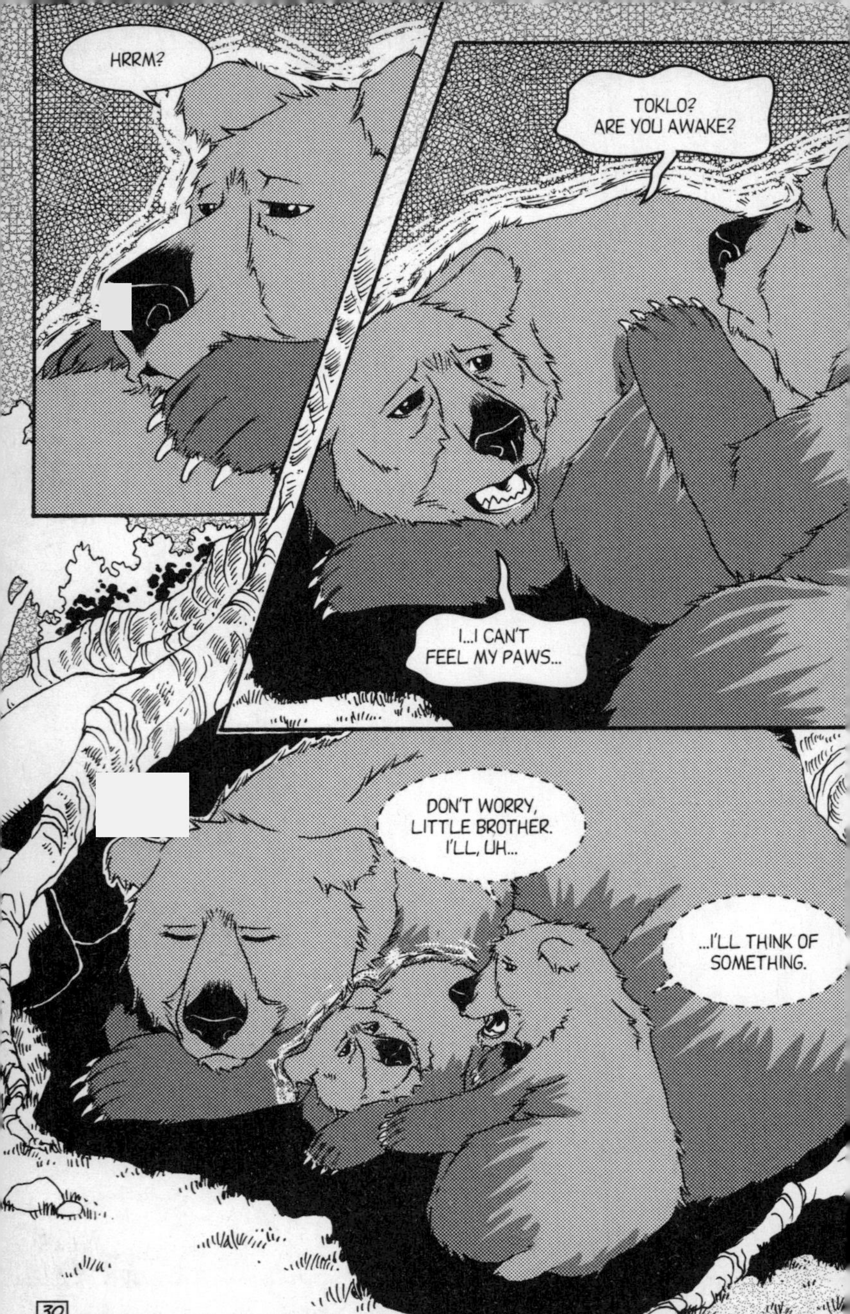
HRRM?
TOKLO? ARE YOU AWAKE?
I...I CAN'T FEEL MY PAWS...
DON'T WORRY, LITTLE BROTHER. I'LL, UH...
...I'LL THINK OF SOMETHING.

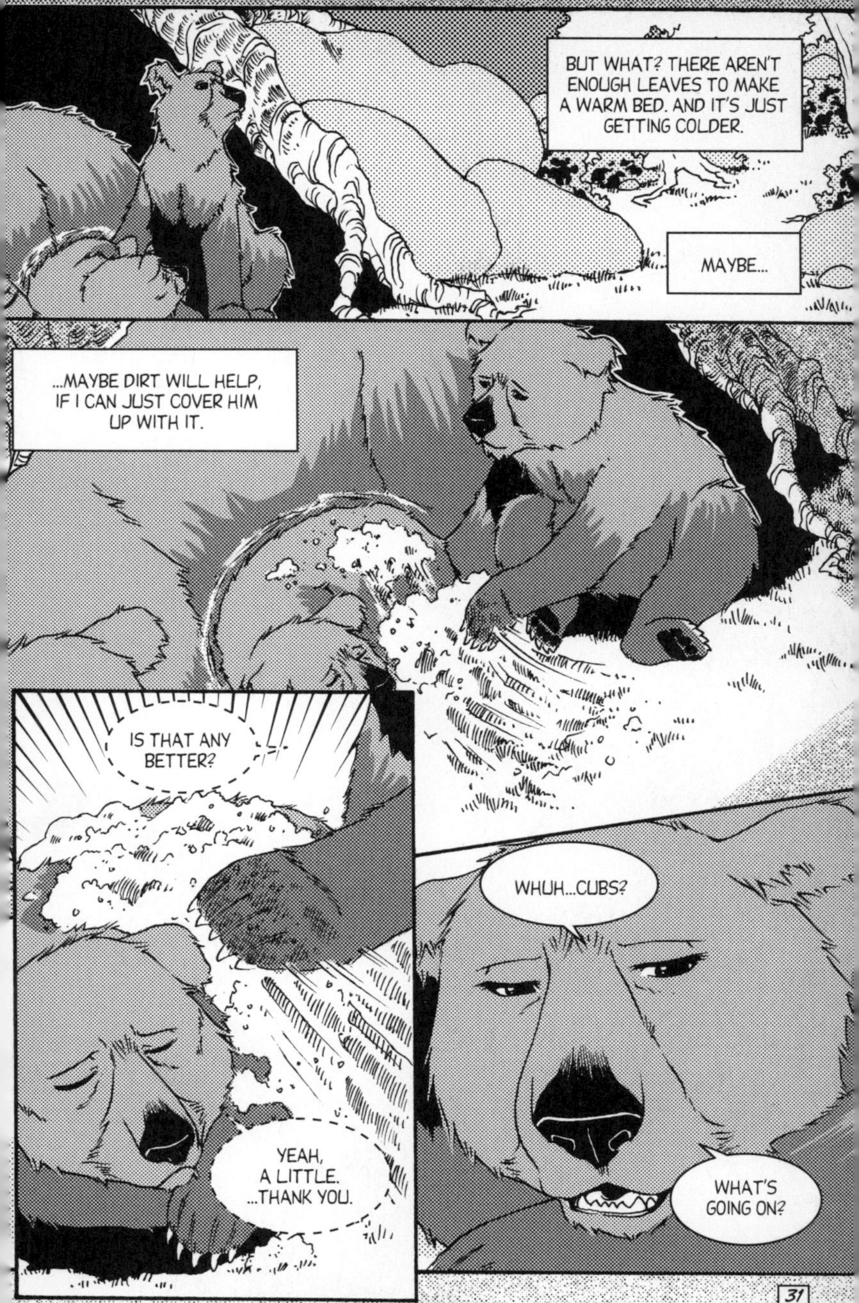
BUT WHAT? THERE AREN'T ENOUGH LEAVES TO MAKE A WARM BED. AND IT'S JUST GETTING COLDER.
MAYBE...
...MAYBE DIRT WILL HELP, IF I CAN JUST COVER HIM UP WITH IT.
IS THAT ANY BETTER?
YEAH, A LITTLE. ...THANK YOU.
WHUH...CUBS?
WHAT'S GOING ON?

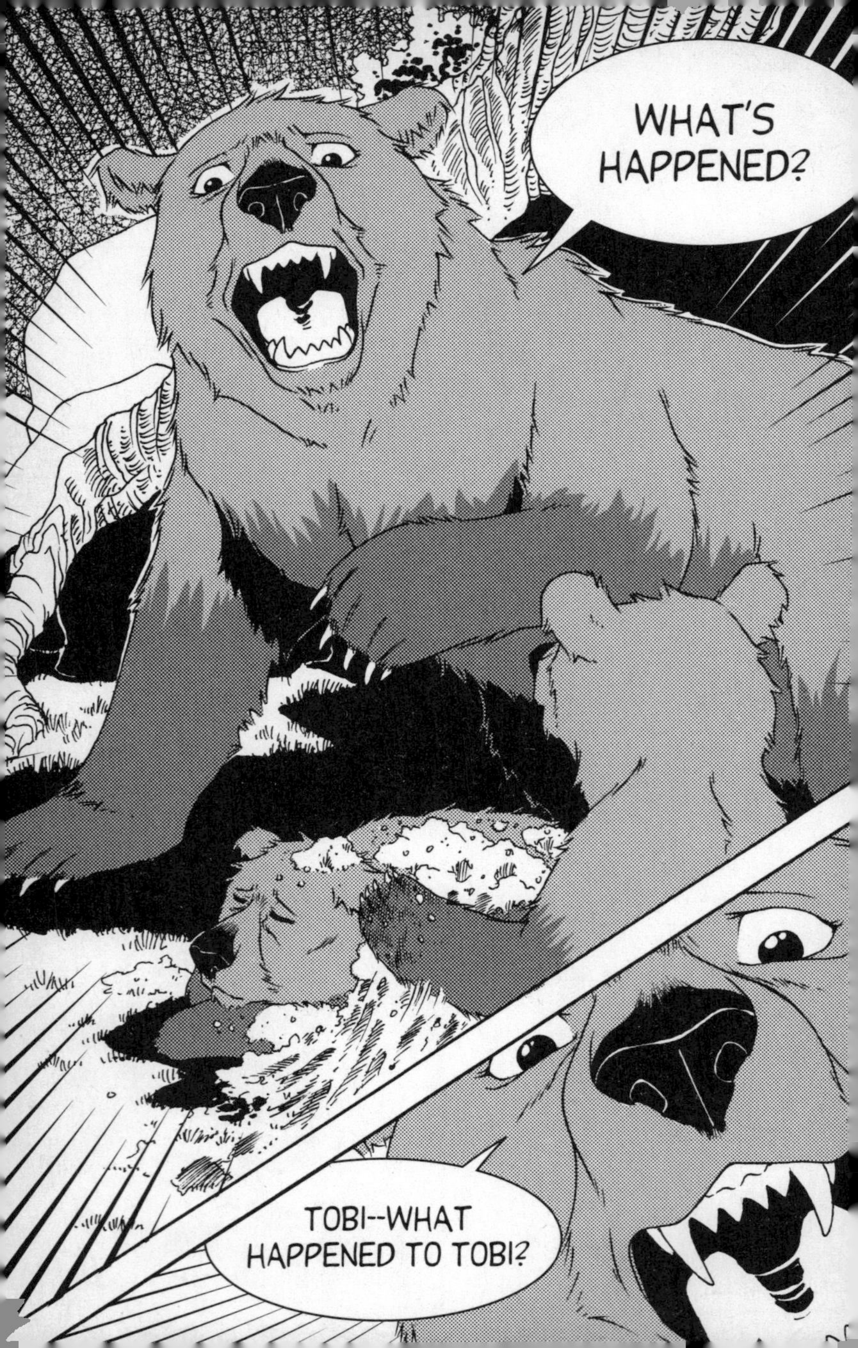
WHAT'S HAPPENED?
TOBI--WHAT HAPPENED TO TOBI?

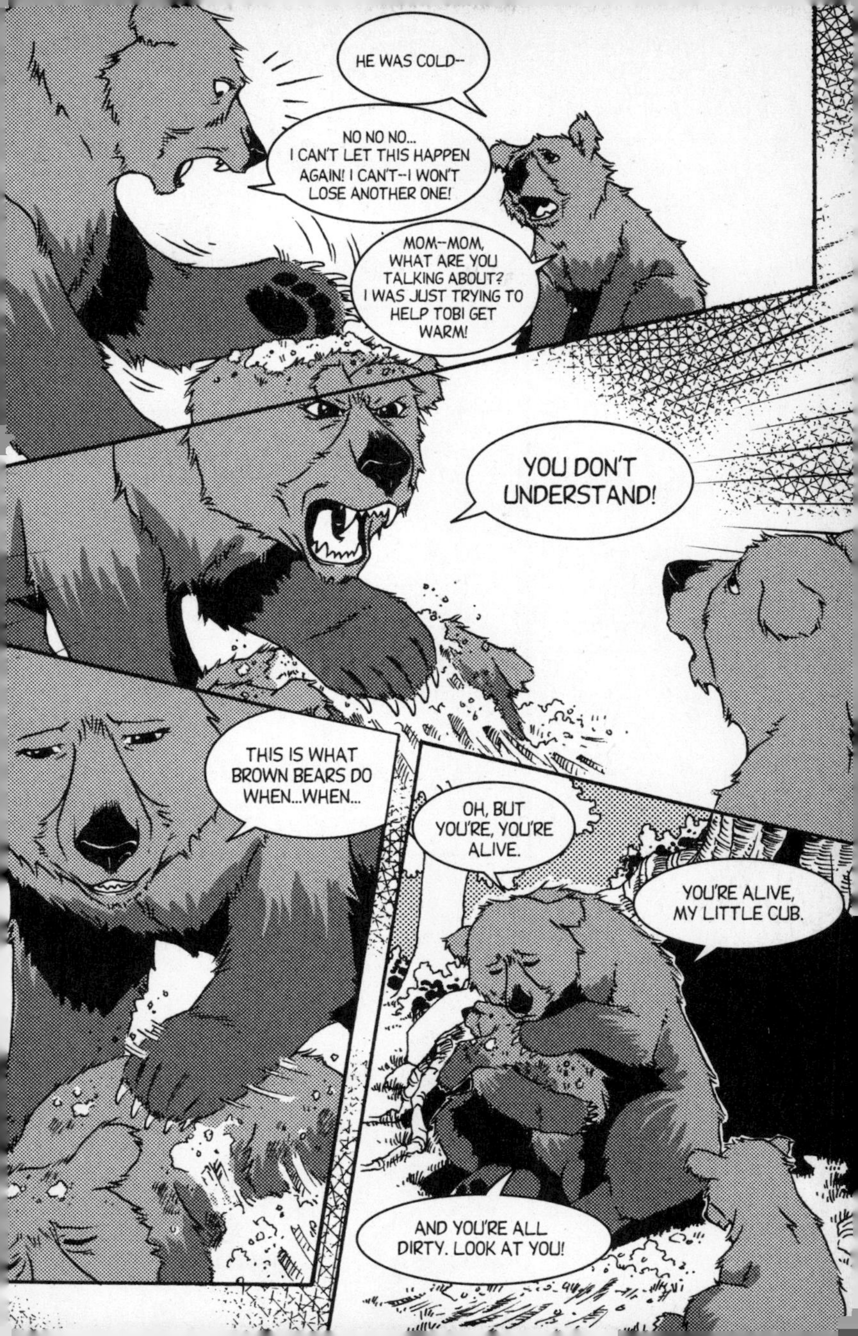
HE WAS COLD--
NO NO NO... I CAN'T LET THIS HAPPEN AGAIN! I CAN'T--I WON'T LOSE ANOTHER ONE!
MOM--MOM, WHAT ARE YOU TALKING ABOUT? I WAS JUST TRYING TO HELP TOBI GET WARM!
YOU DON'T UNDERSTAND!
THIS IS WHAT BROWN BEARS DO WHEN...WHEN...
OH, BUT YOU'RE, YOU'RE ALIVE.
YOU'RE ALIVE, MY LITTLE CUB.
AND YOU'RE ALL DIRTY. LOOK AT YOU!

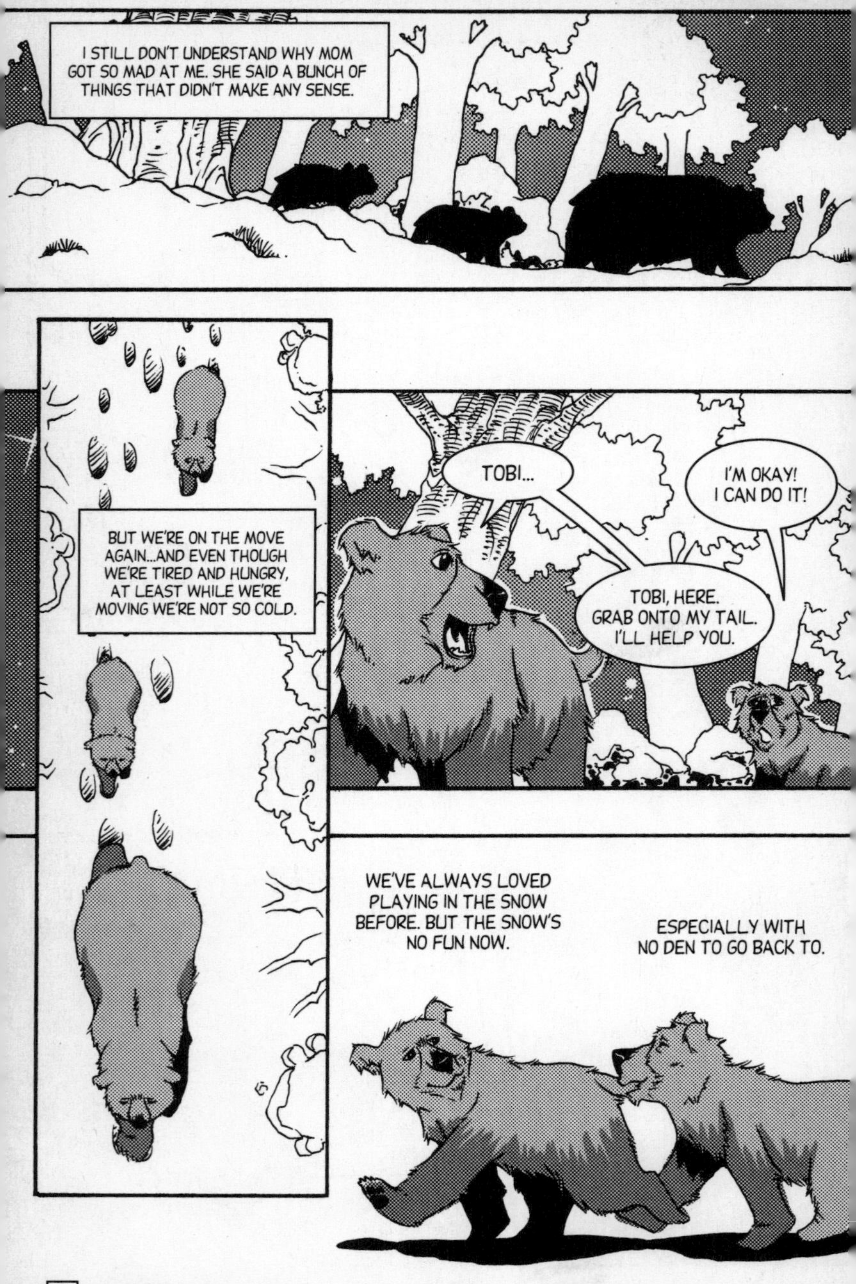

I STILL DON'T UNDERSTAND WHY MOM GOT SO MAD AT ME. SHE SAID A BUNCH OF THINGS THAT DIDN'T MAKE ANY SENSE.
BUT WE'RE ON THE MOVE AGAIN...AND EVEN THOUGH WE'RE TIRED AND HUNGRY, AT LEAST WHILE WE'RE MOVING WE'RE NOT SO COLD.
TOBI...
I'M OKAY! I CAN DO IT!
TOBI, HERE. GRAB ONTO MY TAIL. I'LL HELP YOU.
WE'VE ALWAYS LOVED PLAYING IN THE SNOW BEFORE. BUT THE SNOW'S NO FUN NOW.
ESPECIALLY WITH NO DEN TO GO BACK TO.

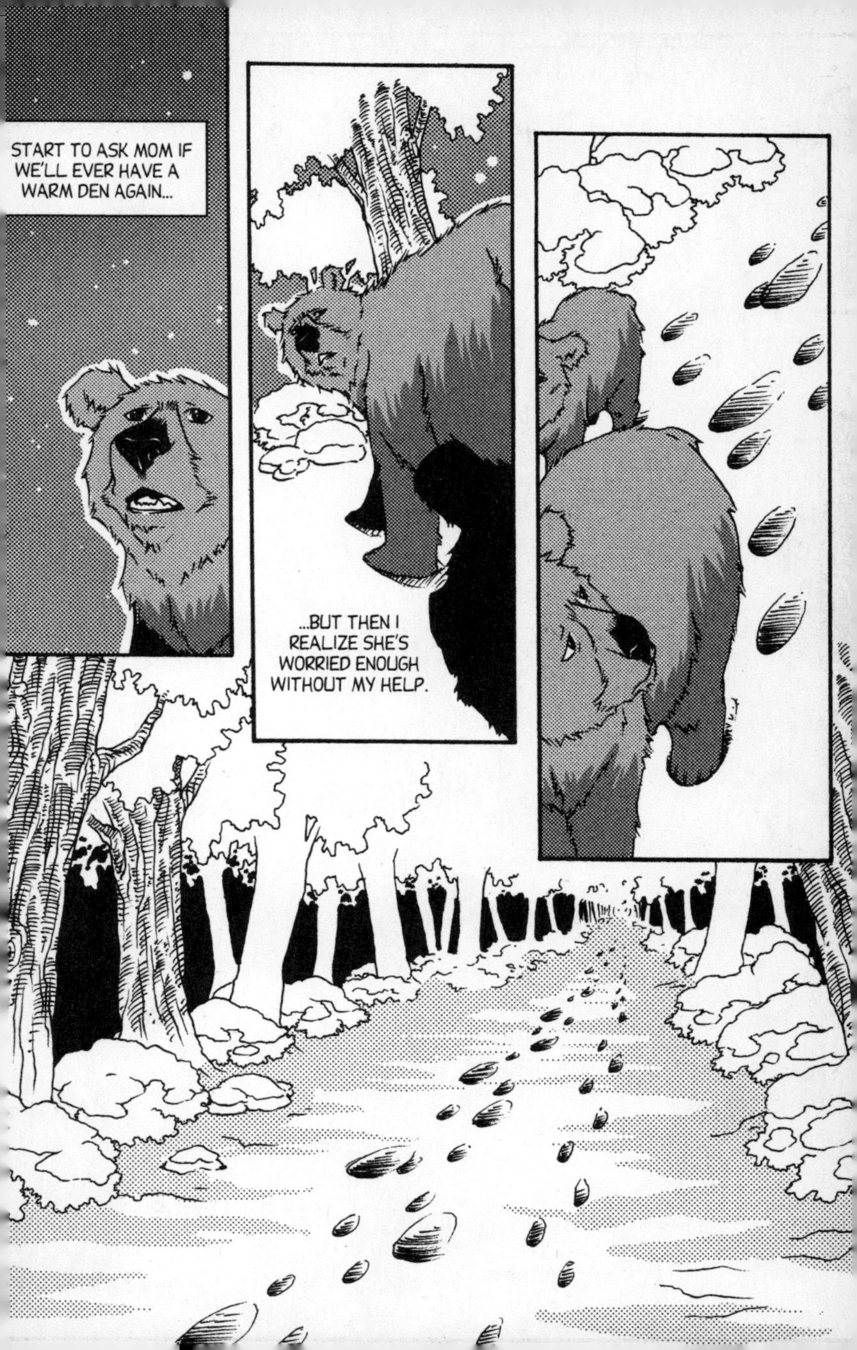
START TO ASK MOM IF WE'LL EVER HAVE A WARM DEN AGAIN...
...BUT THEN I REALIZE SHE'S WORRIED ENOUGH WITHOUT MY HELP.

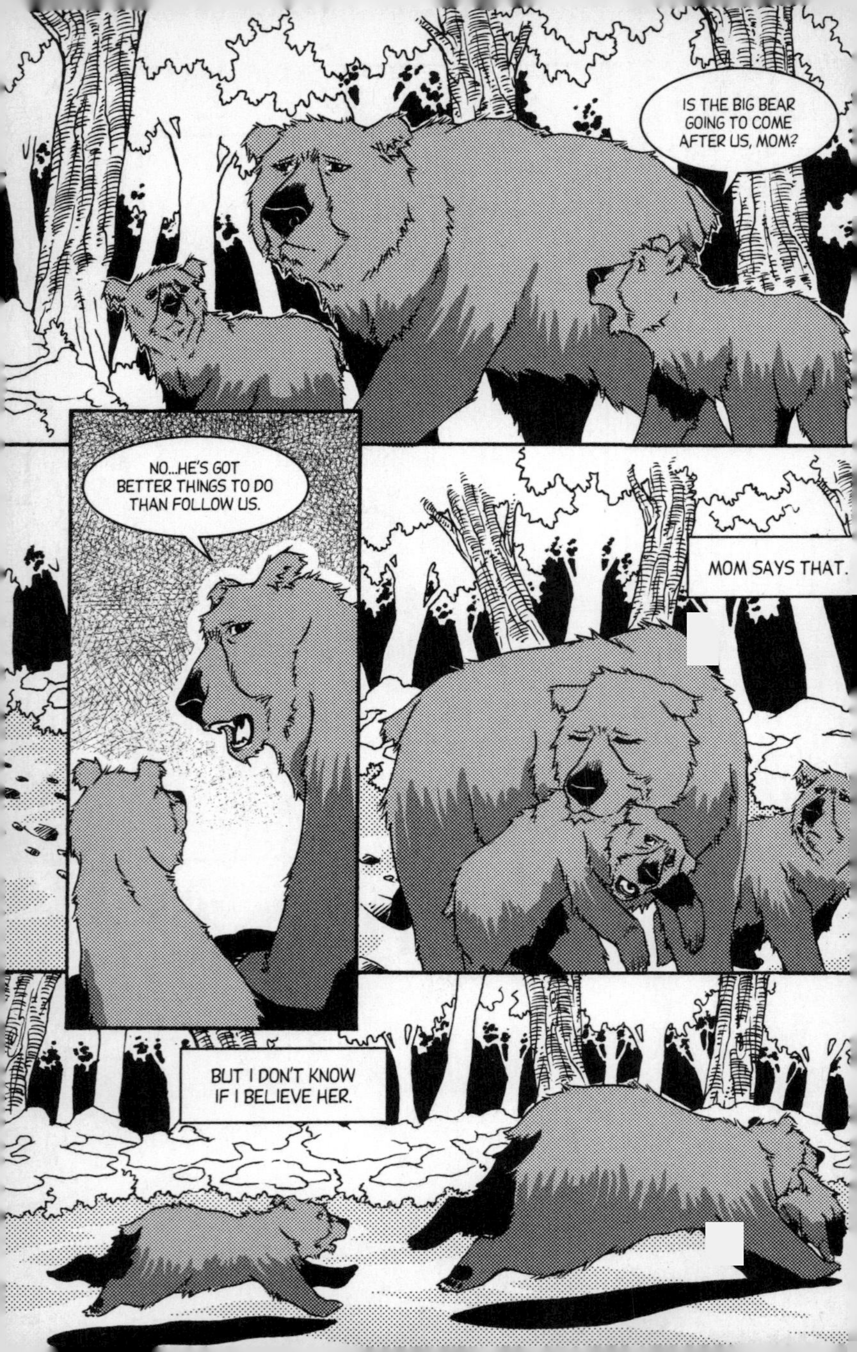
IS THE BIG BEAR GOING TO COME AFTER US, MOM?
NO...HE'S GOT BETTER THINGS TO DO THAN FOLLOW US.
MOM SAYS THAT.
BUT I DON'T KNOW IF I BELIEVE HER.

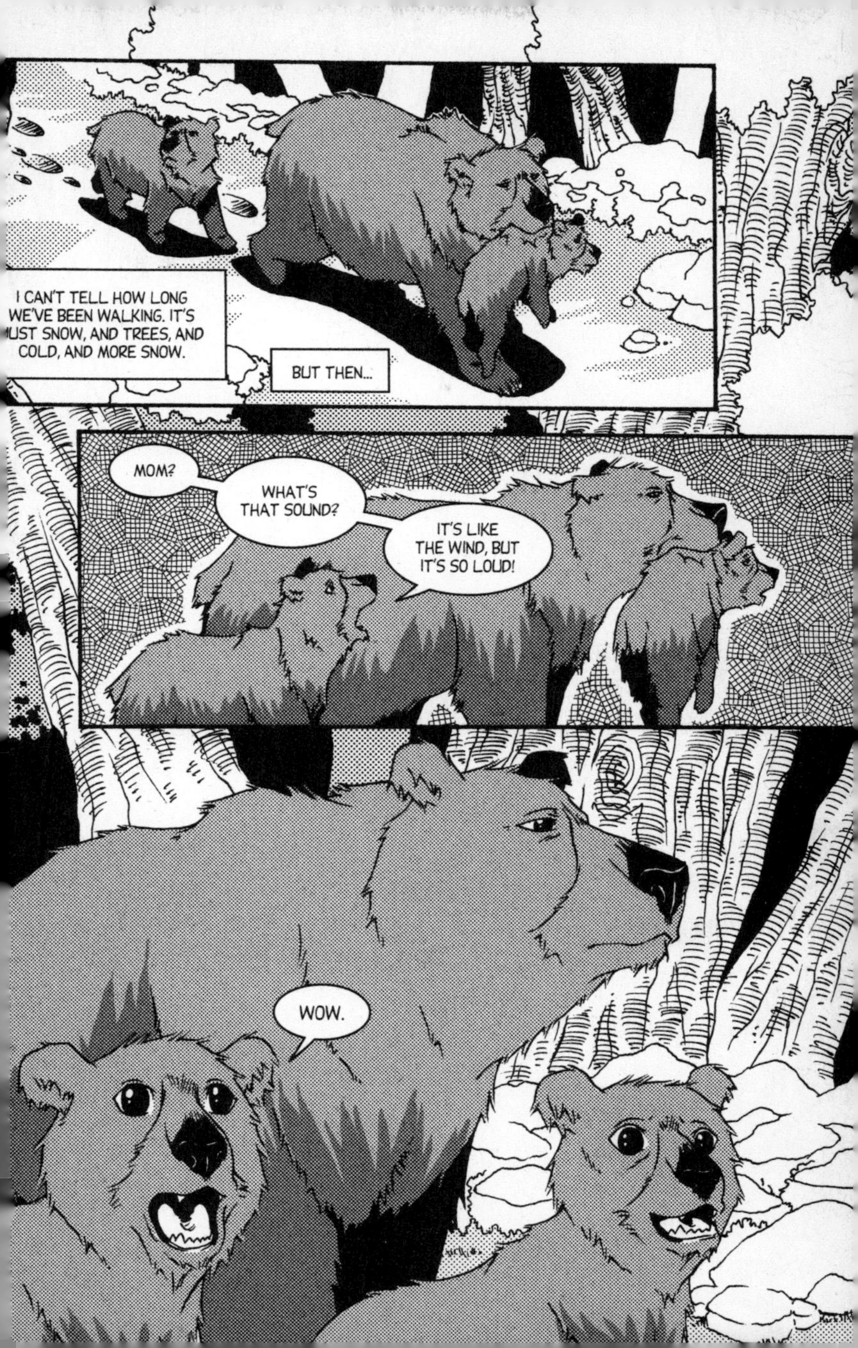
I CAN'T TELL HOW LONG WE'VE BEEN WALKING. IT'S JUST SNOW, AND TREES, AND COLD, AND MORE SNOW.
BUT THEN...
MOM?
WHAT'S THAT SOUND?
IT'S LIKE THE WIND, BUT IT'S SO LOUD!
WOW.

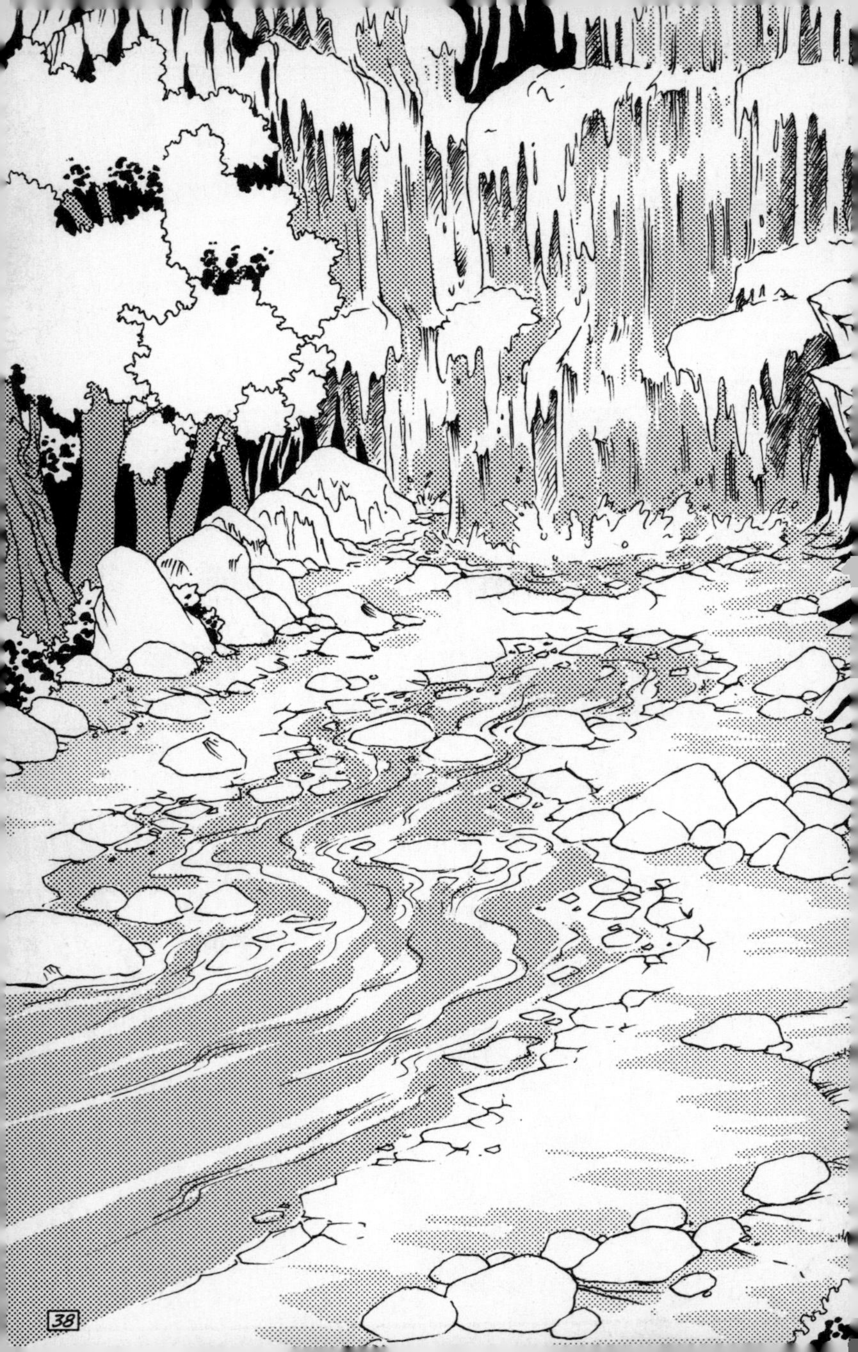

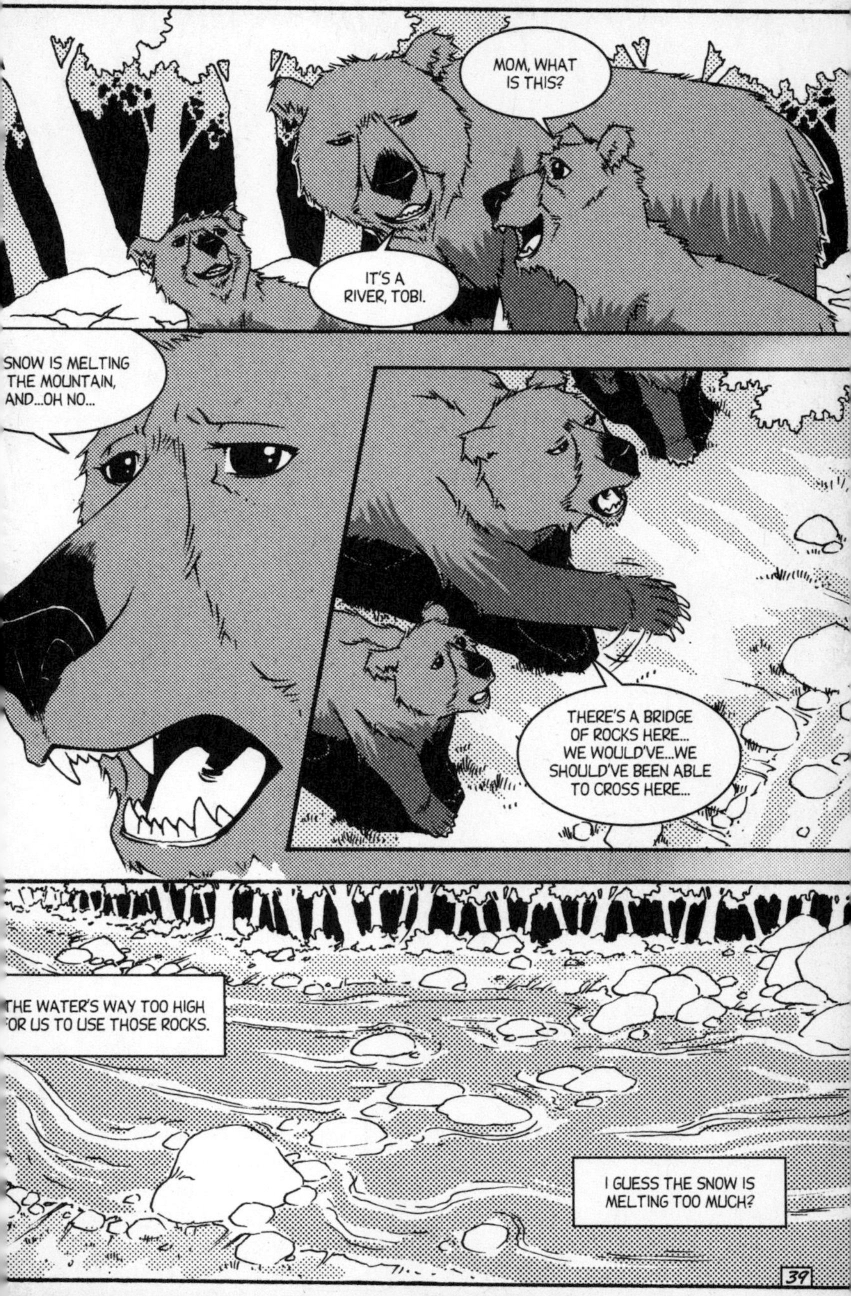
MOM, WHAT IS THIS?
IT'S A RIVER, TOBI.
SNOW IS MELTING THE MOUNTAIN, AND...OH NO...
THERE'S A BRIDGE OF ROCKS HERE... WE WOULD'VE...WE SHOULD'VE BEEN ABLE TO CROSS HERE...
THE WATER'S WAY TOO HIGH FOR US TO USE THOSE ROCKS.
I GUESS THE SNOW IS MELTING TOO MUCH?

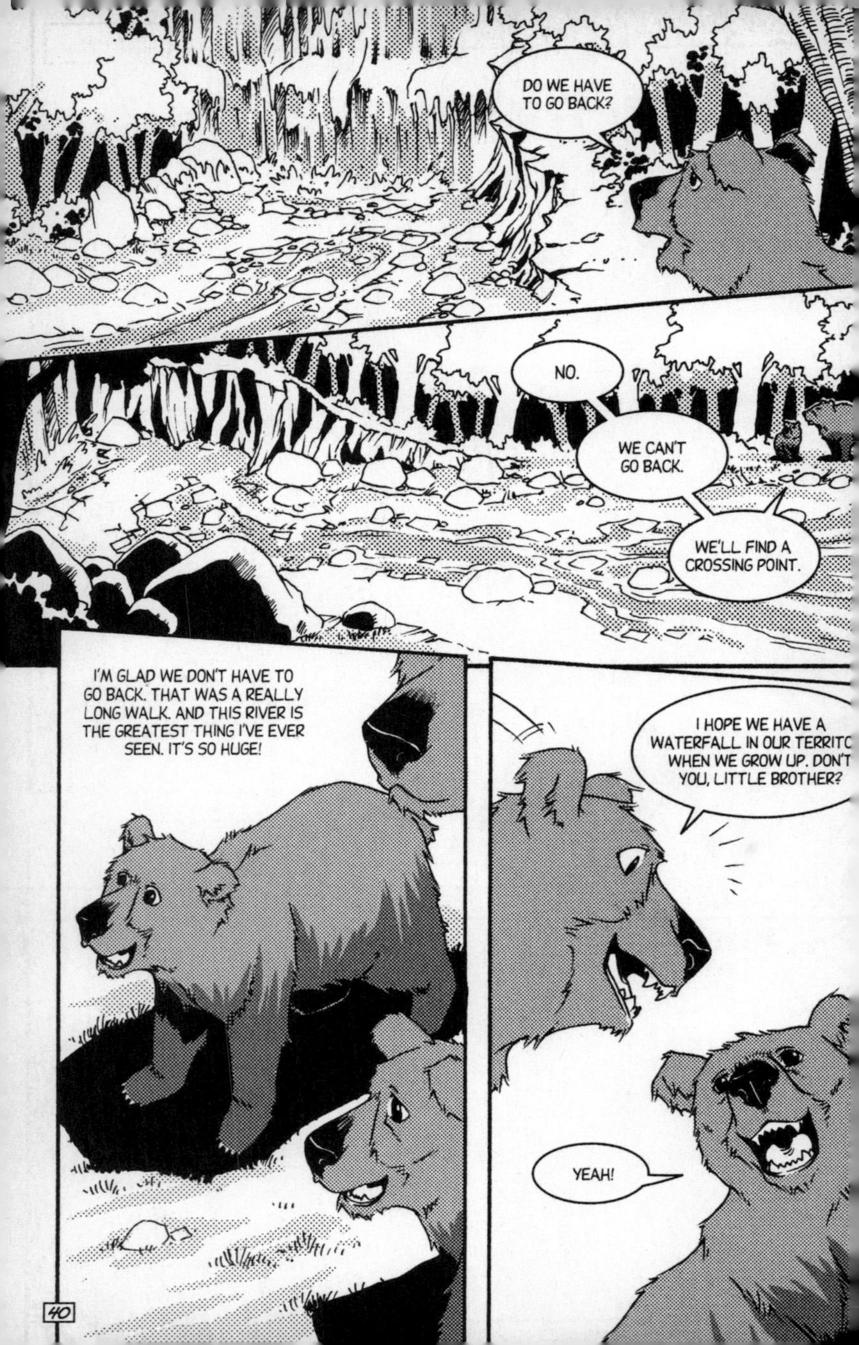
DO WE HAVE TO GO BACK?
NO.
WE CAN'T GO BACK.
WE'LL FIND A CROSSING POINT.
I'M GLAD WE DON'T HAVE TO GO BACK. THAT WAS A REALLY LONG WALK. AND THIS RIVER IS THE GREATEST THING I'VE EVER SEEN. IT'S SO HUGE!
I HOPE WE HAVE A WATERFALL IN OUR TERRITO WHEN WE GROW UP. DON'T YOU, LITTLE BROTHER?
YEAH!

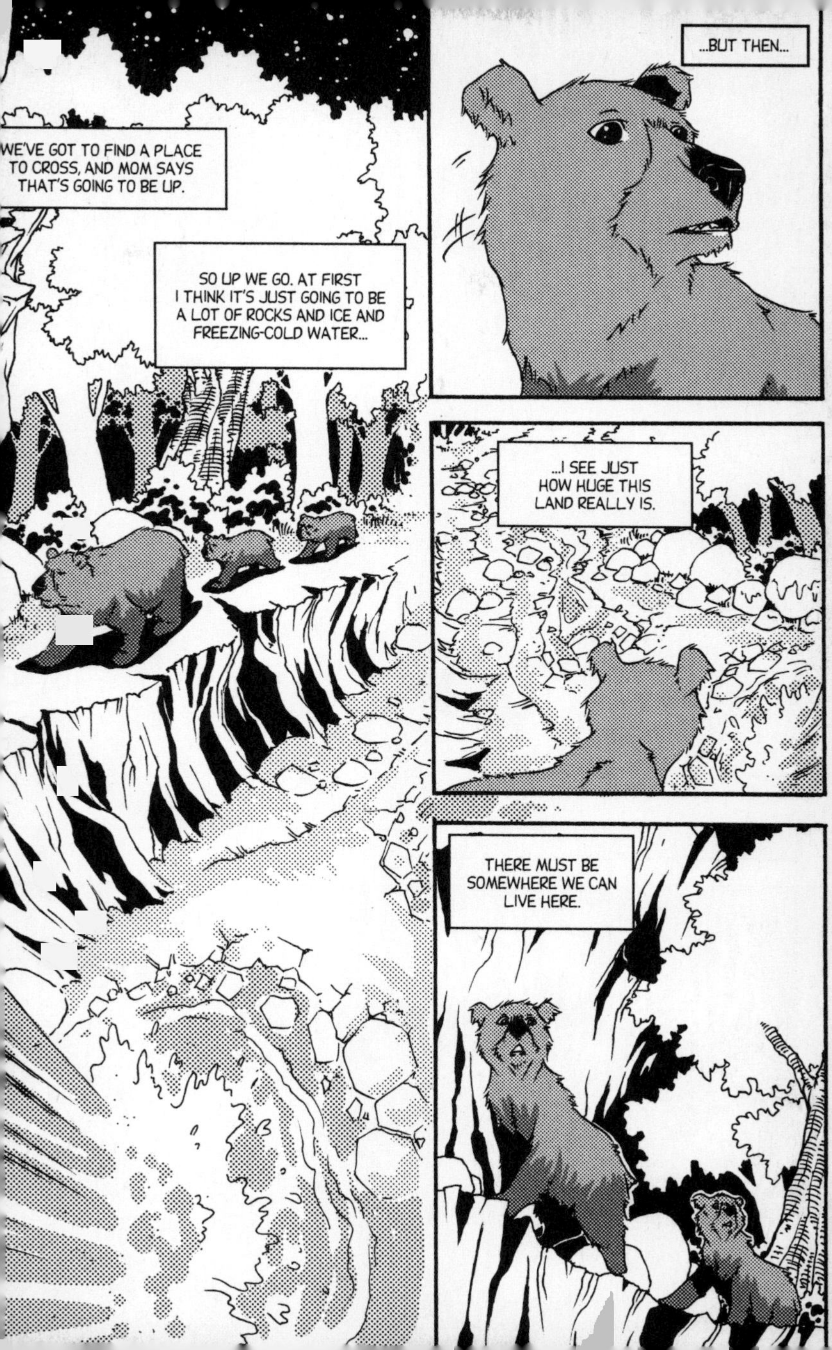
WE'VE GOT TO FIND A PLACE TO CROSS, AND MOM SAYS THAT'S GOING TO BE UP.
SO UP WE GO. AT FIRST I THINK IT'S JUST GOING TO BE A LOT OF ROCKS AND ICE AND FREEZING-COLD WATER...
...BUT THEN...
...I SEE JUST HOW HUGE THIS LAND REALLY IS.
THERE MUST BE SOMEWHERE WE CAN LIVE HERE.

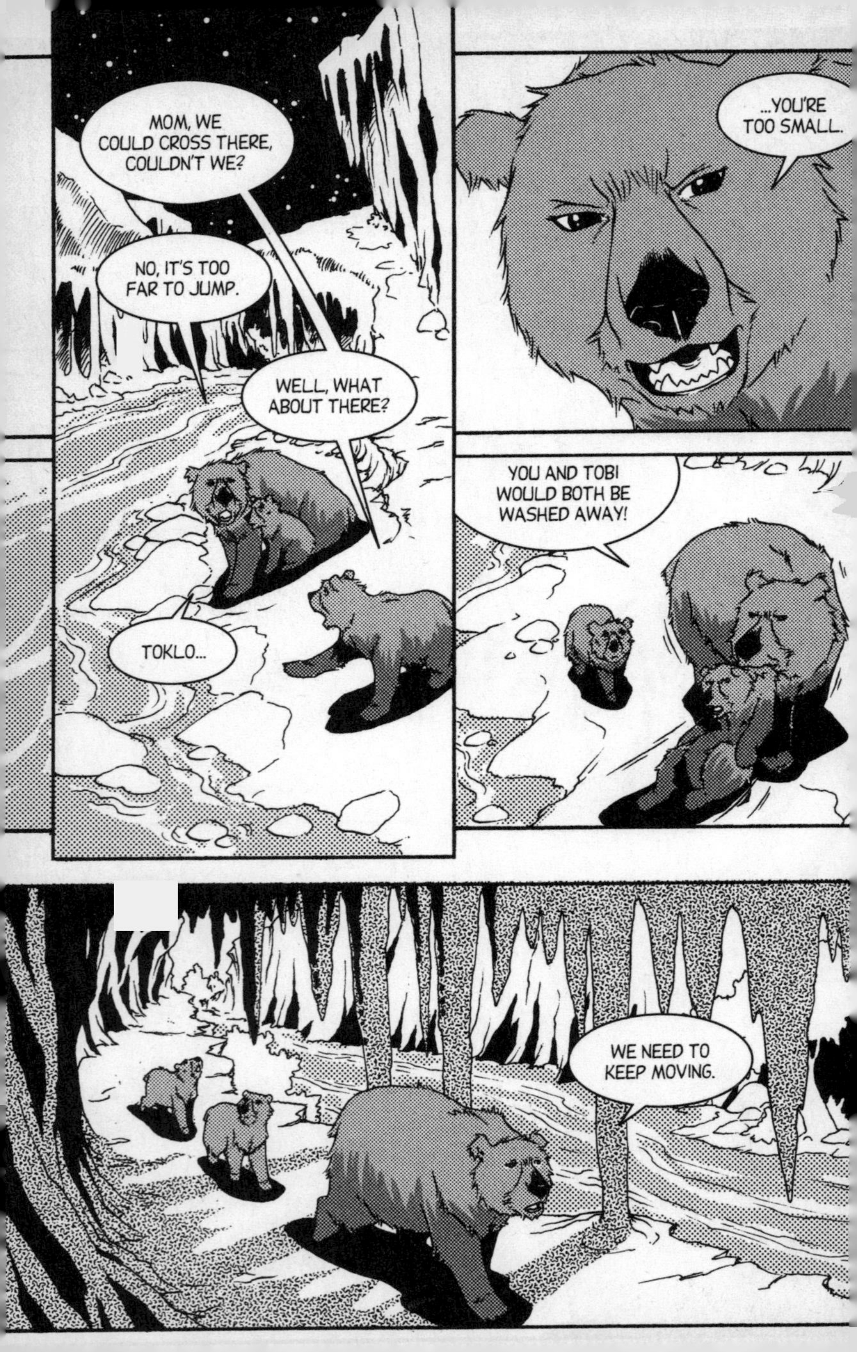
MOM, WE COULD CROSS THERE, COULDN'T WE?
NO, IT'S TOO FAR TO JUMP.
WELL, WHAT ABOUT THERE?
TOKLO...
...YOU'RE TOO SMALL.
YOU AND TOBI WOULD BOTH BE WASHED AWAY!
WE NEED TO KEEP MOVING.

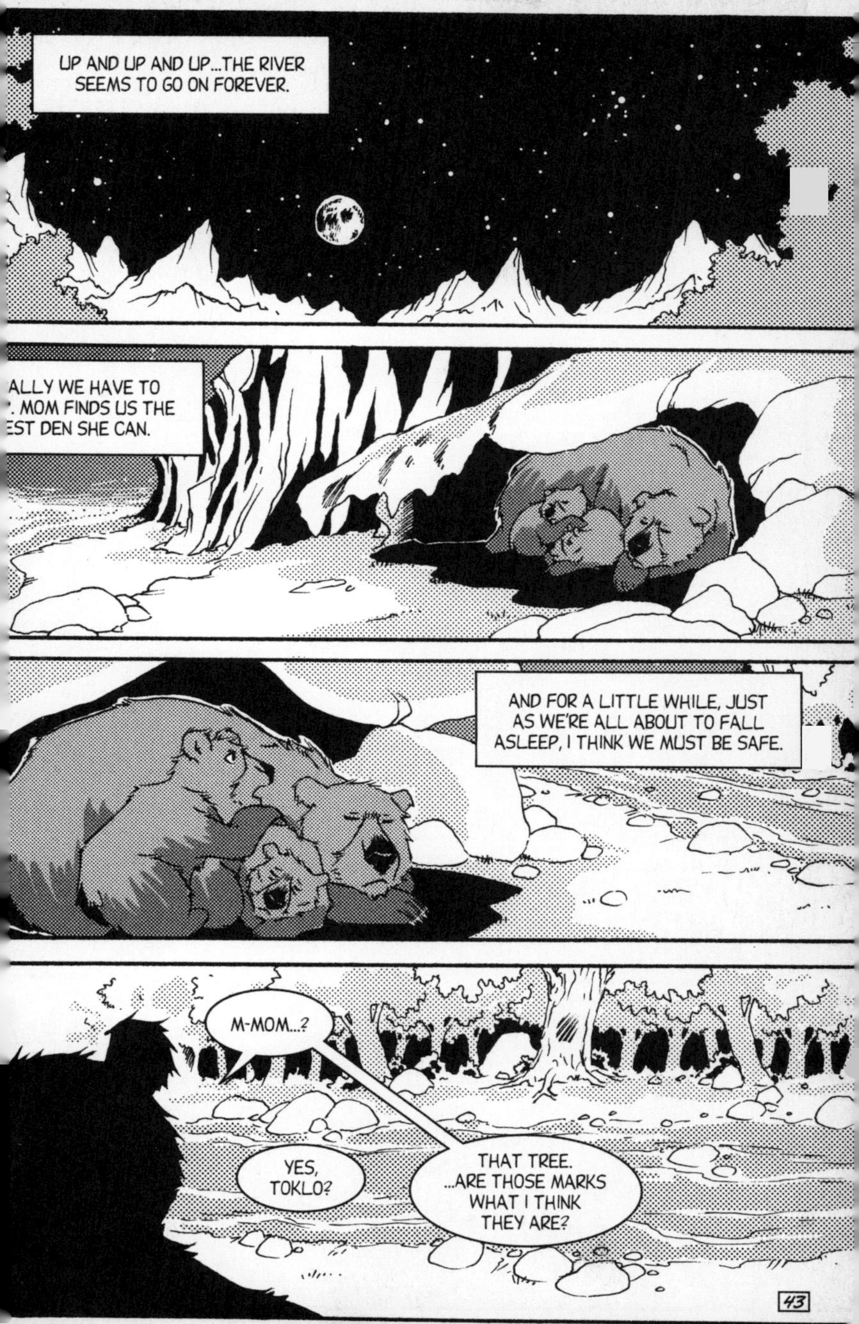
UP AND UP AND UP...THE RIVER SEEMS TO GO ON FOREVER.
ALLY WE HAVE TO
. MOM FINDS US THE
EST DEN SHE CAN.
AND FOR A LITTLE WHILE, JUST AS WE'RE ALL ABOUT TO FALL ASLEEP, I THINK WE MUST BE SAFE.
M-MOM...?
YES, TOKLO?
THAT TREE. ...ARE THOSE MARKS WHAT I THINK THEY ARE?

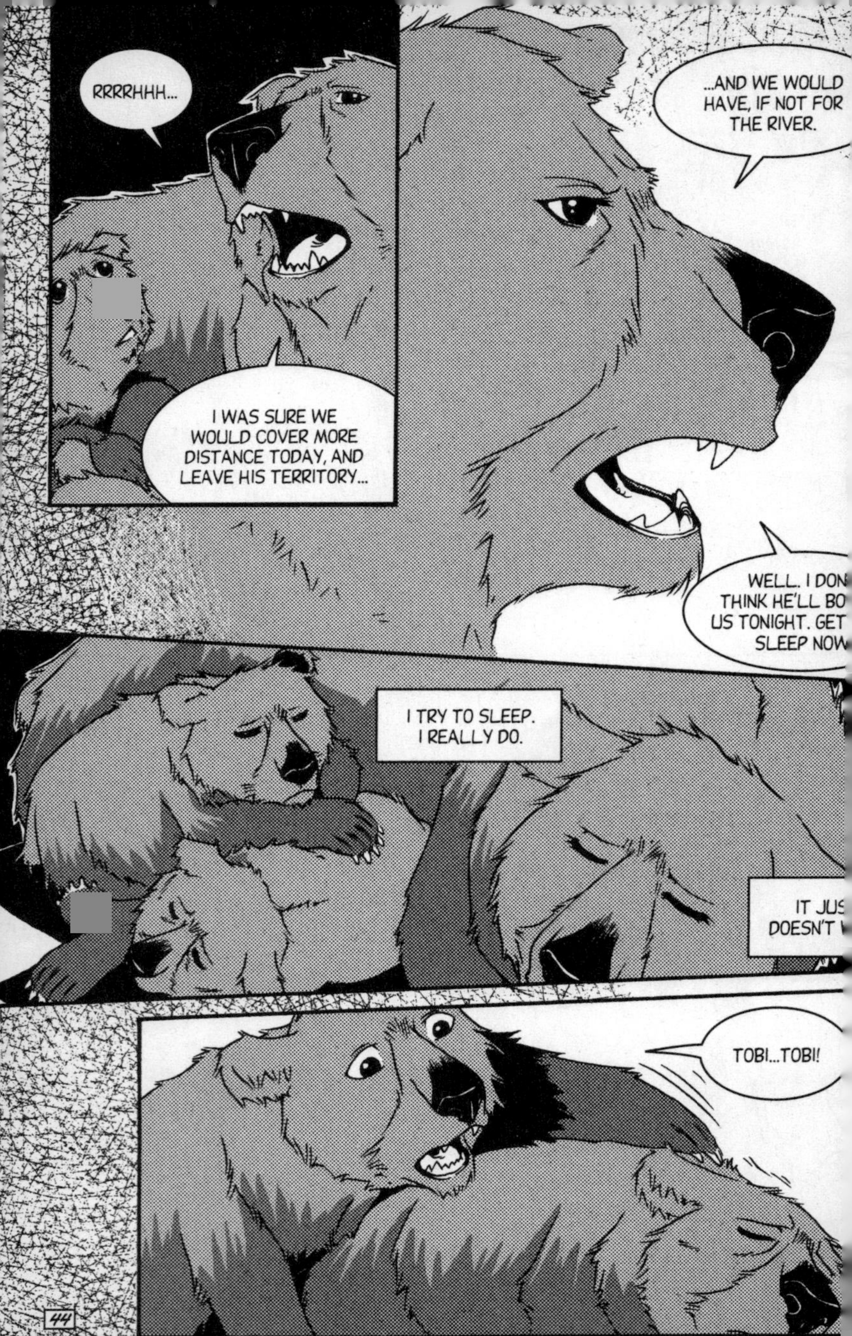
RRRRHHH...
I WAS SURE WE WOULD COVER MORE DISTANCE TODAY, AND LEAVE HIS TERRITORY...
...AND WE WOULD HAVE, IF NOT FOR THE RIVER.
WELL. I DON
THINK HE'LL BO
US TONIGHT. GET
SLEEP NOW
I TRY TO SLEEP. I REALLY DO.
IT JUS
DOESN'T
TOBI...TOBI!

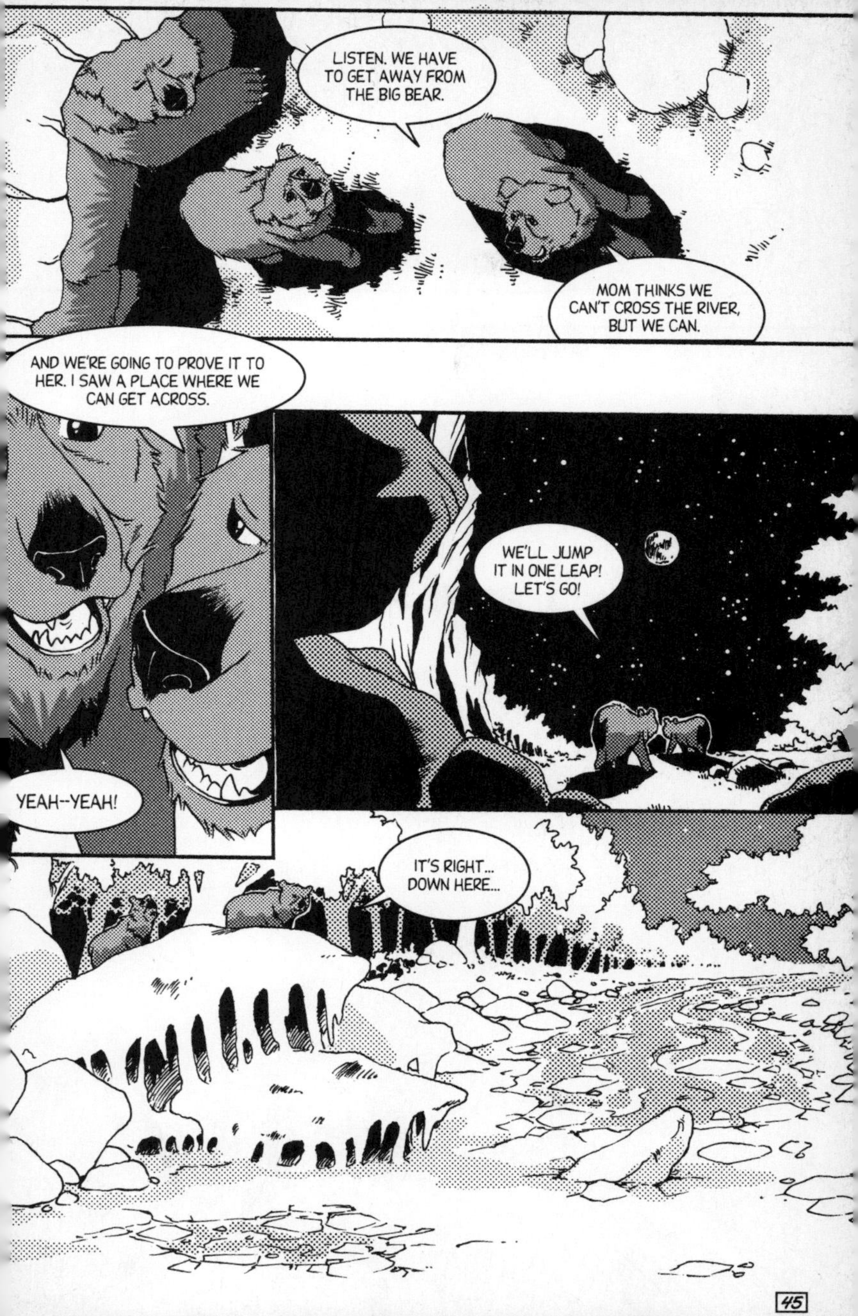
LISTEN. WE HAVE TO GET AWAY FROM THE BIG BEAR.
MOM THINKS WE CAN'T CROSS THE RIVER, BUT WE CAN.
AND WE'RE GOING TO PROVE IT TO HER. I SAW A PLACE WHERE WE CAN GET ACROSS.
YEAH--YEAH!
WE'LL JUMP IT IN ONE LEAP! LET'S GO!
IT'S RIGHT... DOWN HERE...

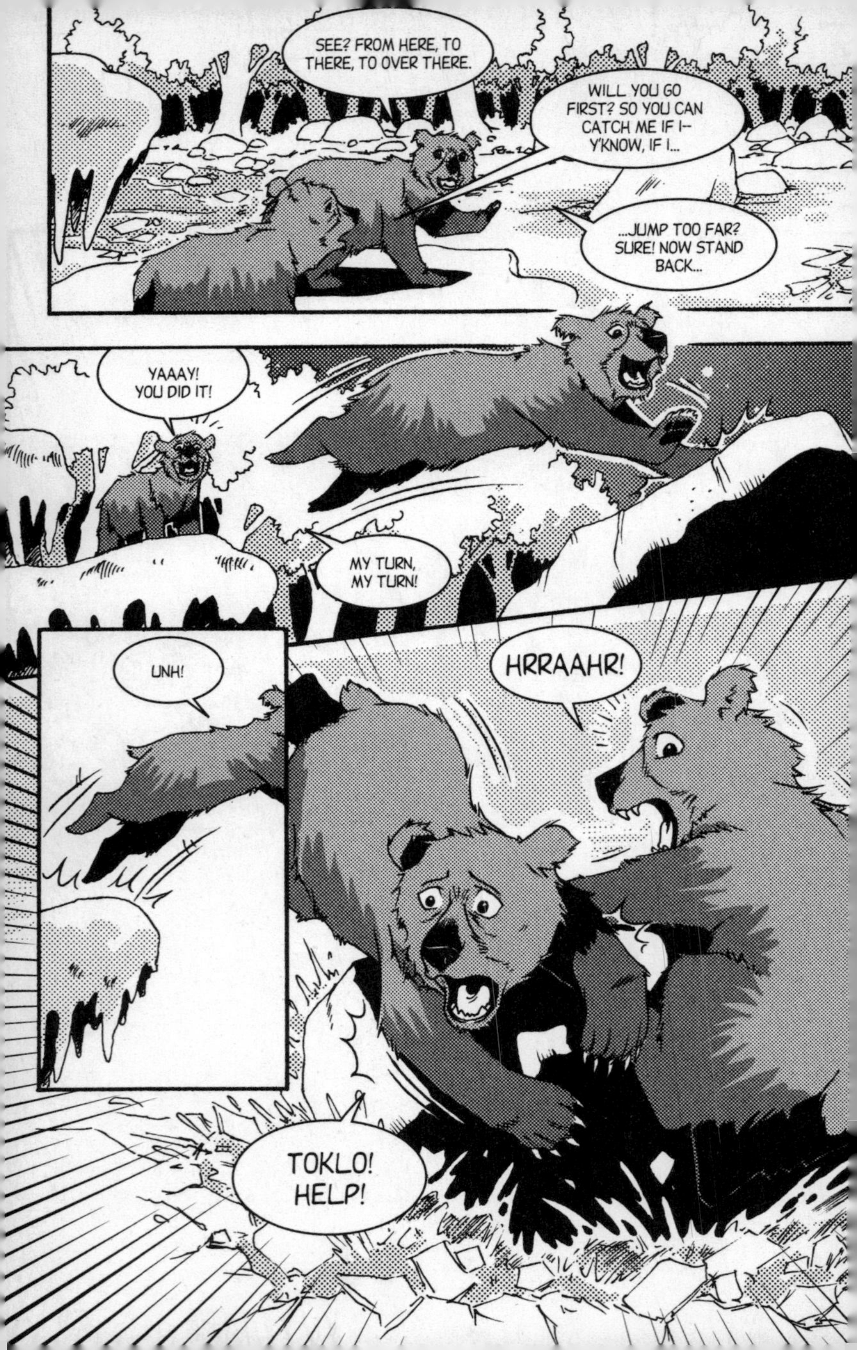

SEE? FROM HERE, TO THERE, TO OVER THERE.
WILL YOU GO FIRST? SO YOU CAN CATCH ME IF I-- Y'KNOW, IF I...
...JUMP TOO FAR? SURE! NOW STAND BACK...
YAAAY! YOU DID IT!
MY TURN, MY TURN!
UNH!
HRRAAHR!
TOKLO! HELP!

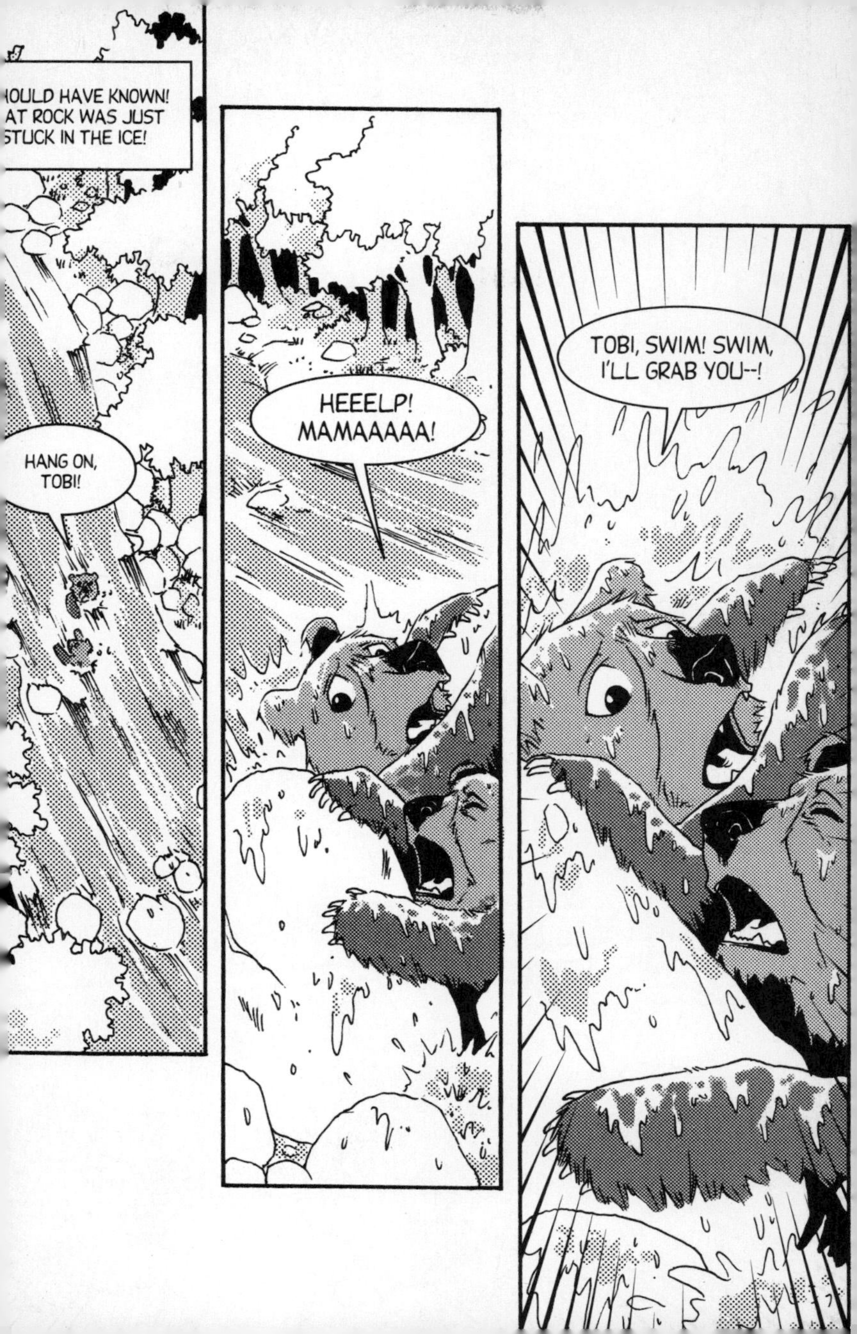

HOULD HAVE KNOWN!
AT ROCK WAS JUST
STUCK IN THE ICE!
HANG ON, TOBI!
HEEELP! MAMAAAAA!
TOBI, SWIM! SWIM, I'LL GRAB YOU--!

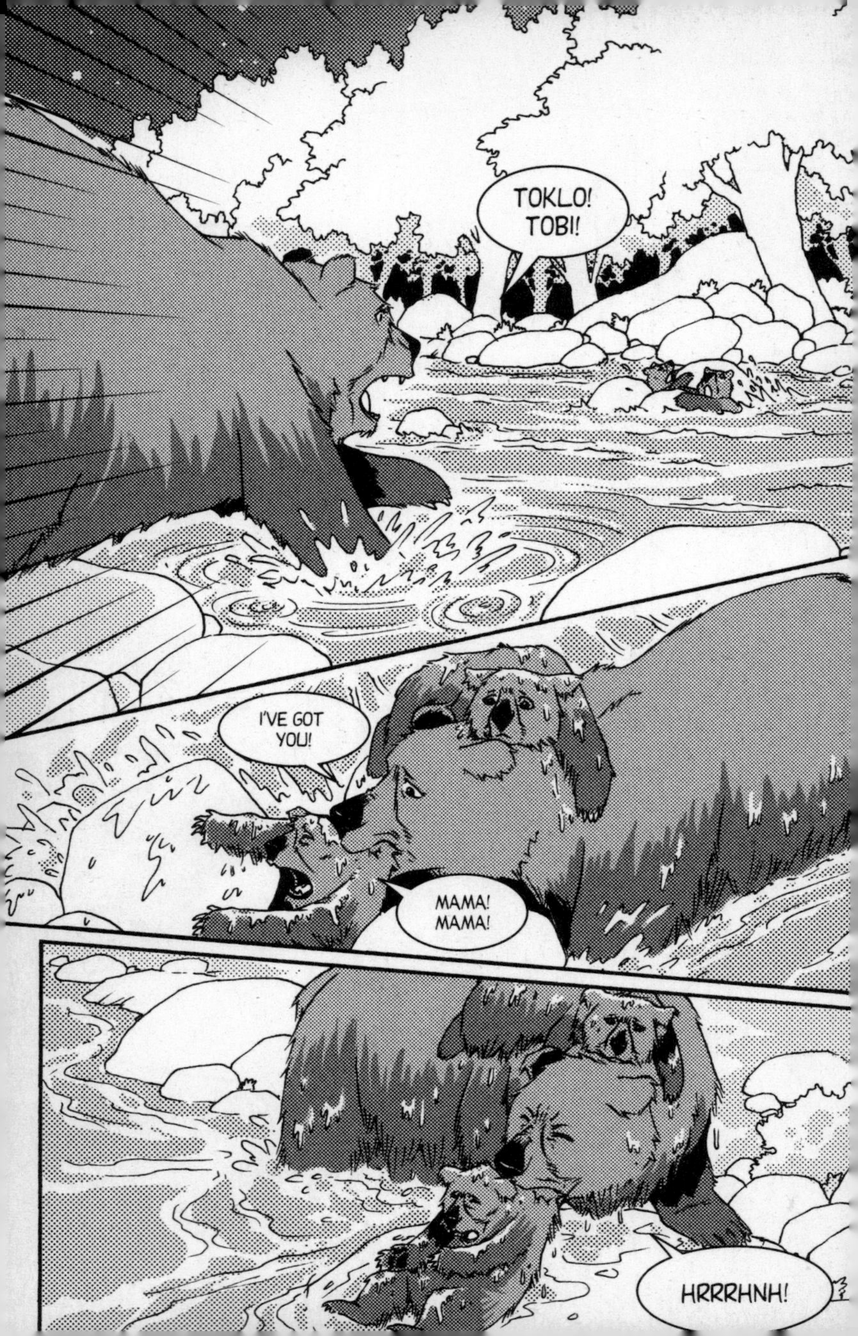
TOKLO! TOBI!
I'VE GOT YOU!
MAMA! MAMA!
HRRRHNH!

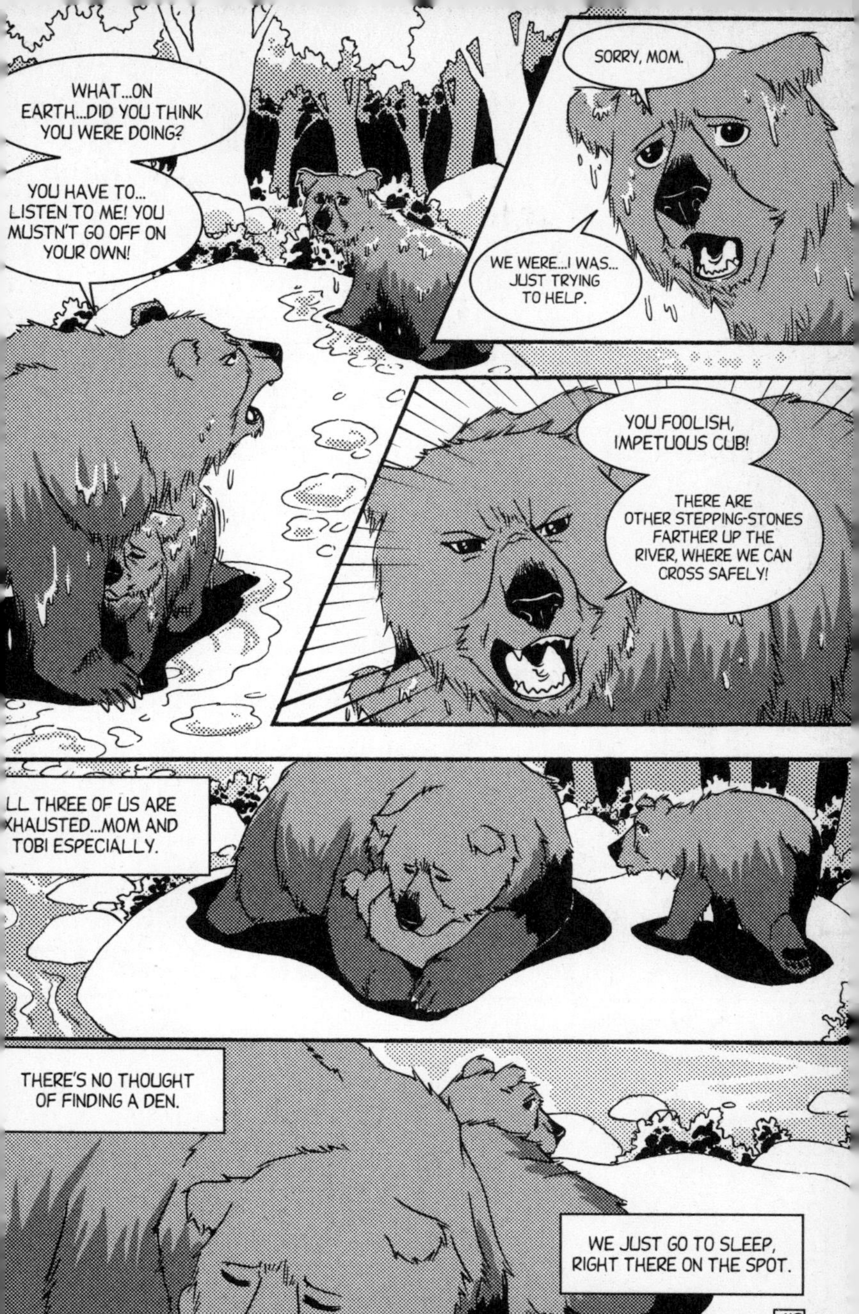
WHAT...ON EARTH...DID YOU THINK YOU WERE DOING?
YOU HAVE TO... LISTEN TO ME! YOU MUSTN'T GO OFF ON YOUR OWN!
SORRY, MOM.
WE WERE...I WAS... JUST TRYING TO HELP.
YOU FOOLISH, IMPETUOUS CUB!
THERE ARE OTHER STEPPING-STONES FARTHER UP THE RIVER, WHERE WE CAN CROSS SAFELY!
LL THREE OF US ARE XHAUSTED...MOM AND TOBI ESPECIALLY.
THERE'S NO THOUGHT OF FINDING A DEN.
WE JUST GO TO SLEEP, RIGHT THERE ON THE SPOT.

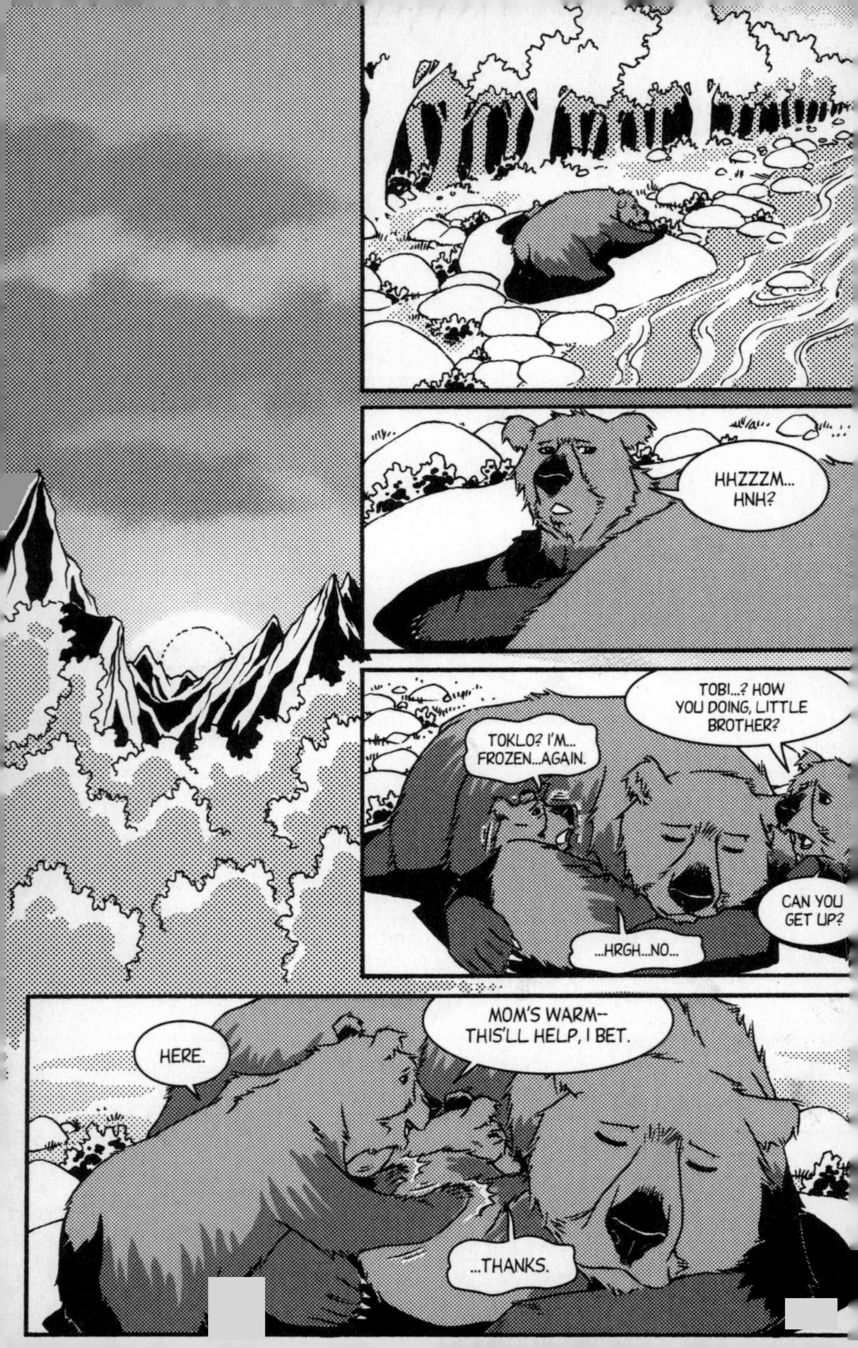
HHZZZM...
HNH?
TOBI...? HOW YOU DOING, LITTLE BROTHER?
TOKLO? I'M... FROZEN...AGAIN.
CAN YOU GET UP?
...HRGH...NO...
HERE.
MOM'S WARM-- THIS'LL HELP, I BET.
...THANKS.

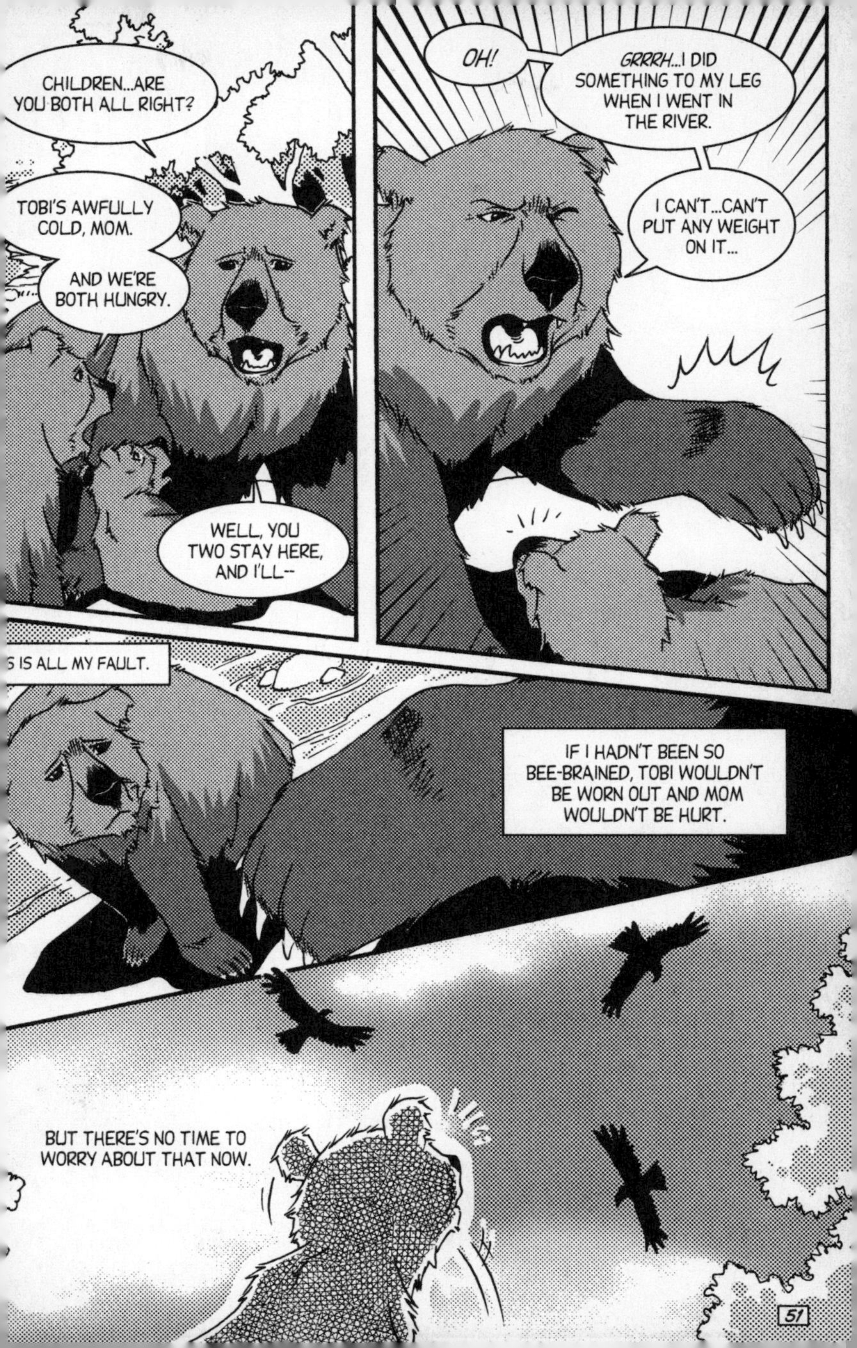
CHILDREN...ARE YOU BOTH ALL RIGHT?
TOBI'S AWFULLY COLD, MOM.
AND WE'RE BOTH HUNGRY.
WELL, YOU TWO STAY HERE, AND I'LL--
OH!
GRRRH...I DID SOMETHING TO MY LEG WHEN I WENT IN THE RIVER.
I CAN'T...CAN'T PUT ANY WEIGHT ON IT...
S IS ALL MY FAULT.
IF I HADN'T BEEN SO BEE-BRAINED, TOBI WOULDN'T BE WORN OUT AND MOM WOULDN'T BE HURT.
BUT THERE'S NO TIME TO WORRY ABOUT THAT NOW.

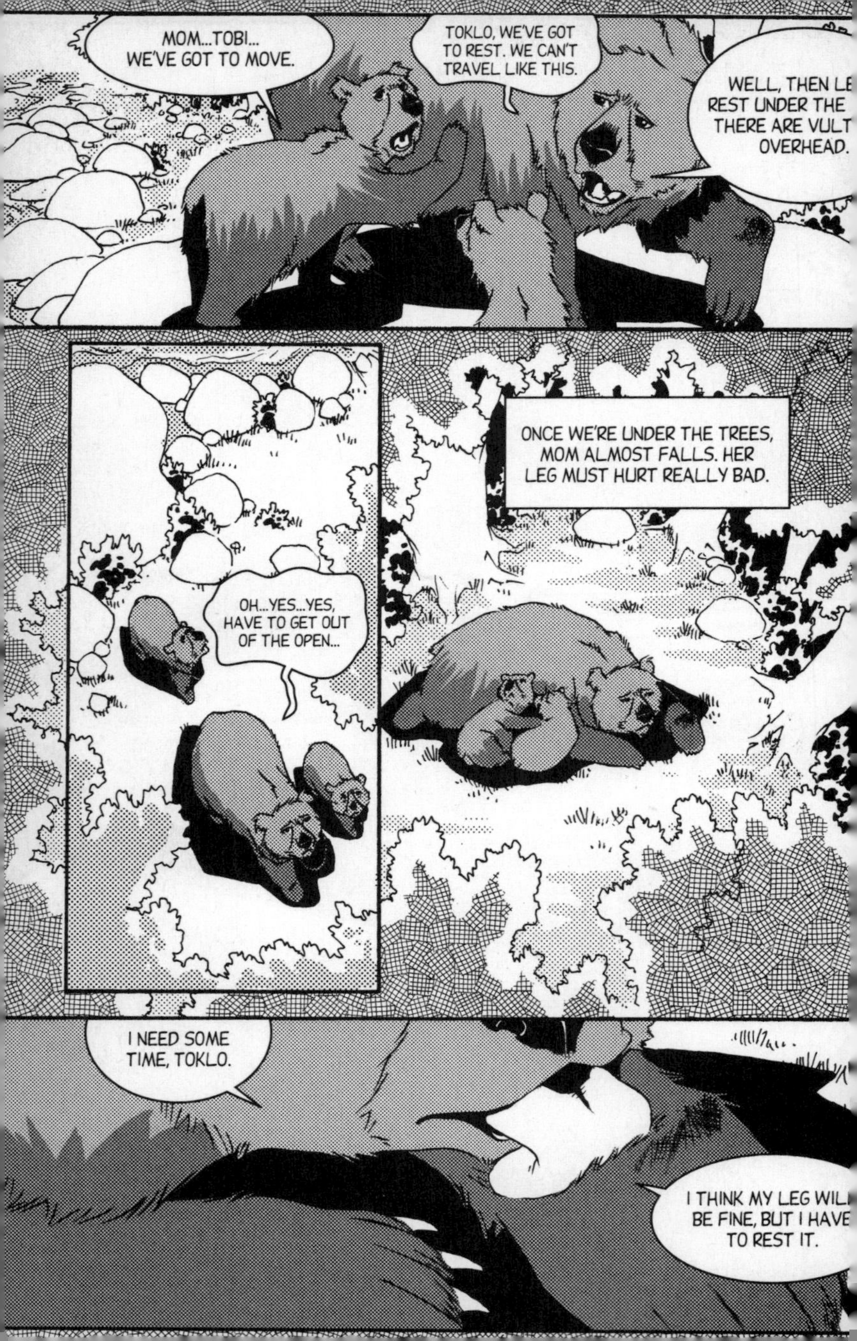
MOM...TOBI... WE'VE GOT TO MOVE.
TOKLO, WE'VE GOT TO REST. WE CAN'T TRAVEL LIKE THIS.
WELL, THEN LE REST UNDER THE THERE ARE VULT OVERHEAD.
OH...YES...YES, HAVE TO GET OUT OF THE OPEN...
ONCE WE'RE UNDER THE TREES, MOM ALMOST FALLS. HER LEG MUST HURT REALLY BAD.
I NEED SOME TIME, TOKLO.
I THINK MY LEG WIL BE FINE, BUT I HAVE TO REST IT.

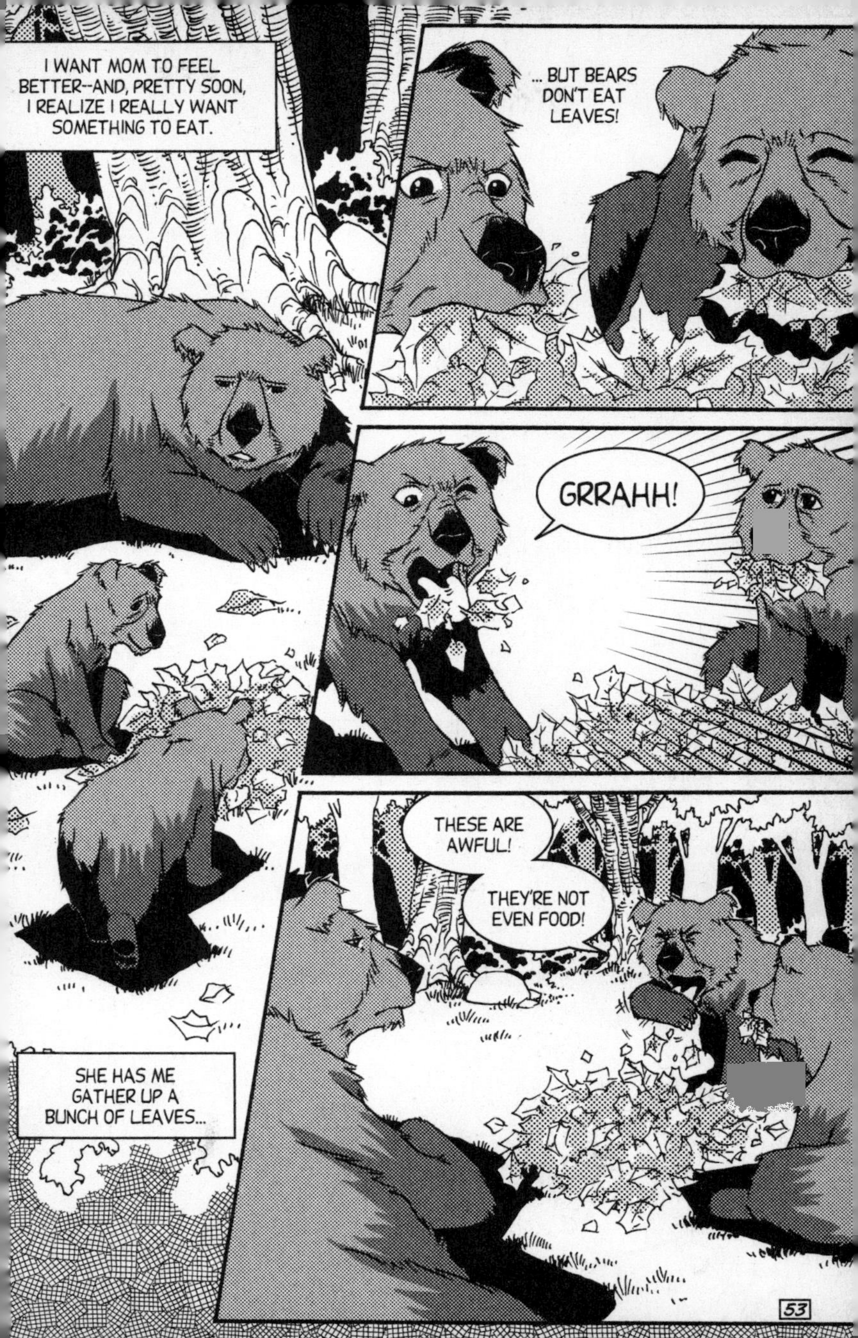
I WANT MOM TO FEEL BETTER--AND, PRETTY SOON, I REALIZE I REALLY WANT SOMETHING TO EAT.
SHE HAS ME GATHER UP A BUNCH OF LEAVES...
... BUT BEARS DON'T EAT LEAVES!
GRRAHH!
THESE ARE AWFUL!
THEY'RE NOT EVEN FOOD!

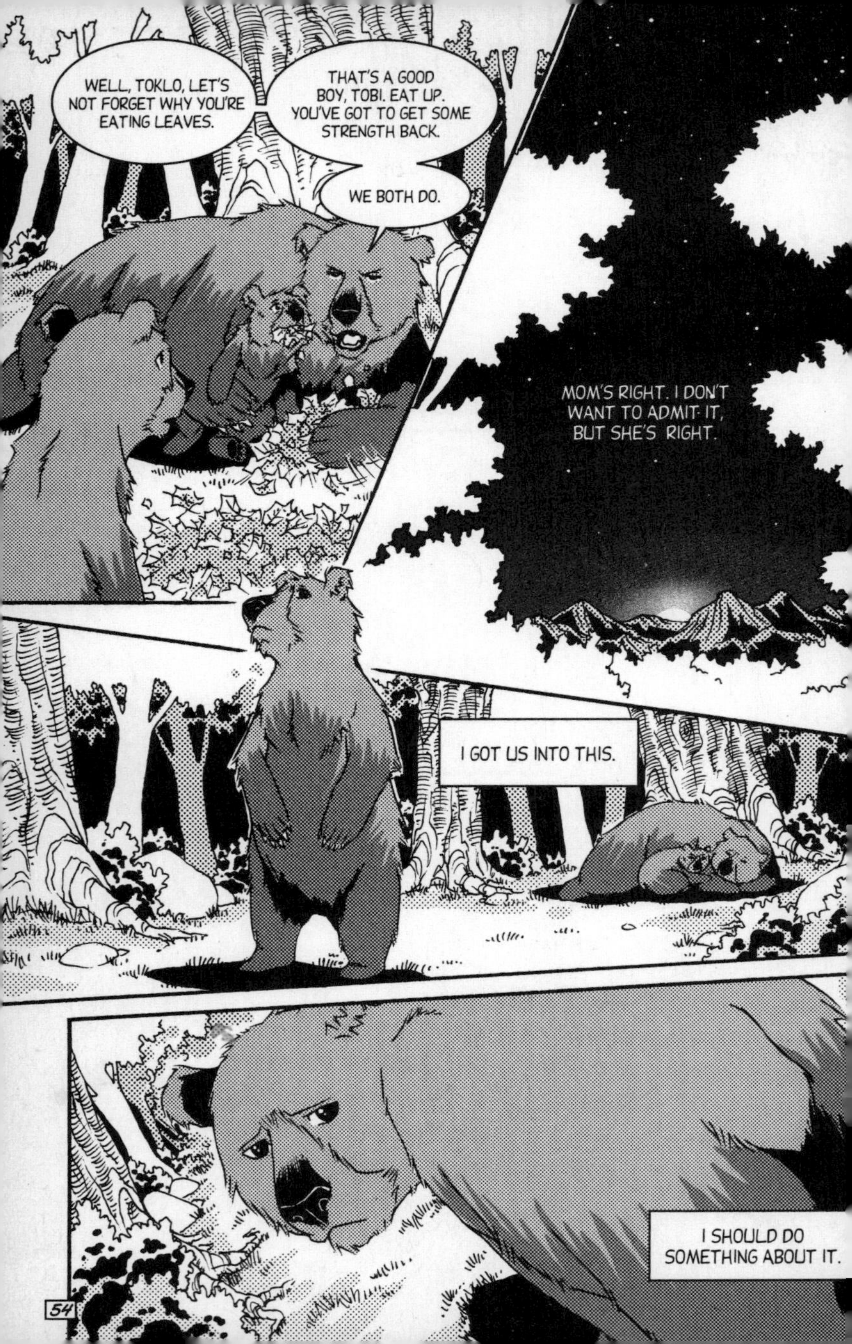
WELL, TOKLO, LET'S NOT FORGET WHY YOU'RE EATING LEAVES.
THAT'S A GOOD BOY, TOBI. EAT UP. YOU'VE GOT TO GET SOME STRENGTH BACK.
WE BOTH DO.
MOM'S RIGHT. I DON'T WANT TO ADMIT IT, BUT SHE'S RIGHT.
I GOT US INTO THIS.
I SHOULD DO SOMETHING ABOUT IT.

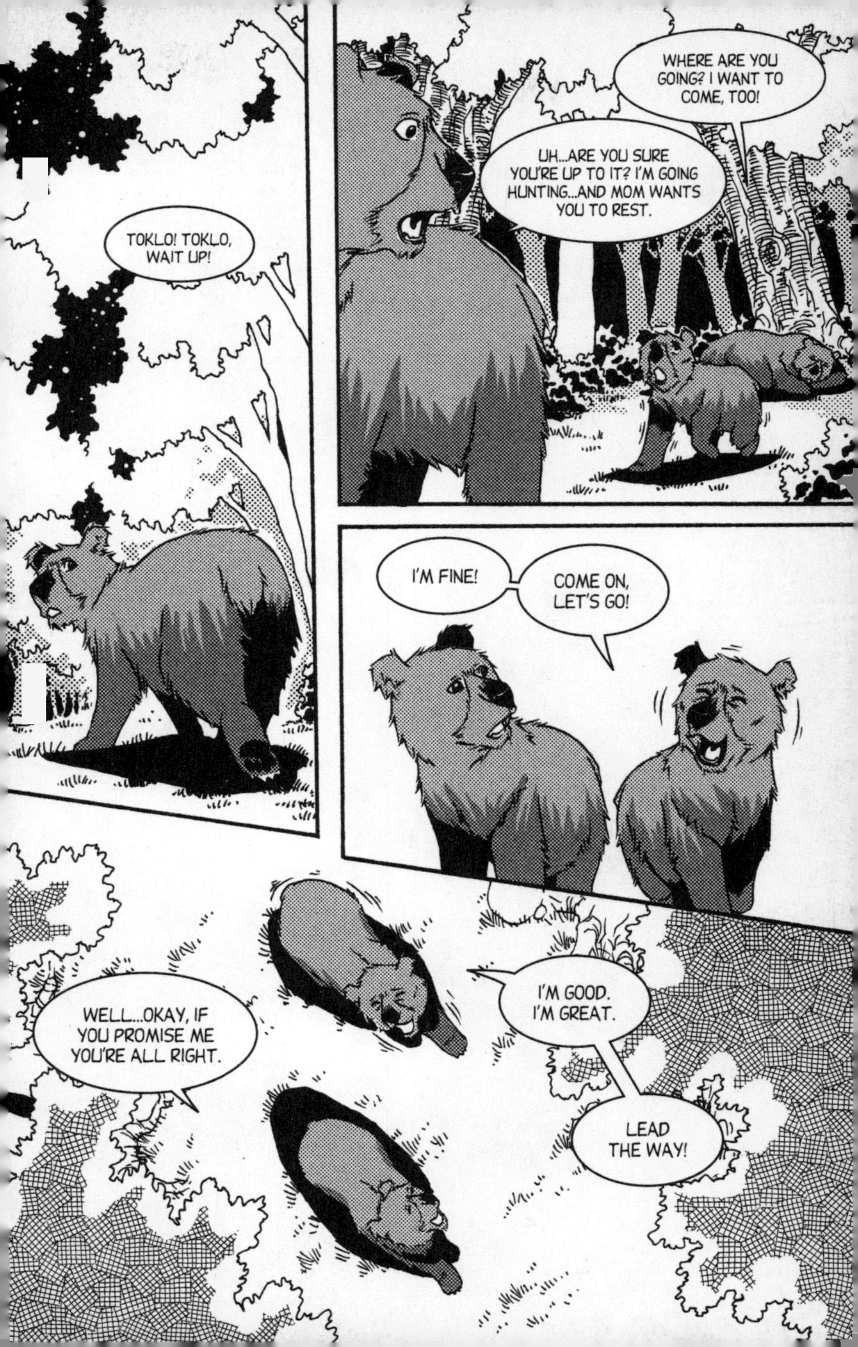
TOKLO! TOKLO, WAIT UP!
WHERE ARE YOU GOING? I WANT TO COME, TOO!
UH...ARE YOU SURE YOU'RE UP TO IT? I'M GOING HUNTING...AND MOM WANTS YOU TO REST.
I'M FINE!
COME ON, LET'S GO!
WELL...OKAY, IF YOU PROMISE ME YOU'RE ALL RIGHT.
I'M GOOD. I'M GREAT.
LEAD THE WAY!

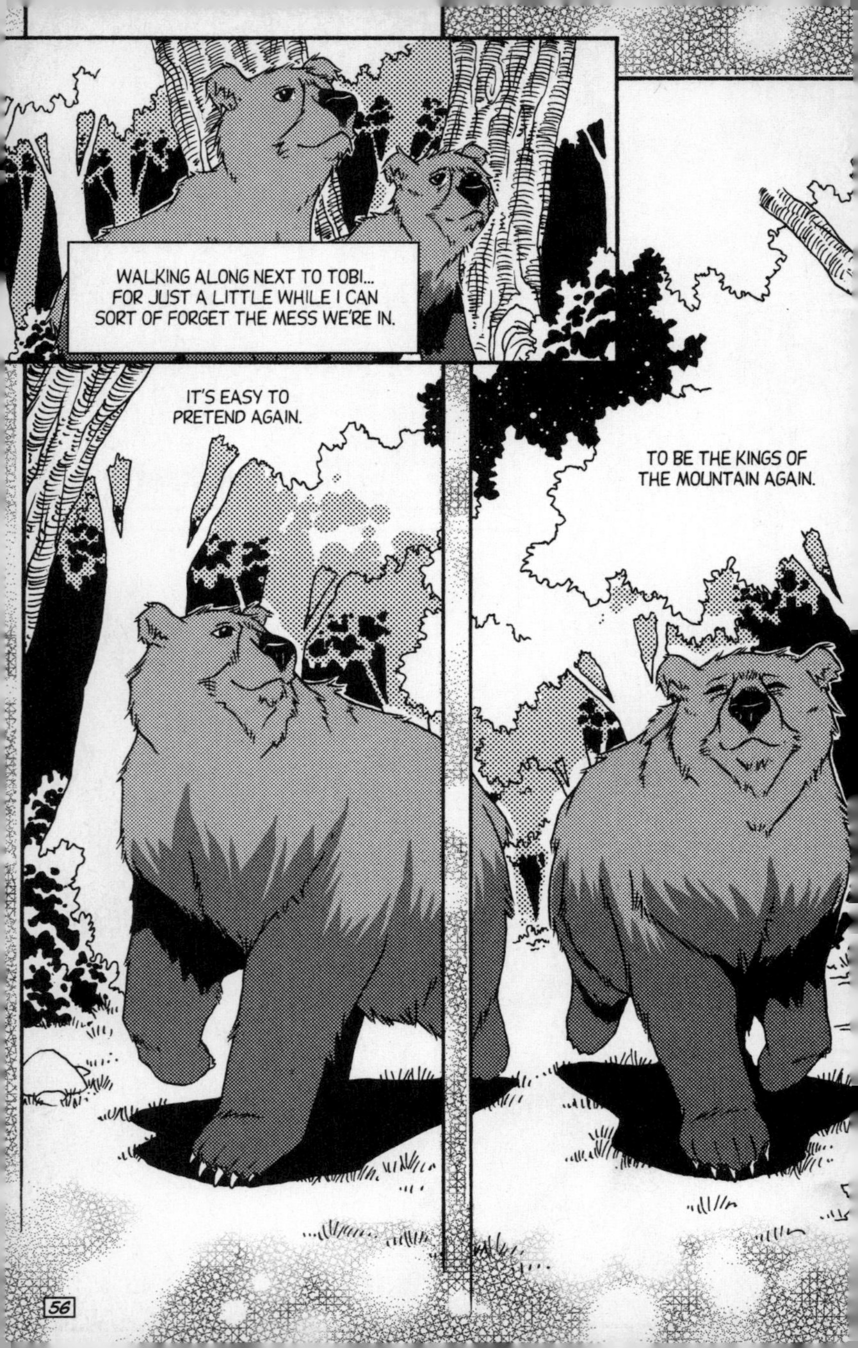
WALKING ALONG NEXT TO TOBI... FOR JUST A LITTLE WHILE I CAN SORT OF FORGET THE MESS WE'RE IN.
IT'S EASY TO PRETEND AGAIN.
TO BE THE KINGS OF THE MOUNTAIN AGAIN.

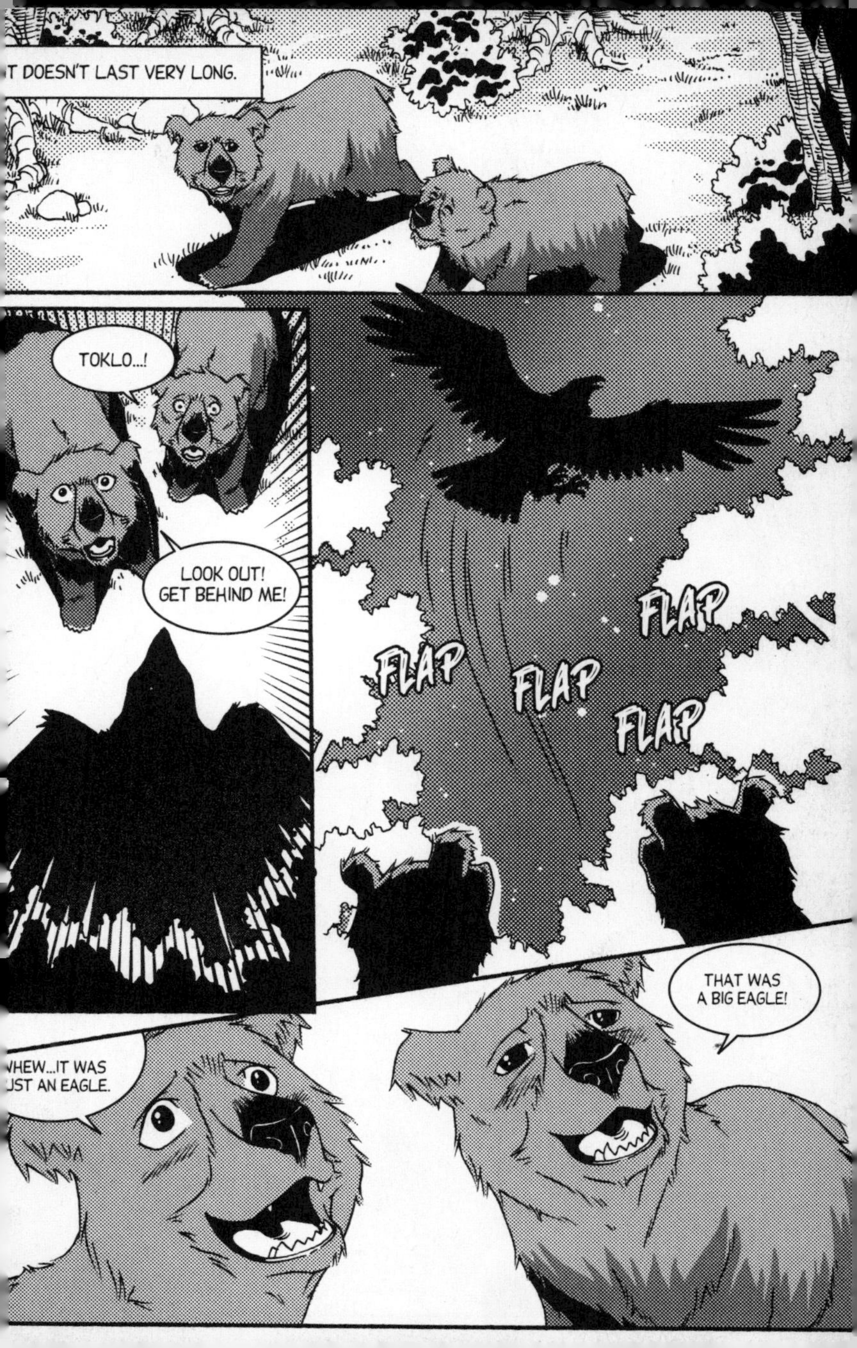

T DOESN'T LAST VERY LONG.
TOKLO...!
LOOK OUT! GET BEHIND ME!
FLAP
FLAP
FLAP
FLAP
WHEW...IT WAS JUST AN EAGLE.
THAT WAS A BIG EAGLE!

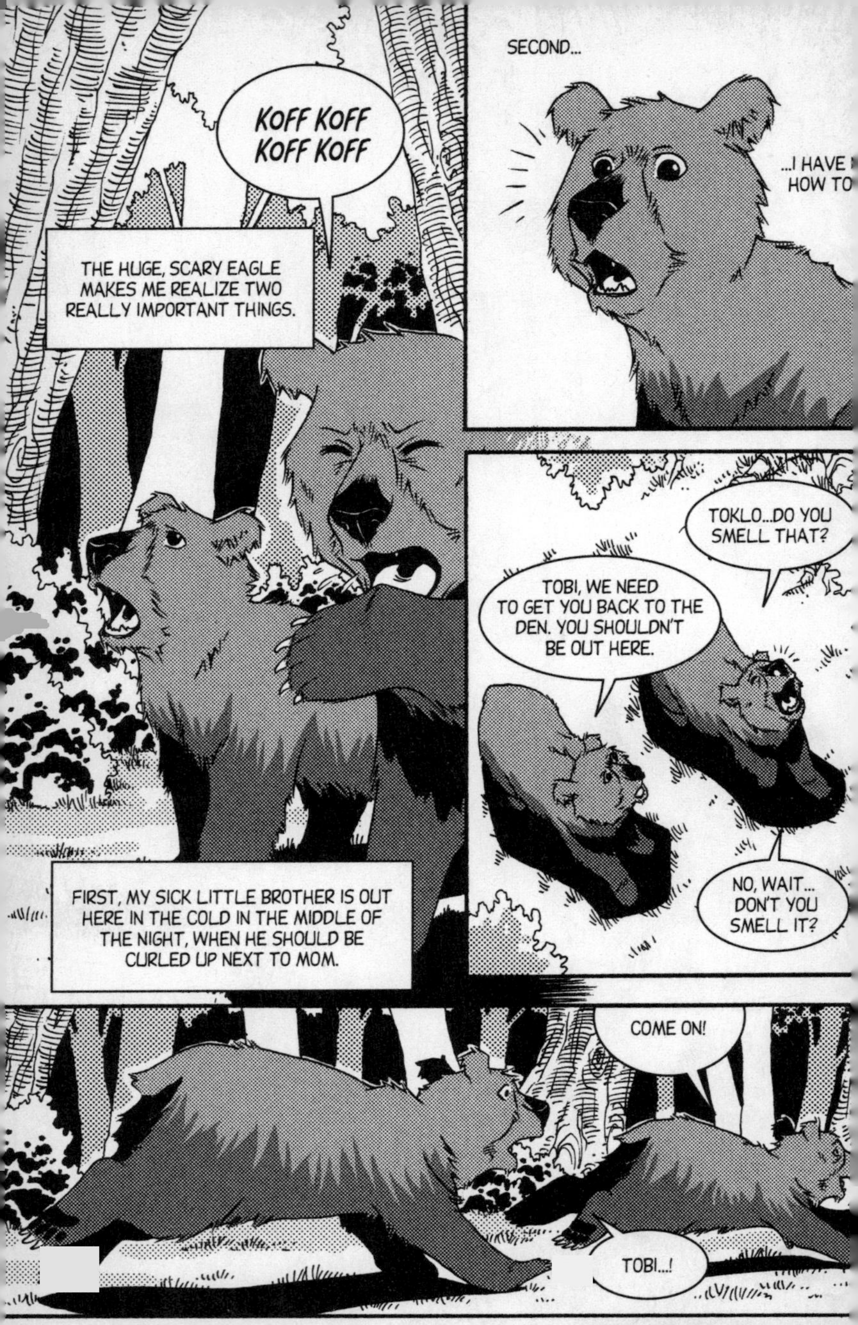
KOFF KOFF KOFF KOFF
THE HUGE, SCARY EAGLE MAKES ME REALIZE TWO REALLY IMPORTANT THINGS.
FIRST, MY SICK LITTLE BROTHER IS OUT HERE IN THE COLD IN THE MIDDLE OF THE NIGHT, WHEN HE SHOULD BE CURLED UP NEXT TO MOM.
SECOND...
...I HAVE
HOW TO
TOKLO...DO YOU SMELL THAT?
TOBI, WE NEED TO GET YOU BACK TO THE DEN. YOU SHOULDN'T BE OUT HERE.
NO, WAIT... DON'T YOU SMELL IT?
COME ON!
TOBI...!

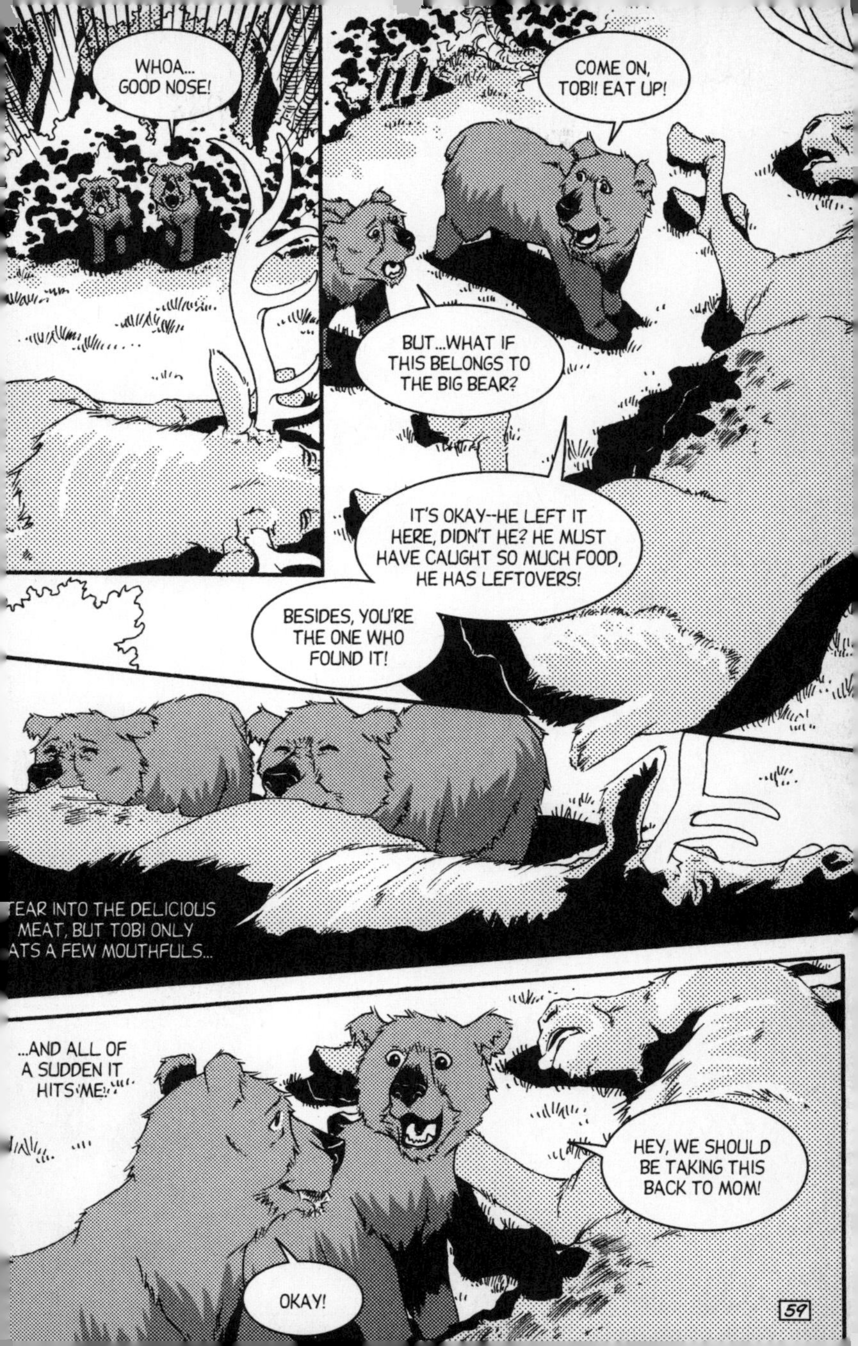
WHOA... GOOD NOSE!
COME ON, TOBI! EAT UP!
BUT...WHAT IF THIS BELONGS TO THE BIG BEAR?
IT'S OKAY--HE LEFT IT HERE, DIDN'T HE? HE MUST HAVE CAUGHT SO MUCH FOOD, HE HAS LEFTOVERS!
BESIDES, YOU'RE THE ONE WHO FOUND IT!
TEAR INTO THE DELICIOUS MEAT, BUT TOBI ONLY ATS A FEW MOUTHFULS...
...AND ALL OF A SUDDEN IT HITS ME.
HEY, WE SHOULD BE TAKING THIS BACK TO MOM!
OKAY!

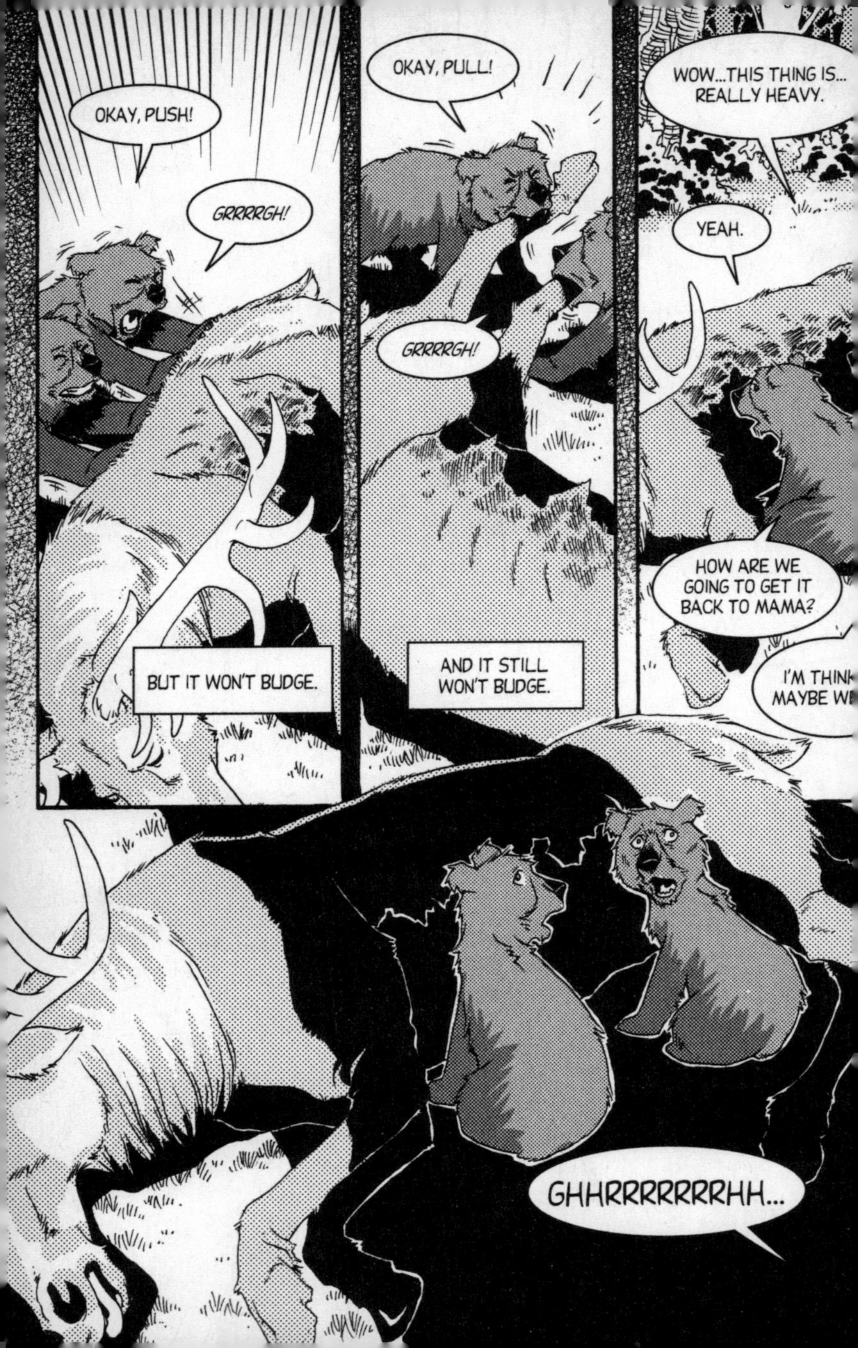
OKAY, PUSH!
GRRRRGH!
BUT IT WON'T BUDGE.
OKAY, PULL!
GRRRRGH!
AND IT STILL WON'T BUDGE.
WOW...THIS THING IS... REALLY HEAVY.
YEAH.
HOW ARE WE GOING TO GET IT BACK TO MAMA?
GHHRRRRRRRHH...

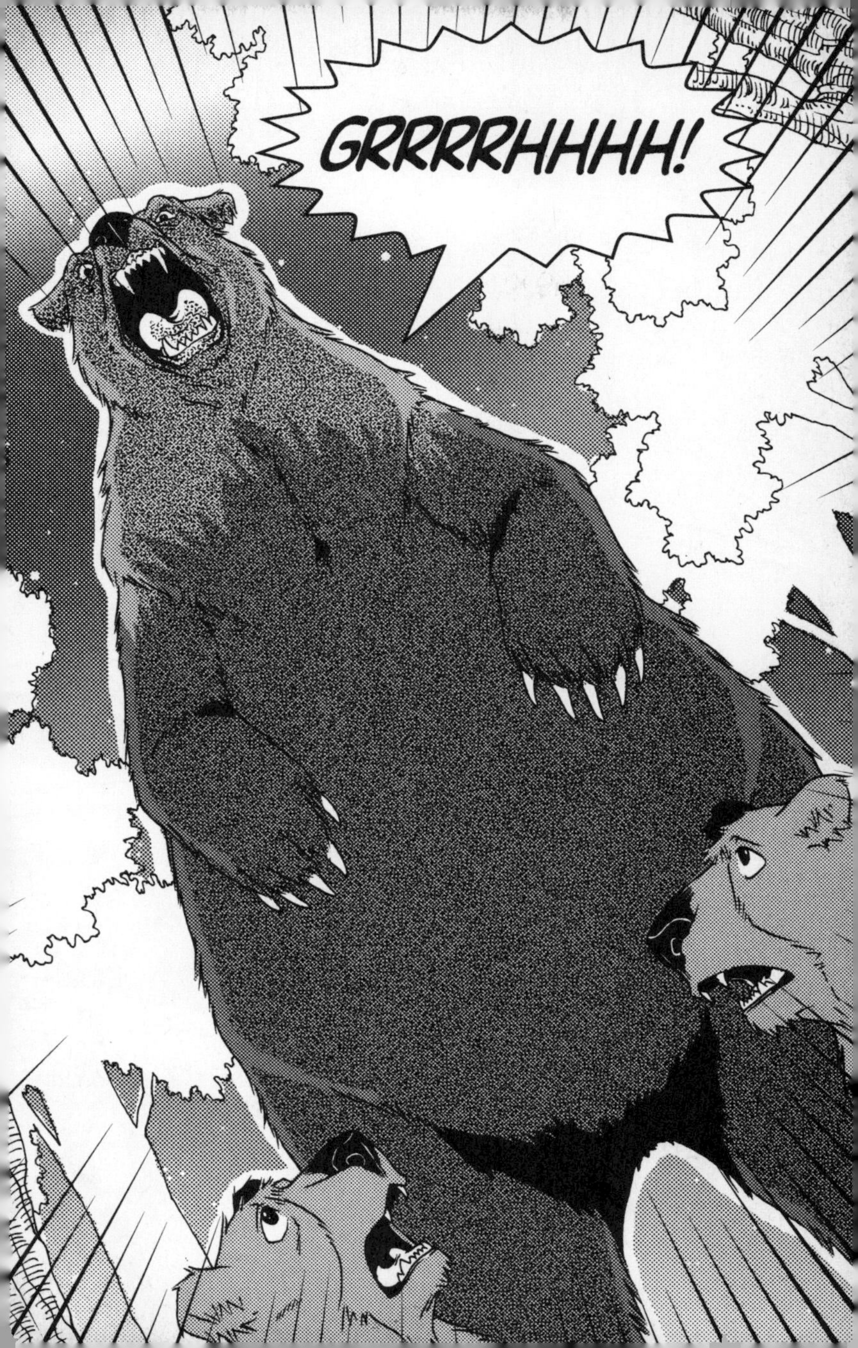
GRRRRHHHH!

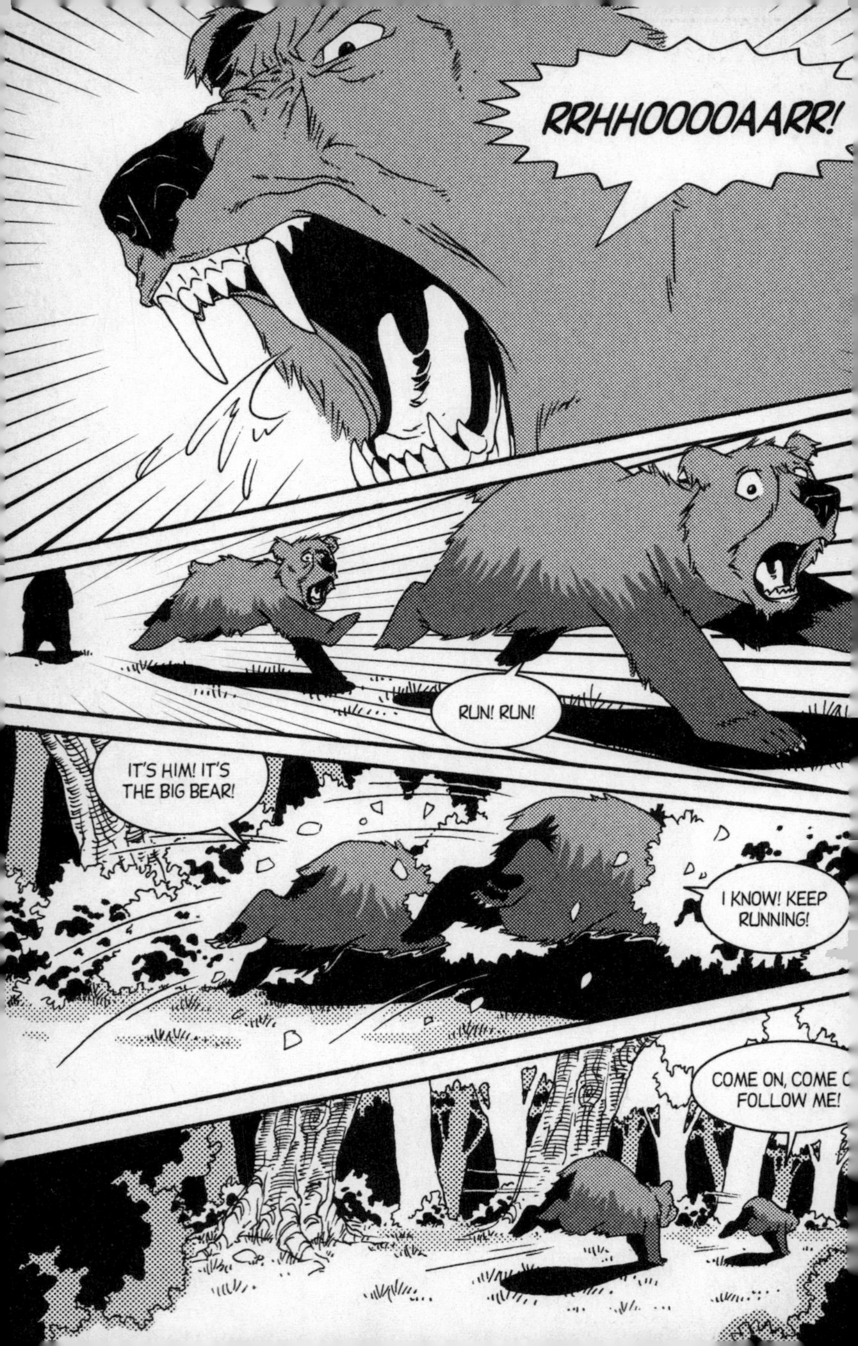
RRHHOOOOAARR!
RUN! RUN!
IT'S HIM! IT'S THE BIG BEAR!
I KNOW! KEEP RUNNING!
COME ON, COME C
FOLLOW ME!

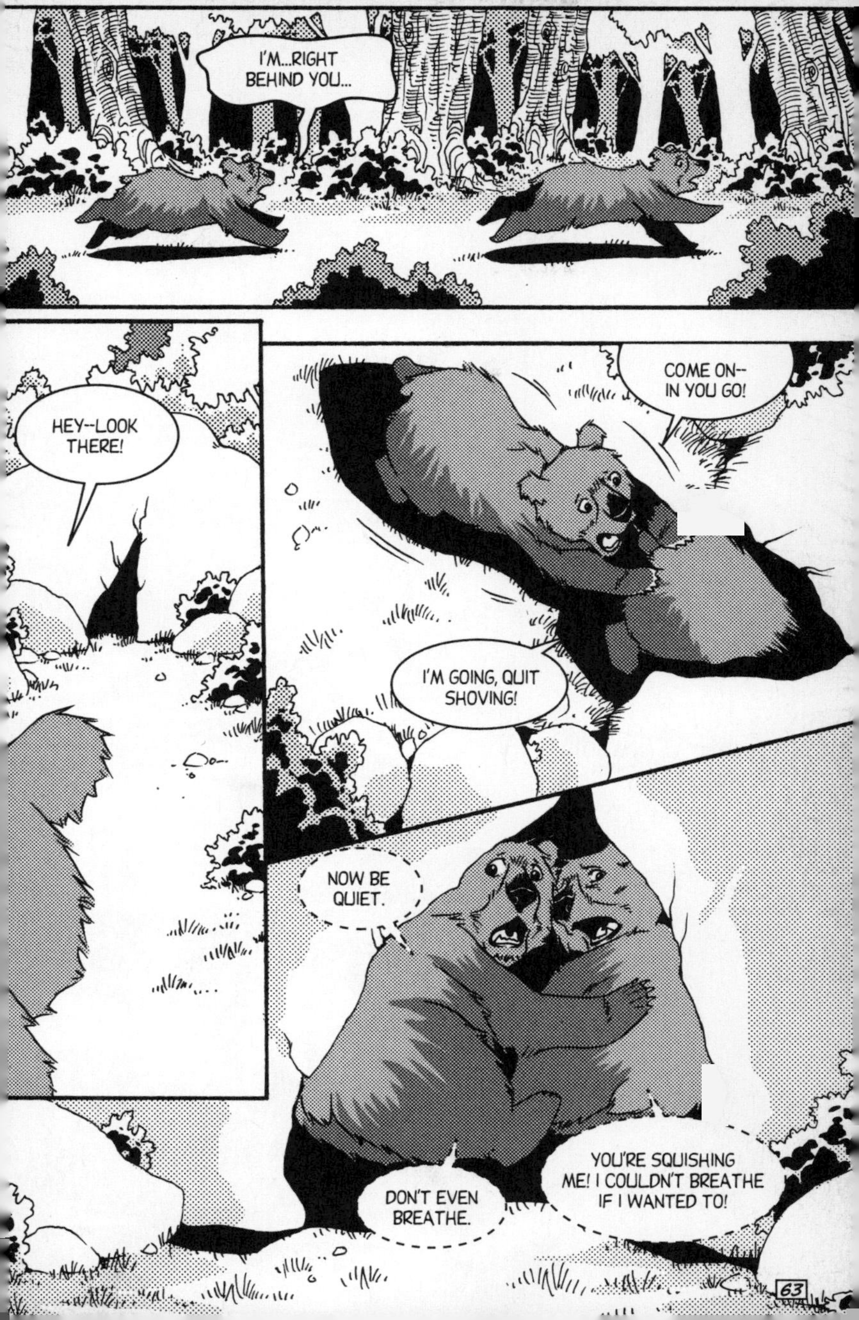
I'M...RIGHT BEHIND YOU...
HEY--LOOK THERE!
COME ON-- IN YOU GO!
I'M GOING, QUIT SHOVING!
NOW BE QUIET.
DON'T EVEN BREATHE.
YOU'RE SQUISHING ME! I COULDN'T BREATHE IF I WANTED TO!

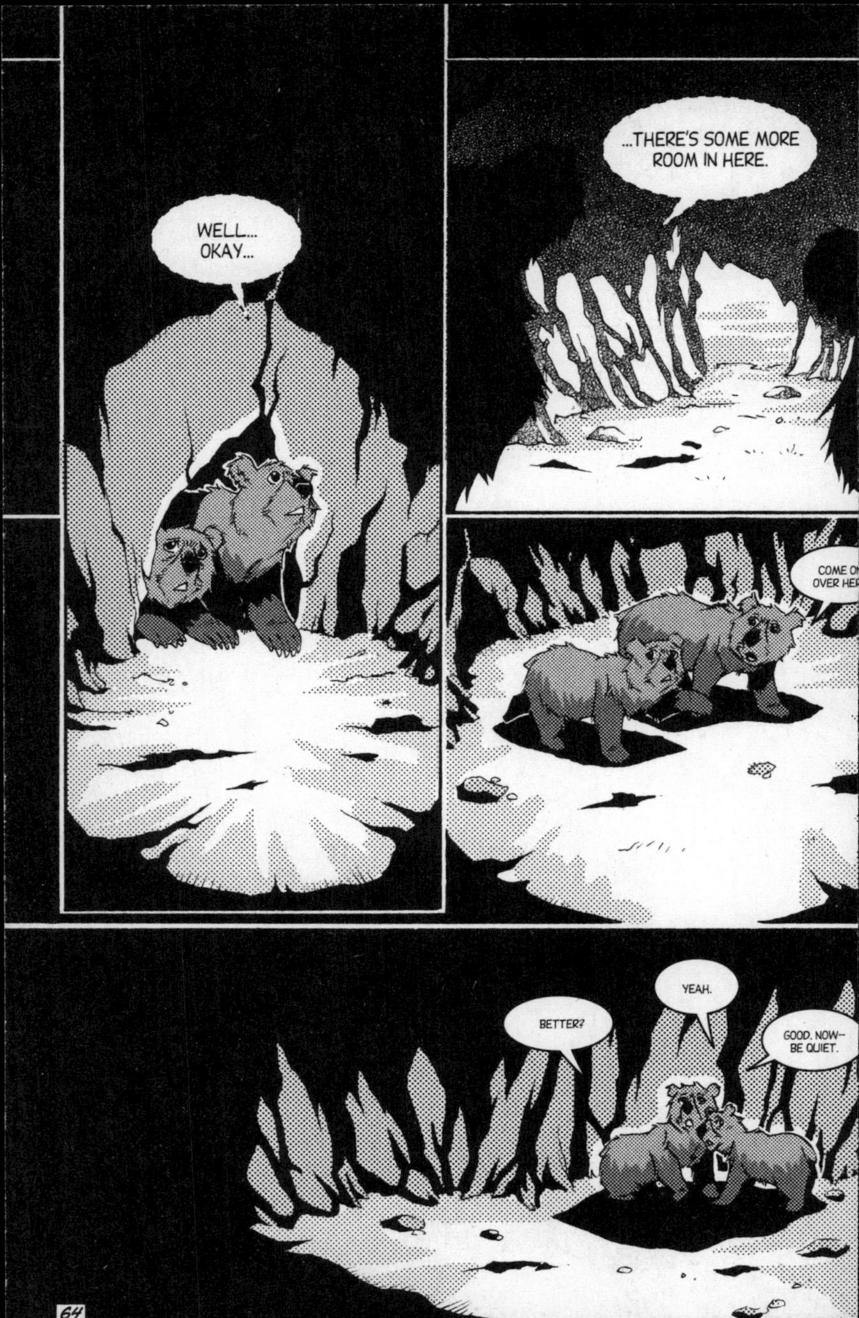
WELL... OKAY...
...THERE'S SOME MORE ROOM IN HERE.
BETTER?
YEAH.
GOOD. NOW— BE QUIET.

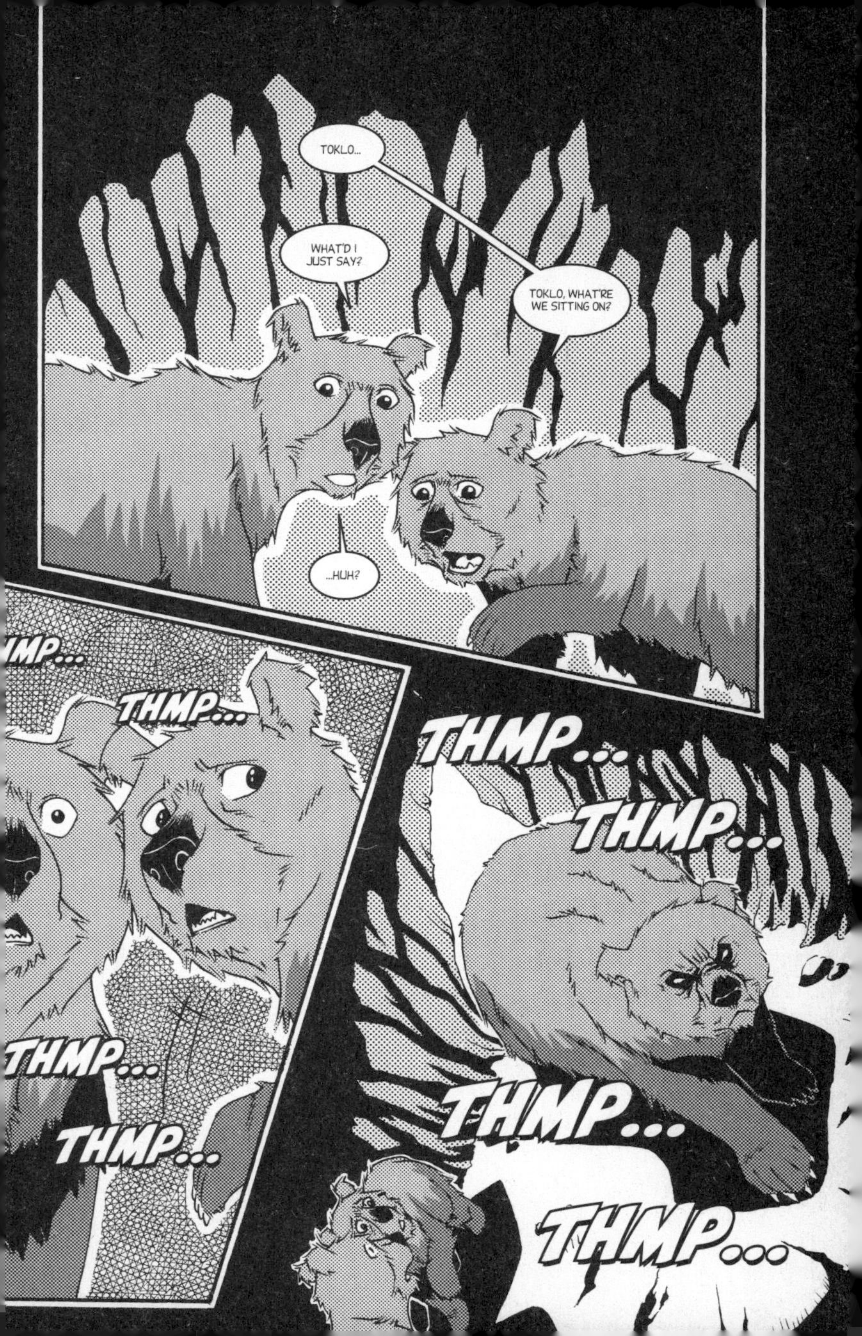
TOKLO...
WHAT'D I JUST SAY?
TOKLO, WHAT'RE WE SITTING ON?
...HUH?
THMP...
THMP...
THMP...
THMP...
THMP...
THMP...
THMP...
THMP...

I CAN'T BELIEVE IT. EVEN WHILE I CAN FEEL TOBI SHIVERING, I CAN'T BELIEVE IT.

OF ALL THE HIDING PLACES ON THE WHOLE MOUNTAIN, WE PICK THE BIG BEAR'S DEN!

BUT WHY HE KNOW HERE? DOESN'T SMELL

THAT'S I FINA UNDERS WHEN I F NOTIC

THE BIG BEAR DOESN'T SMELL US 'CAUSE THE WHOLE CAVE IS FILLED WITH A HORRIBLE STENCH.

THAT'S TOBI WAS TO TELL

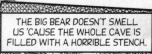

THE FL OF THE C COVERED BONE

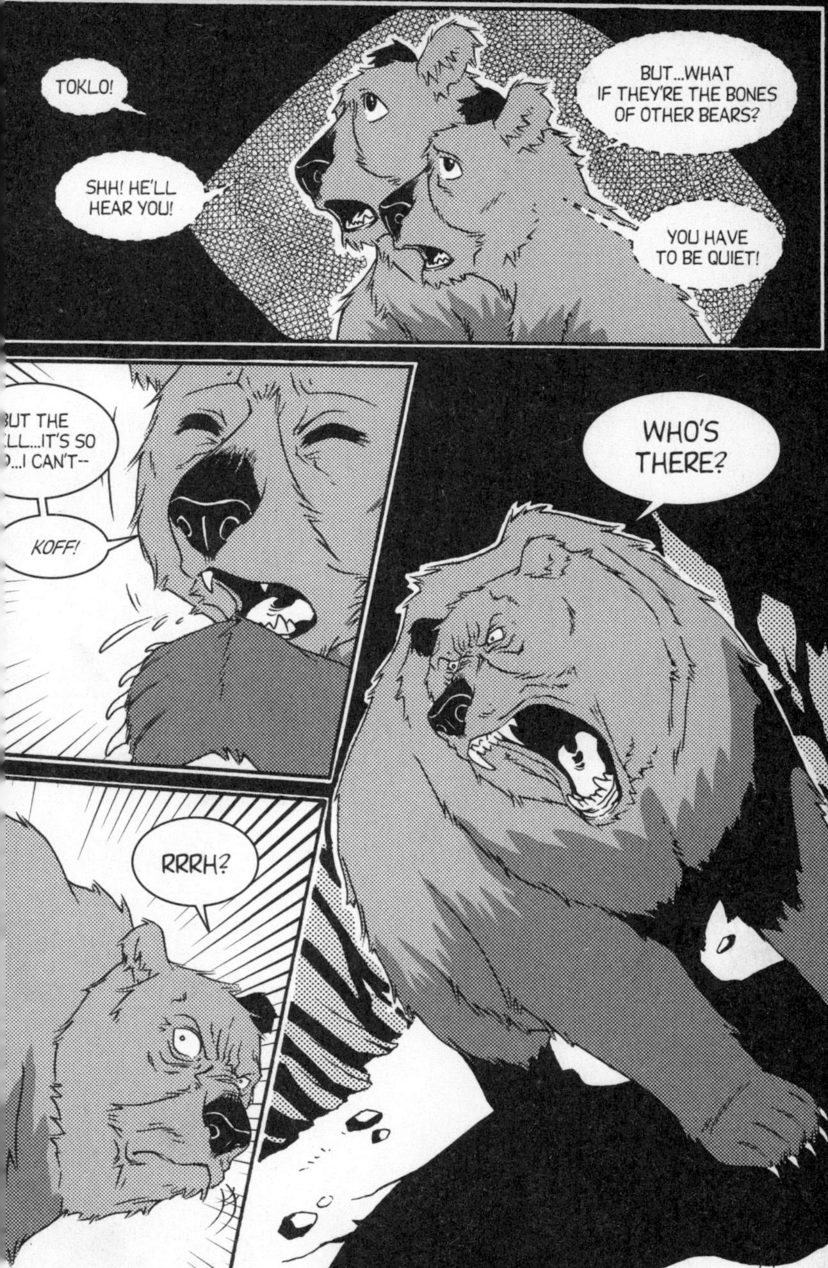
TOKLO!
BUT...WHAT IF THEY'RE THE BONES OF OTHER BEARS?
SHH! HE'LL HEAR YOU!
YOU HAVE TO BE QUIET!
UT THE LL...IT'S SO ...I CAN'T--
KOFF!
WHO'S THERE?
RRRH?

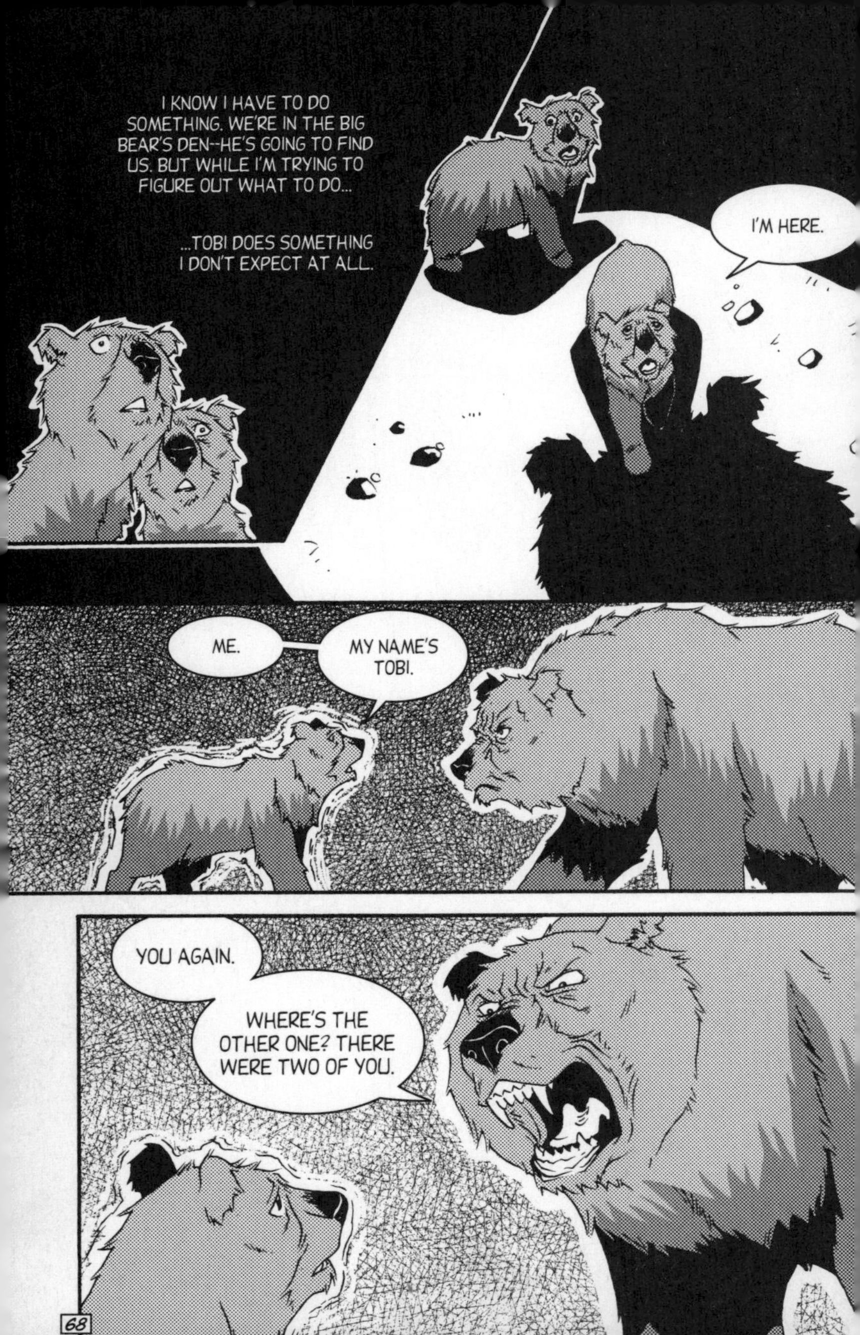
I KNOW I HAVE TO DO SOMETHING. WE'RE IN THE BIG BEAR'S DEN--HE'S GOING TO FIND US. BUT WHILE I'M TRYING TO FIGURE OUT WHAT TO DO...
...TOBI DOES SOMETHING I DON'T EXPECT AT ALL.
I'M HERE.
ME.
MY NAME'S TOBI.
YOU AGAIN.
WHERE'S THE OTHER ONE? THERE WERE TWO OF YOU.

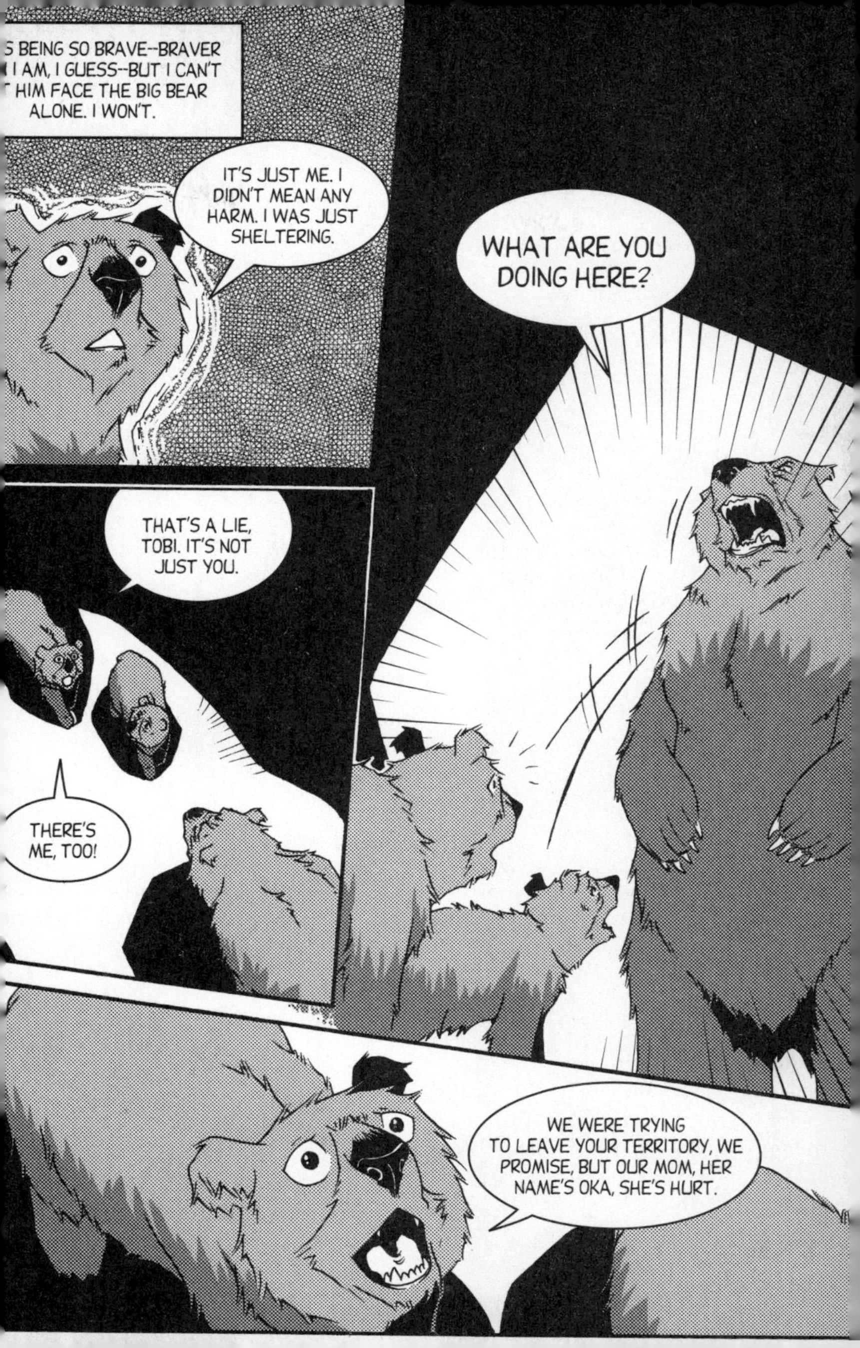
S BEING SO BRAVE--BRAVER I AM, I GUESS--BUT I CAN'T T HIM FACE THE BIG BEAR ALONE. I WON'T.
IT'S JUST ME. I DIDN'T MEAN ANY HARM. I WAS JUST SHELTERING.
WHAT ARE YOU DOING HERE?
THAT'S A LIE, TOBI. IT'S NOT JUST YOU.
THERE'S ME, TOO!
WE WERE TRYING TO LEAVE YOUR TERRITORY, WE PROMISE, BUT OUR MOM, HER NAME'S OKA, SHE'S HURT.

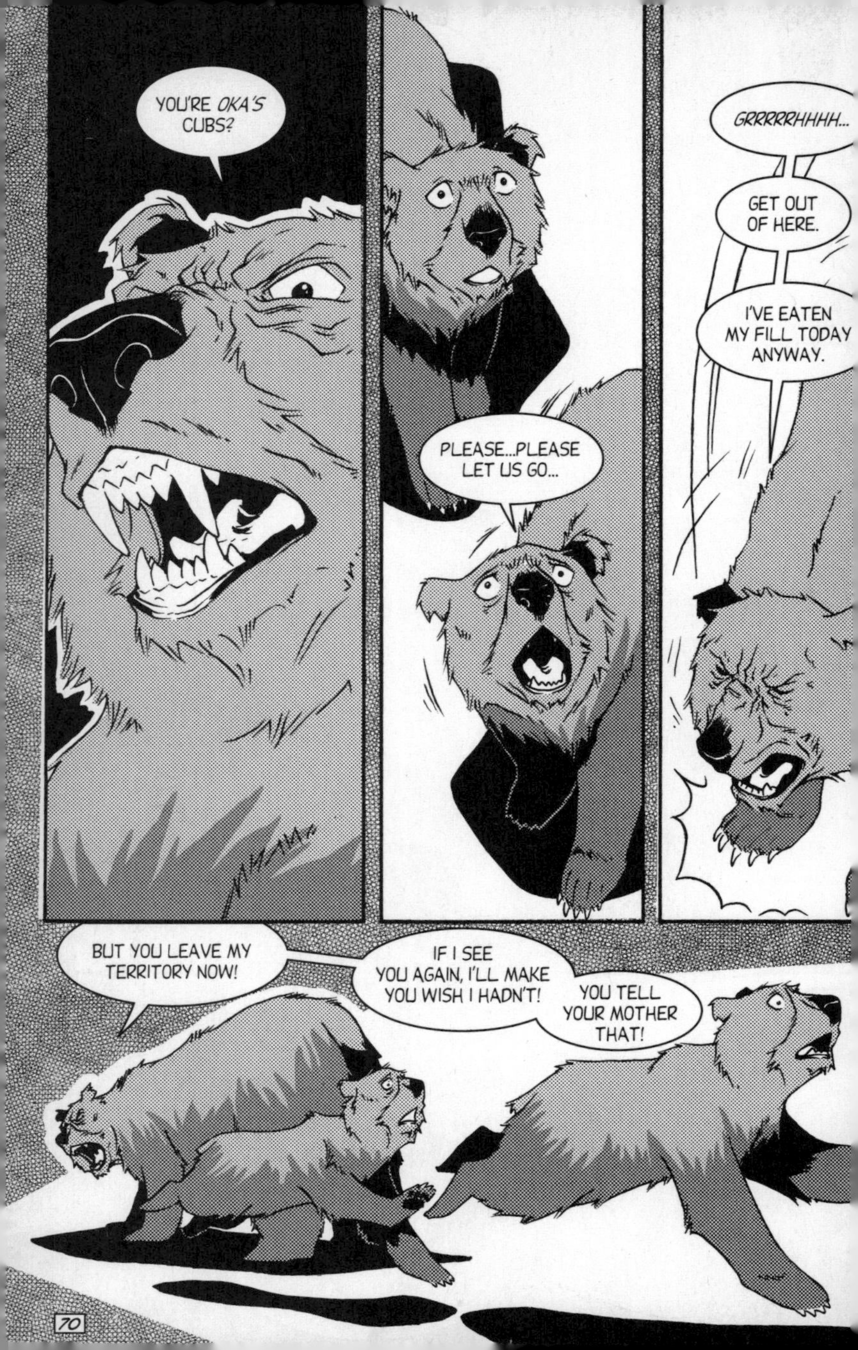

YOU'RE *OKA'S* CUBS?
PLEASE...PLEASE LET US GO...
GRRRRRHHHH...
GET OUT OF HERE.
I'VE EATEN MY FILL TODAY ANYWAY.
BUT YOU LEAVE MY TERRITORY NOW!
IF I SEE YOU AGAIN, I'LL MAKE YOU WISH I HADN'T!
YOU TELL YOUR MOTHER THAT!

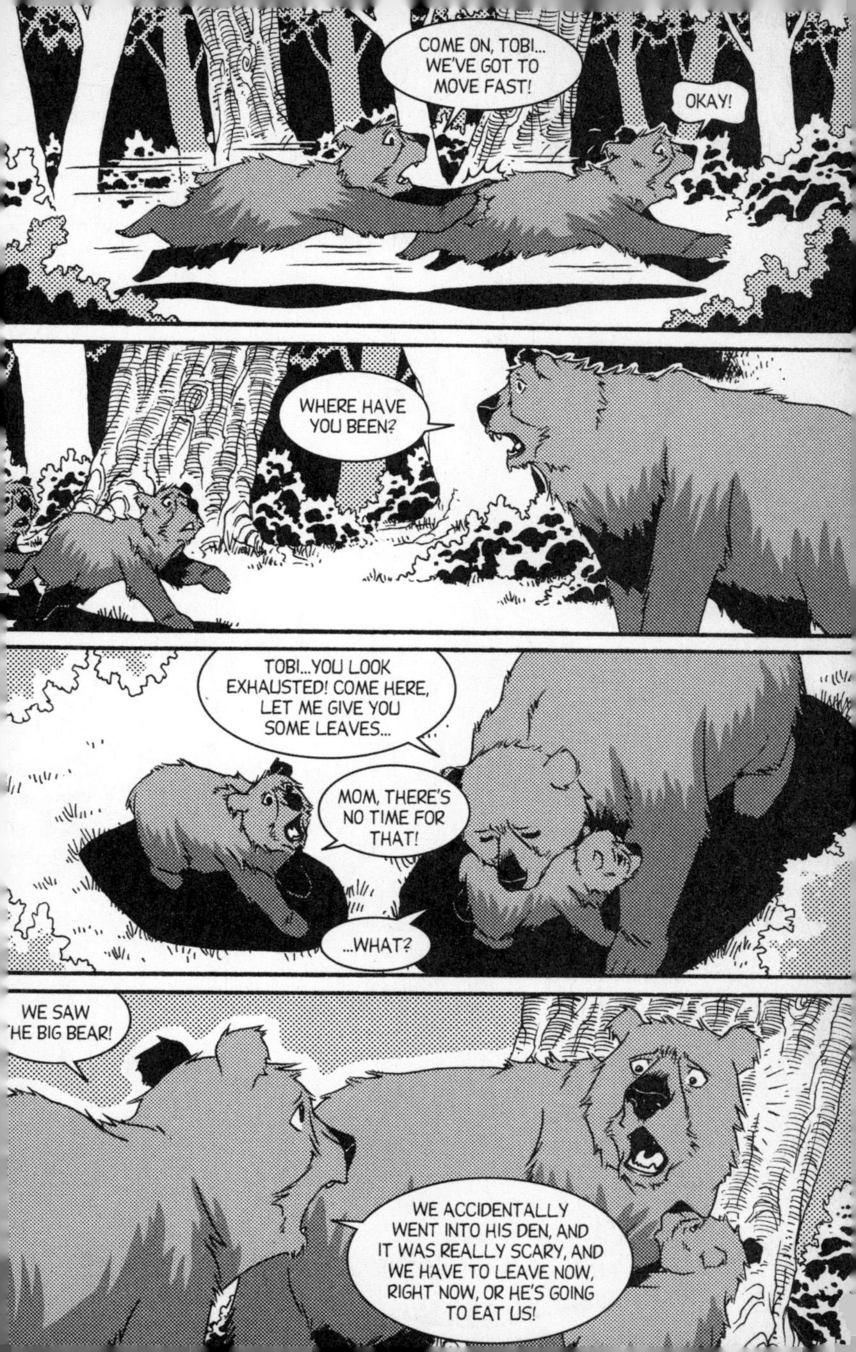
COME ON, TOBI... WE'VE GOT TO MOVE FAST!
OKAY!
WHERE HAVE YOU BEEN?
TOBI...YOU LOOK EXHAUSTED! COME HERE, LET ME GIVE YOU SOME LEAVES...
MOM, THERE'S NO TIME FOR THAT!
...WHAT?
WE SAW THE BIG BEAR!
WE ACCIDENTALLY WENT INTO HIS DEN, AND IT WAS REALLY SCARY, AND WE HAVE TO LEAVE NOW, RIGHT NOW, OR HE'S GOING TO EAT US!

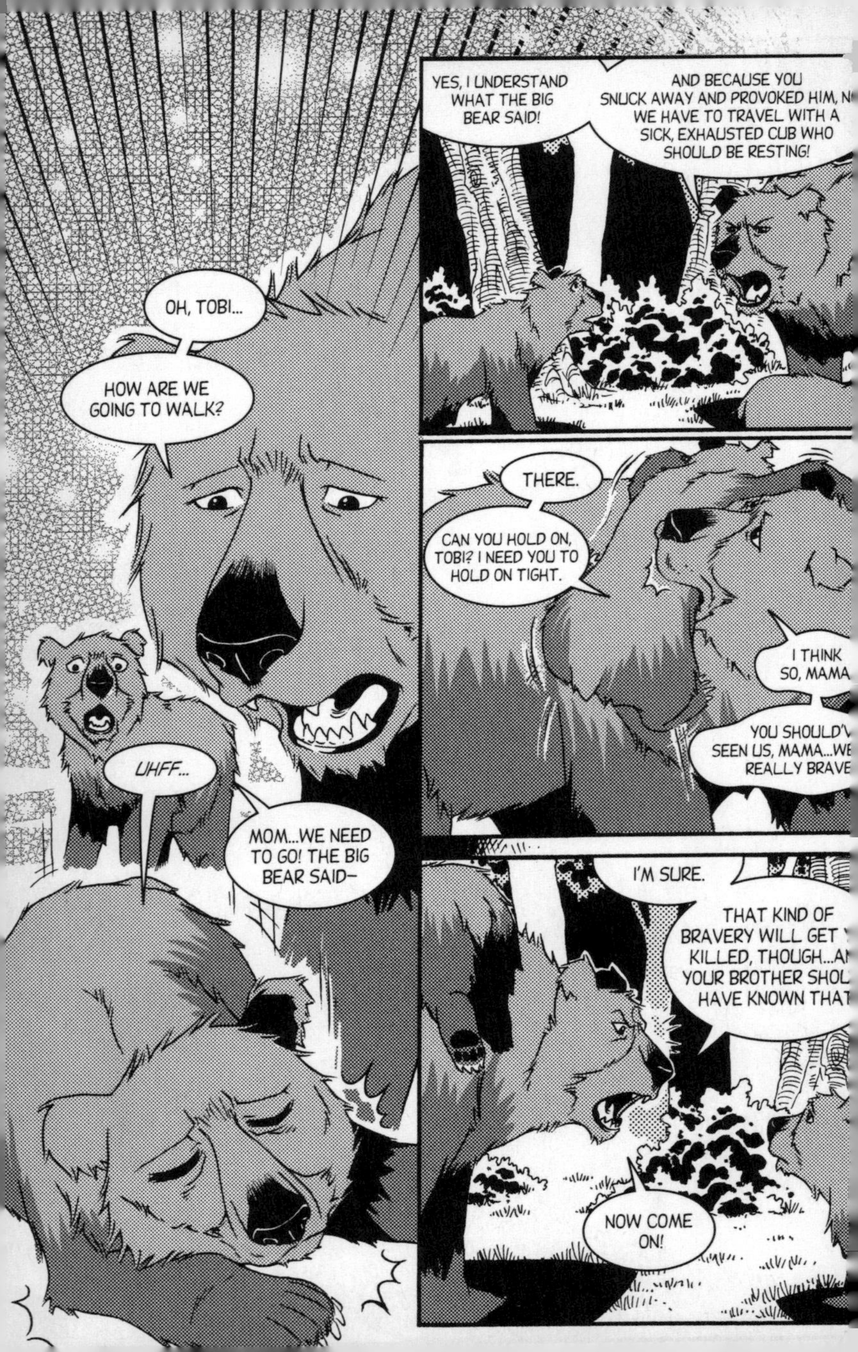
OH, TOBI...
HOW ARE WE GOING TO WALK?
UHFF...
MOM...WE NEED TO GO! THE BIG BEAR SAID—
YES, I UNDERSTAND WHAT THE BIG BEAR SAID!
AND BECAUSE YOU SNUCK AWAY AND PROVOKED HIM, N
WE HAVE TO TRAVEL WITH A SICK, EXHAUSTED CUB WHO SHOULD BE RESTING!
THERE.
CAN YOU HOLD ON, TOBI? I NEED YOU TO HOLD ON TIGHT.
I THINK SO, MAMA
YOU SHOULD'V SEEN US, MAMA...WE REALLY BRAVE
I'M SURE.
THAT KIND OF BRAVERY WILL GET KILLED, THOUGH...A YOUR BROTHER SHO HAVE KNOWN THAT
NOW COME ON!

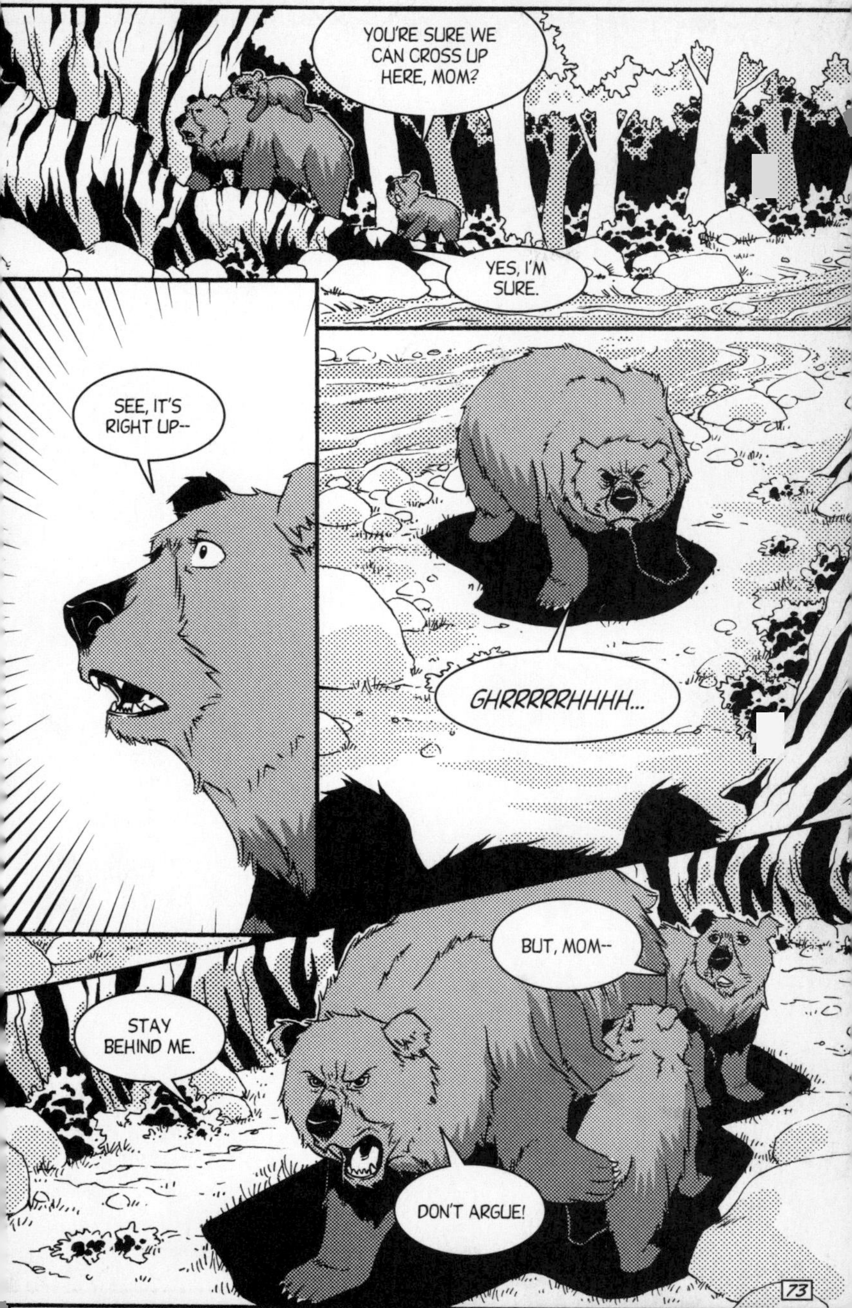
YOU'RE SURE WE CAN CROSS UP HERE, MOM?
YES, I'M SURE.
SEE, IT'S RIGHT UP--
GHRRRRRHHHH...
BUT, MOM--
STAY BEHIND ME.
DON'T ARGUE!

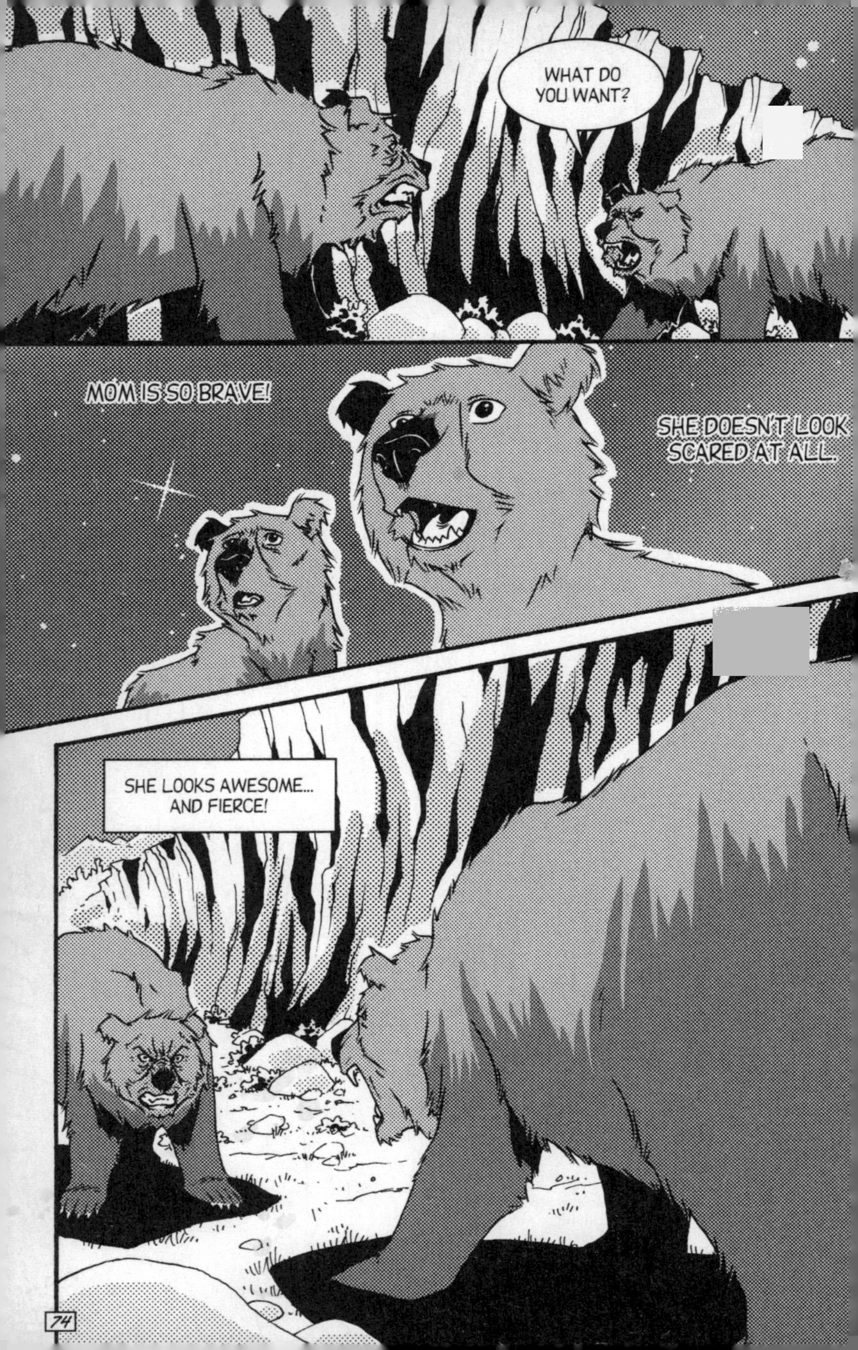
WHAT DO YOU WANT?
MOM IS SO BRAVE!
SHE DOESN'T LOOK SCARED AT ALL.
SHE LOOKS AWESOME... AND FIERCE!

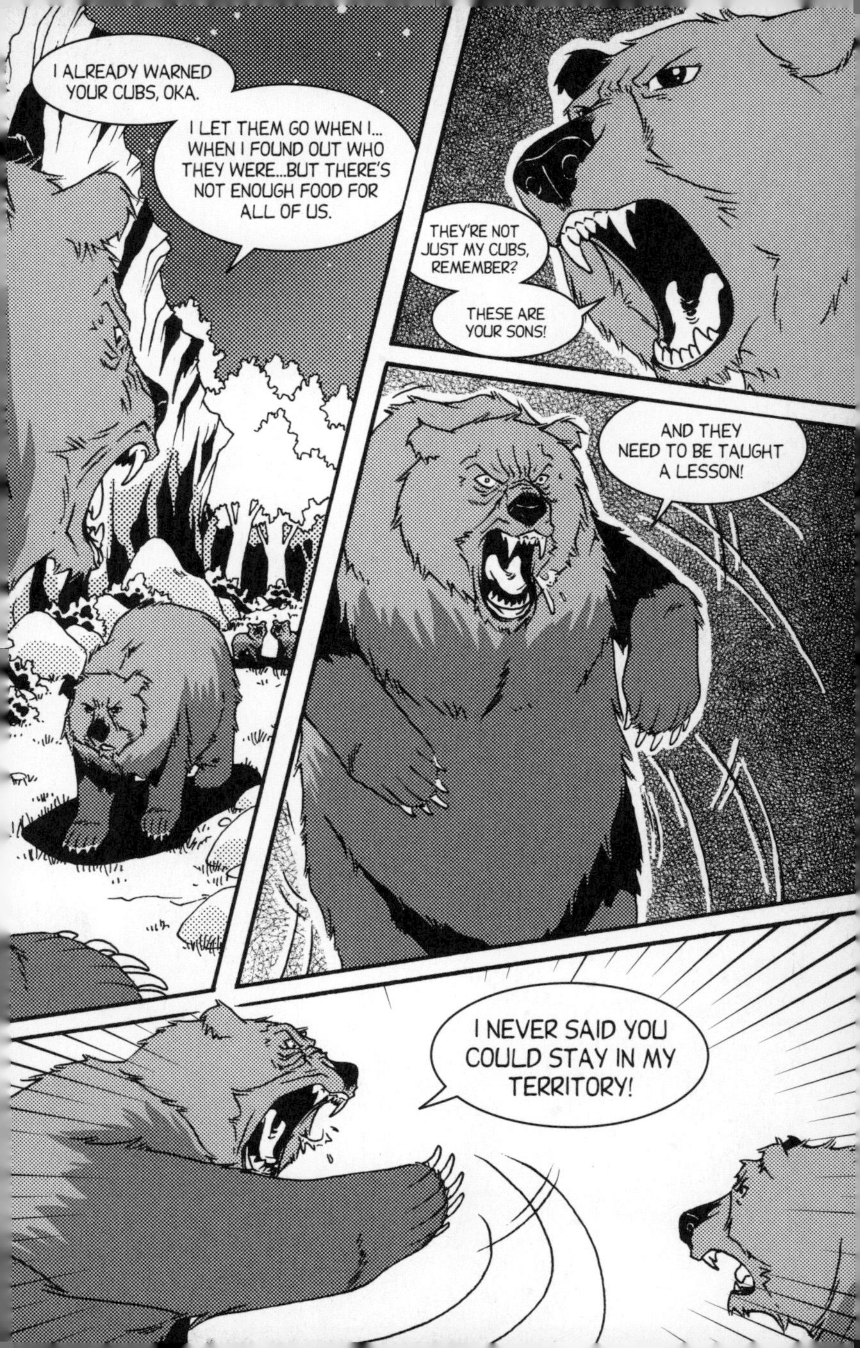
I ALREADY WARNED YOUR CUBS, OKA.
I LET THEM GO WHEN I... WHEN I FOUND OUT WHO THEY WERE...BUT THERE'S NOT ENOUGH FOOD FOR ALL OF US.
THEY'RE NOT JUST MY CUBS, REMEMBER?
THESE ARE YOUR SONS!
AND THEY NEED TO BE TAUGHT A LESSON!
I NEVER SAID YOU COULD STAY IN MY TERRITORY!

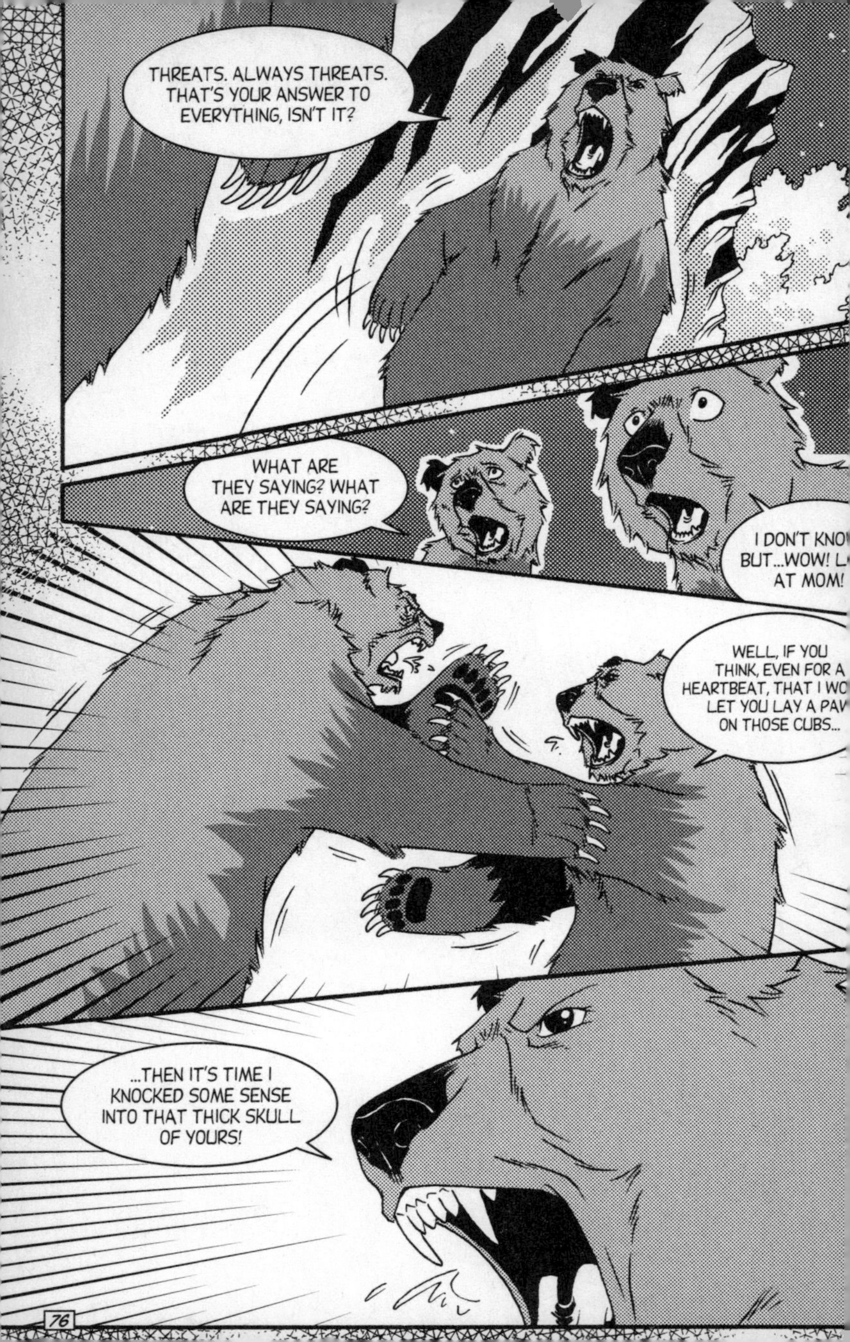
THREATS. ALWAYS THREATS. THAT'S YOUR ANSWER TO EVERYTHING, ISN'T IT?
WHAT ARE THEY SAYING? WHAT ARE THEY SAYING?
I DON'T KNO BUT...WOW! L AT MOM!
WELL, IF YOU THINK, EVEN FOR A HEARTBEAT, THAT I WO LET YOU LAY A PAW ON THOSE CUBS...
...THEN IT'S TIME I KNOCKED SOME SENSE INTO THAT THICK SKULL OF YOURS!

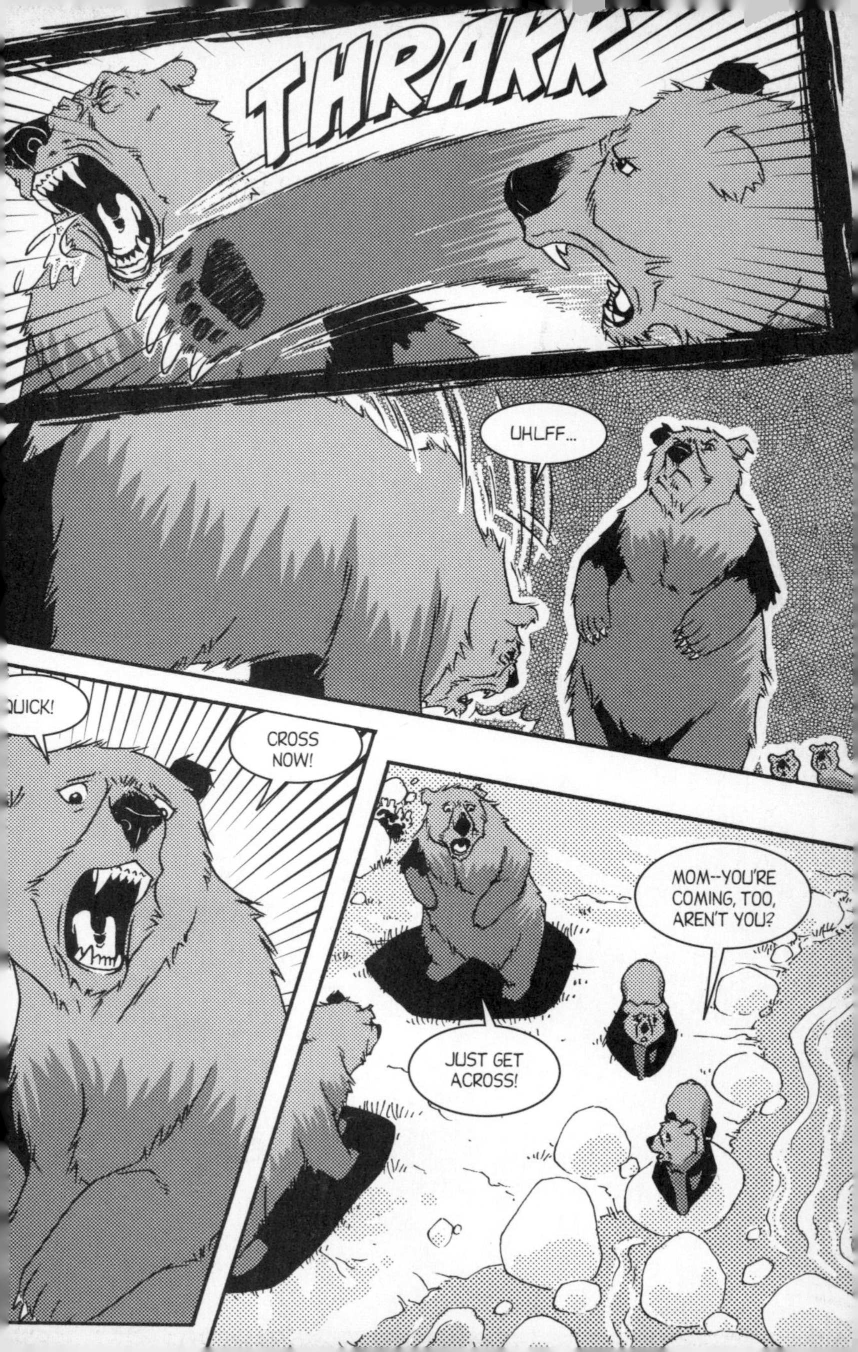
THRAKK
UHLFF...
QUICK!
CROSS NOW!
MOM--YOU'RE COMING, TOO, AREN'T YOU?
JUST GET ACROSS!

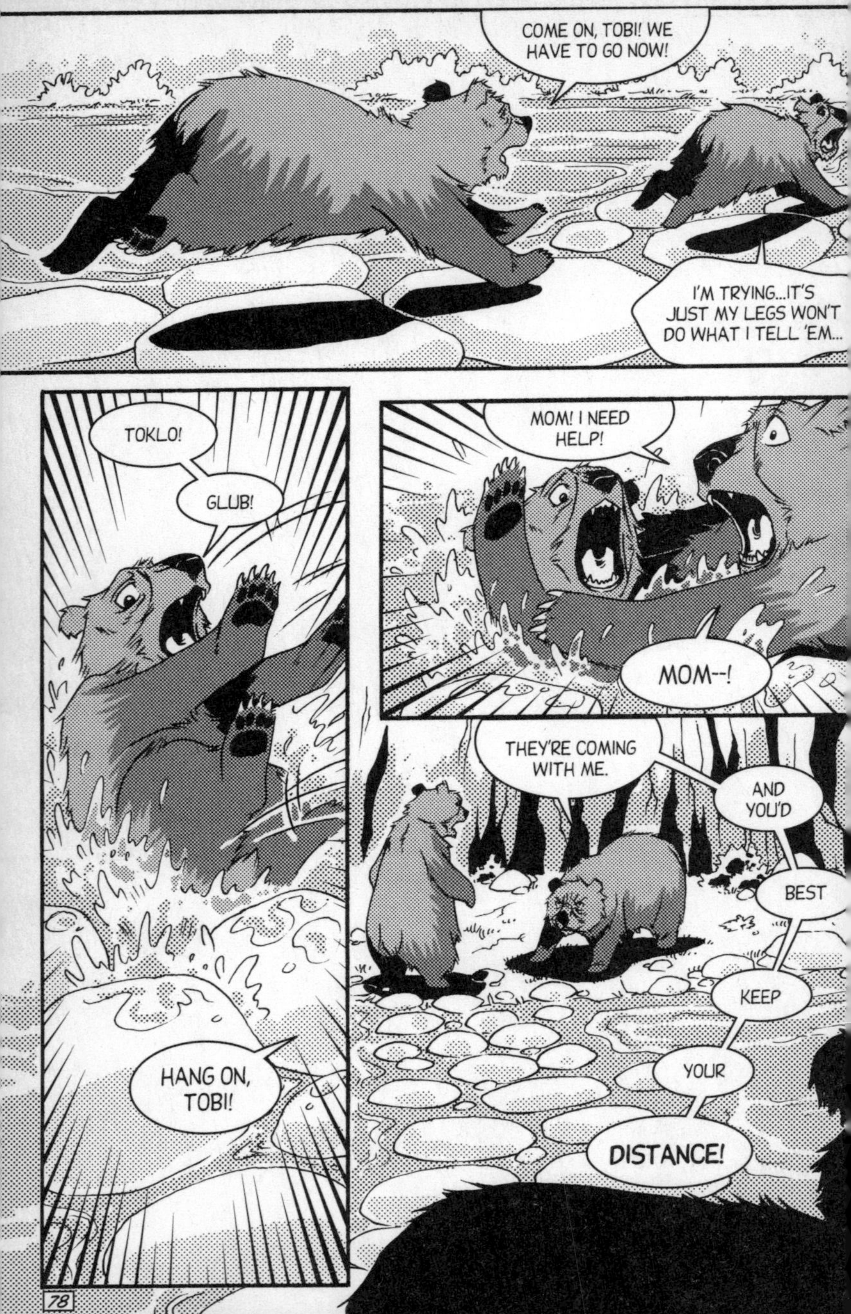
COME ON, TOBI! WE HAVE TO GO NOW!
I'M TRYING...IT'S JUST MY LEGS WON'T DO WHAT I TELL 'EM...
TOKLO!
GLUB!
HANG ON, TOBI!
MOM! I NEED HELP!
MOM--!
THEY'RE COMING WITH ME.
AND YOU'D
BEST
KEEP
YOUR
DISTANCE!

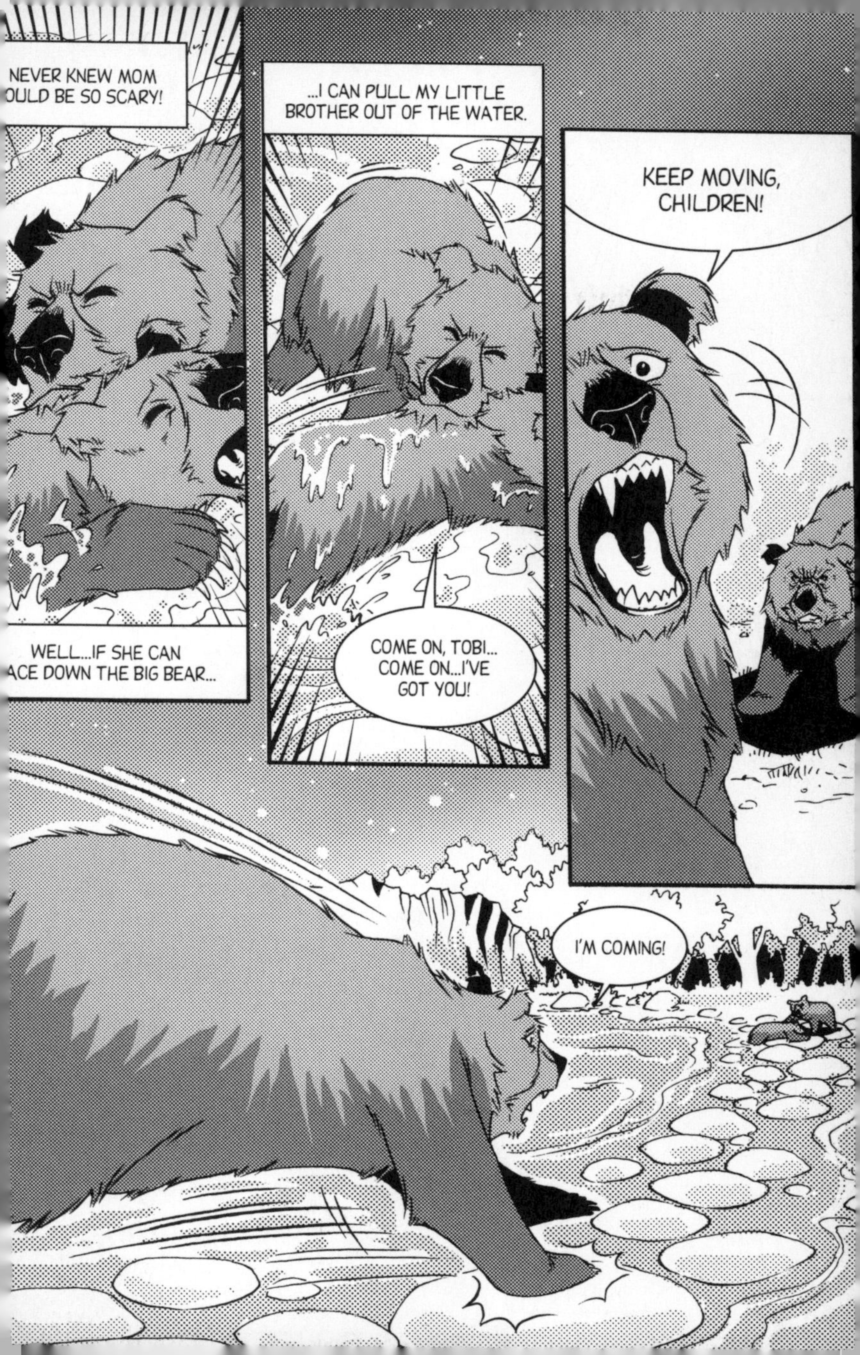
NEVER KNEW MOM
OULD BE SO SCARY!
WELL...IF SHE CAN
ACE DOWN THE BIG BEAR...
...I CAN PULL MY LITTLE BROTHER OUT OF THE WATER.
COME ON, TOBI... COME ON...I'VE GOT YOU!
KEEP MOVING, CHILDREN!
I'M COMING!

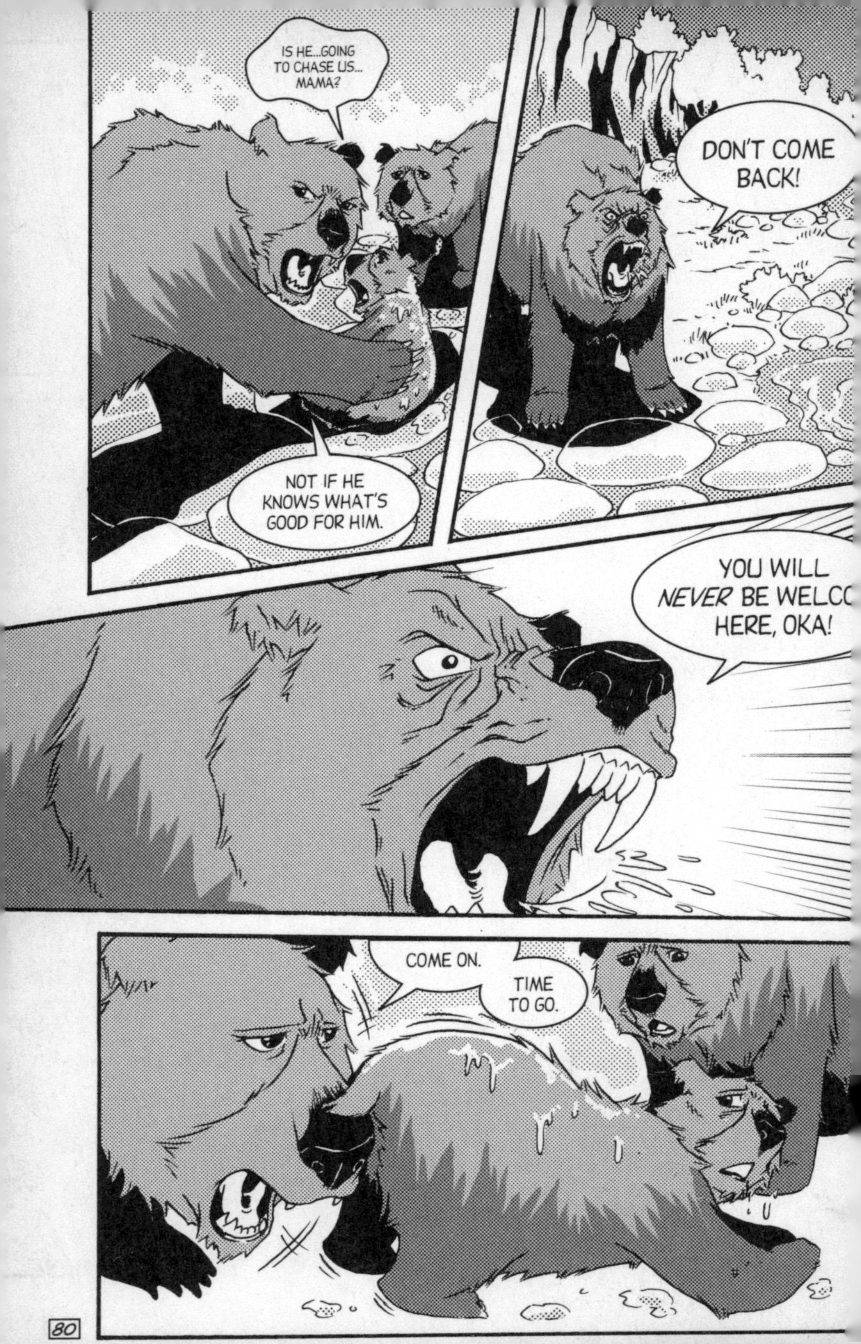
IS HE...GOING TO CHASE US... MAMA?
NOT IF HE KNOWS WHAT'S GOOD FOR HIM.
DON'T COME BACK!
YOU WILL *NEVER* BE WELCO
HERE, OKA!
COME ON.
TIME TO GO.

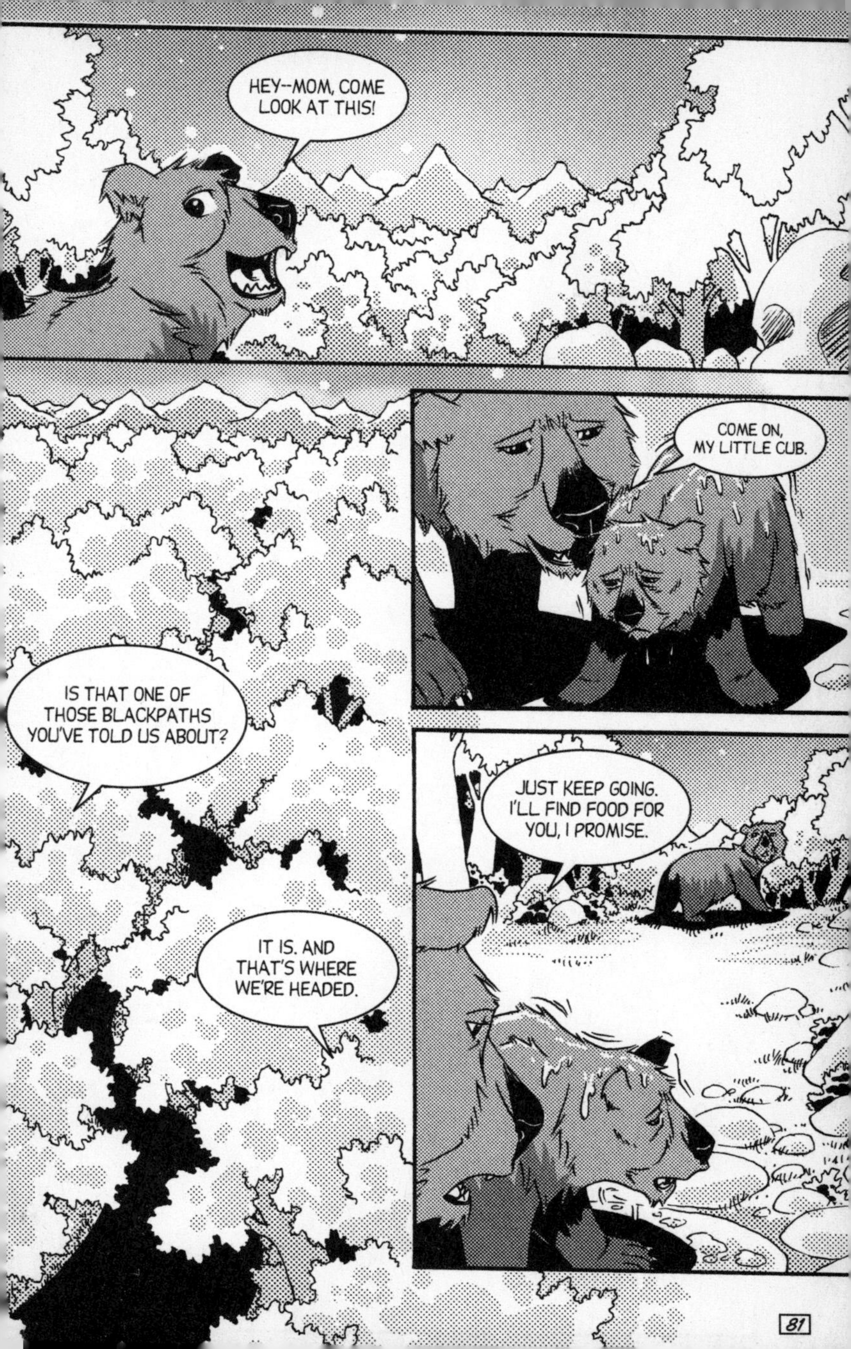
HEY--MOM, COME LOOK AT THIS!
IS THAT ONE OF THOSE BLACKPATHS YOU'VE TOLD US ABOUT?
IT IS. AND THAT'S WHERE WE'RE HEADED.
COME ON, MY LITTLE CUB.
JUST KEEP GOING. I'LL FIND FOOD FOR YOU, I PROMISE.

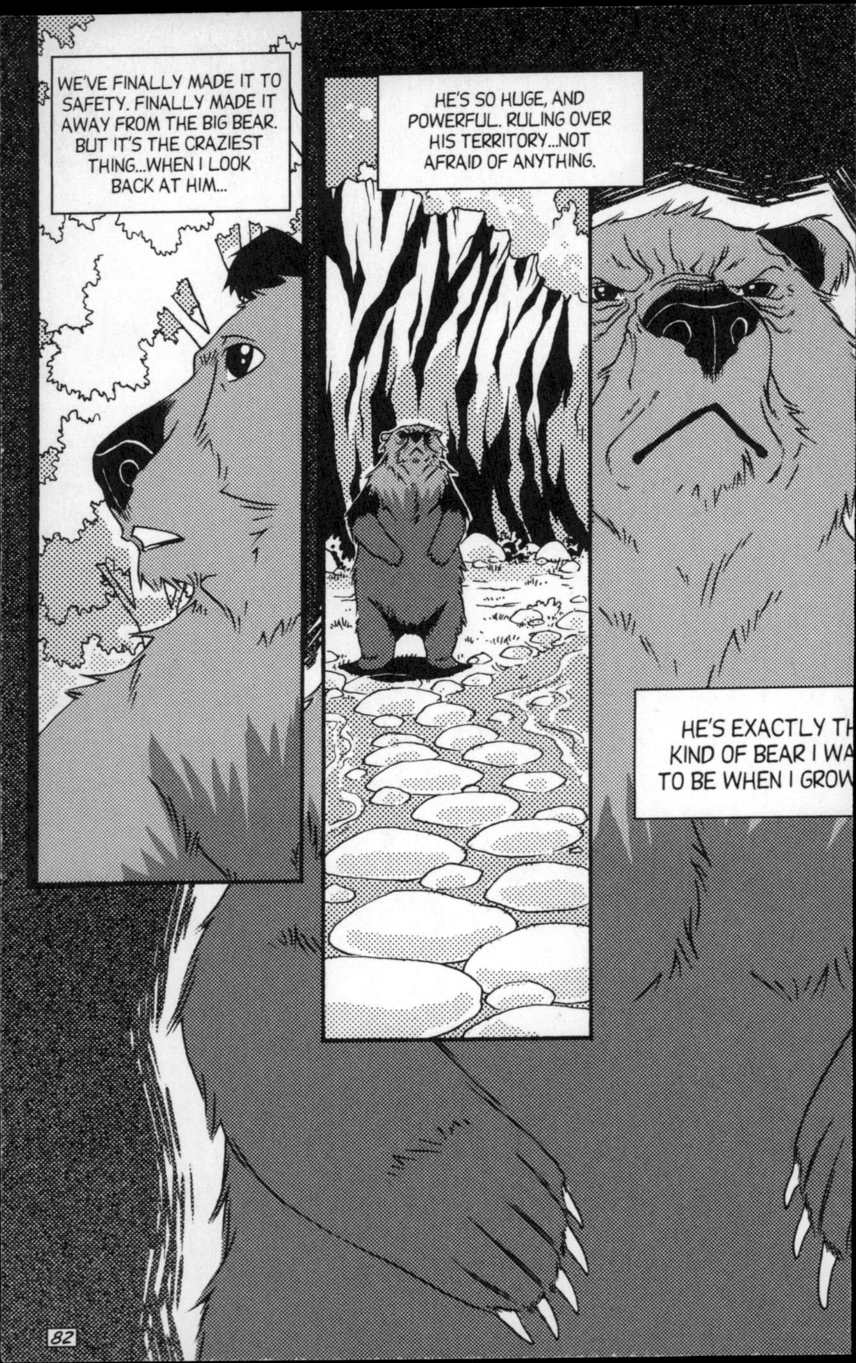
WE'VE FINALLY MADE IT TO SAFETY. FINALLY MADE IT AWAY FROM THE BIG BEAR. BUT IT'S THE CRAZIEST THING...WHEN I LOOK BACK AT HIM...
HE'S SO HUGE, AND POWERFUL. RULING OVER HIS TERRITORY...NOT AFRAID OF ANYTHING.
HE'S EXACTLY TH
KIND OF BEAR I WA
TO BE WHEN I GROW

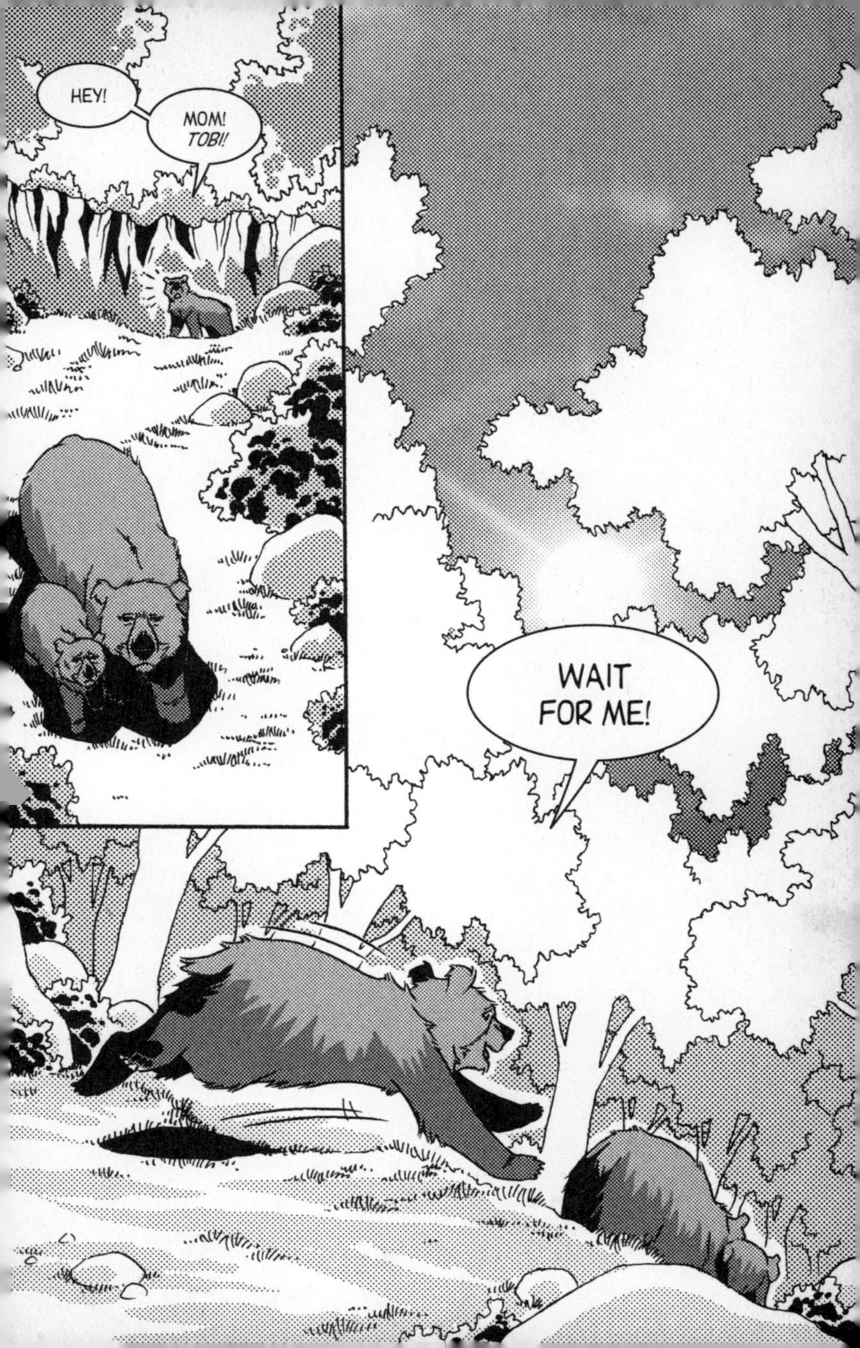
HEY!
MOM! *TOBI!*
WAIT FOR ME!

ERIN HUNTER

is inspired by a fascination with the ferocity of the natural world. As well as having great respect for nature in all its forms, Erin enjoys creating rich mythical explanations for animal behavior. She is also the author of the Warriors series.

Visit Erin Hunter online at www.warriorcats.com and www.seekerbears.com.

For exclusive information on your favorite authors and artists, visit www.authortracker.com.

DON'T MISS THE SECOND
SEEKERS MANGA:

KALLIK'S ADVENTURE

lar bear cub Kallik and her brother, Taqqiq, live in a cozy den
stled into the side of a snowy hill. Their mother, Nisa, tells
em endless stories of the outside world and Kallik and Taqqiq
n't wait to explore everything. Nisa says they're too little to
ve the den, but that won't stop them from sneaking out and
ving all sorts of thrilling adventures on their own!

TURN THE PAGE FOR A SNEAK PEEK AT

SEEKERS

THE QUEST BEGINS

SEEKERS

THE QUEST BEGINS

CHAPTER ONE

Kallik

"*A long, long time ago, long* before bears walked the earth, a frozen sea shattered into pieces, scattering tiny bits of ice across the darkness of the sky. Each of those pieces of ice contains the spirit of a bear, and if you are good, and brave, and strong, one day your spirit will join them."

Kallik leaned against her mother's hind leg, listening to the story she had heard so many times before. Beside her, her brother, Taqqiq, stretched, batting at the snowy walls of the den with his paws. He was always restless when the weather trapped them inside.

"When you look carefully at the sky," Kallik's mother continued, "you can see a pattern of stars in the shape of the Great Bear, Silaluk. She is running around and around the Pathway Star."

"Why is she running?" Kallik chipped in. She knew the answer but this was the part of the story where she always asked.

"Because it is snow-sky and she is hunting. With her quick and powerful claws, she hunts seal and beluga whale. She is the greatest of all hunters on the ice."

Kallik loved hearing about Silaluk's strength.

"But then the ice melts," Nisa said in a hushed voice. "And she can't hunt anymore. She gets hungrier and hungrier, but she has to keep running because three hunters pursue her: Robin, Chickadee, and Moose Bird. They chase her for many moons, all through the warm days, until the end of burn-sky. Then, as the warmth begins to leave the earth, they finally catch up to her.

"They gather around her and strike the fatal blow with their spears. The heart's blood of the Great Bear falls to the ground and everywhere it falls the leaves on the trees turn red and yellow. Some of the blood falls on Robin's chest, and that is why the bird has a red breast."

"Does the Great Bear die?" breathed Taqqiq.

"She does," Nisa replied. Kallik shivered. Every time she heard this story it frightened her all over again. Her mother went on.

"But then snow-sky returns, bringing back the ice. Silaluk is reborn and the ice-hunt begins all over again, season after season."

Kallik snuggled into her mother's soft white fur. The walls of the den curved up and around them, making a sheltering cave of snow that Kallik could barely glimpse in the dark, although it was only a few pawlengths from her nose. Outside a fierce wind howled across the ice, sending tendrils of freezing air through the entrance tunnel into their den. Kallik was glad they didn't have to be out there tonight.

Inside the den, she and her brother were warm and safe. Kallik wondered if Silaluk had ever had a mother and brother, or a den where she could hide from the storms. If the Great Bear had a family to keep her safe, maybe she wouldn't have to run from the hunters. Kallik knew her mother would protect her from anything scary until she was big enough and strong enough and smart enough to protect herself.

Taqqiq batted at Kallik's nose with his large furry paw. "Kallik's scared," he teased. She could make out his eyes gleaming in the darkness.

"Am not!" Kallik protested.

"She thinks robins and chickadees are going to come after her," Taqqiq said with an amused rumble.

"No, I don't!" Kallik growled, digging her claws into the snow. "That's not why I'm scared!"

"Ha! You *are* scared! I knew it!"

Nisa nudged Kallik gently with her muzzle. "Why are you frightened, little one? You've heard the legend of the Great Bear many times before."

"I know," Kallik said. "It's just . . . it reminds me that soon snow-sky will be over, and the snow and ice will all melt away.

And then we won't be able to hunt anymore, and we'll be hungry all the time. Right? Isn't that what happens during burn-sky?"

Kallik's mother sighed, her massive shoulders shifting under her snow-white pelt. "Oh, my little star," she murmured. "I didn't mean to worry you." She touched her black nose to Kallik's. "You haven't lived through a burn-sky yet, Kallik. It's not as terrible as it sounds. We'll find a way to survive, even if it means eating berries and grass for a little while."

"What is berries and grass?" Kallik asked.

Taqqiq wrinkled his muzzle. "Does it taste as good as seals?"

"No," Nisa said, "but berries and grass will keep you alive, which is the important thing. I'll show them to you when we reach land." She fell silent. For a few heartbeats, all Kallik could hear was the thin wail of the wind battering at the snowy walls.

She pressed closer to her mother, feeling the warmth radiating from her skin. "Are you sad?" she whispered.

Nisa touched Kallik with her muzzle again. "Don't be afraid," she said, a note of determination in her voice. "Remember the story of the Great Bear. No matter what happens, the ice will always return. And all the bears gather on the edge of the sea to meet it. Silaluk will always get back on her paws. She's a survivor, and so are we."

"I can survive anything!" Taqqiq boasted, puffing up his fur. "I'll fight a walrus! I'll swim across an ocean! I'll battle all the white bears we meet!"

"I'm sure you will, dear. But why don't you start by going to sleep?" Nisa suggested.

As Taqqiq circled and scuffled in the snow beside her, making himself comfortable, Kallik rested her chin on her mother's back and closed her eyes. Her mother was right; she didn't need to be afraid. As long as she was with her family, she'd always be safe and warm, like she was right now in their den.

Kallik woke to an eerie silence. Faint light filtered through the walls, casting pale blue and pink shadows on her mother and brother as they slept. At first she thought her ears must be full of snow, but when she shook her head, Nisa grunted in her sleep, and Kallik realized that it was quiet because the storm had finally passed.

"Hey," she said, poking her brother with her nose. "Hey, Taqqiq, wake up. The storm has stopped."

Taqqiq lifted his head with a bleary expression. The fur on one side of his muzzle was flattened, making him look lopsided.

Kallik barked with laughter. "Come on, you big, lazy seal," she said. "Let's go play outside."

"All right!" Taqqiq said, scrambling to his paws.

"Not without me watching you," their mother muttered with her eyes still closed. Kallik jumped. She'd thought Nisa was asleep.

"We won't go far," Kallik promised. "We'll stay right next to the den. Please can we go outside?"

Nisa huffed and the fur on her back quivered like a breeze was passing over it. "Let's all go out," she said. She pushed herself to her massive paws and turned around carefully in the small space, bundling her cubs to one side.

Sniffing cautiously, she nosed her way down the entrance tunnel, brushing away snow that the storm had piled up.

Kallik could see tension in her mother's hindquarters. "I don't know why she's so careful," she whispered to her brother. "Aren't white bears the biggest, scariest animals on the ice? Nothing would dare attack us!"

"Except maybe a bigger white bear, seal-brain!" Taqqiq retorted. "Maybe you haven't noticed how little you are."

Kallik bristled. "I may not be as big as you," she growled, "but I'm just as fierce!"

"Let's find out!" Taqqiq challenged as their mother finally padded out of the tunnel. He sprinted after her, sliding down the slope of the tunnel and scrambling out into the snow.

Kallik leaped to her paws and chased him. A clump of snow fell on her muzzle on her way out of the tunnel and she shook her head vigorously to get it off. The fresh, cold air tingled in her nostrils, full of the scent of fish and ice and faraway clouds. Kallik felt the last of her sleepiness melt away. The ice was where she belonged, not underground, buried alive. She batted a chunk of snow at Taqqiq, who dodged away with a yelp.

He chased her in a circle until she dove into the fresh snow, digging up clumps with her long claws and breathing in the sparkling whiteness. Nisa sat watching them, chuffing occasionally and sniffing the air with a wary expression.

"I'm coming for you," Taqqiq growled at Kallik, crouching low to the ground. "I'm a ferocious walrus, swimming through the water to get you." He pushed himself through the snow with his paws. Kallik braced herself to jump away, but before she could move, he leaped forward and bowled her over. They rolled through the snow, squalling excitedly, until Kallik managed to wriggle free.

"Ha!" she cried.

"Roar!" Taqqiq bellowed. "The walrus is really angry now!" He dug his paws into the snow, kicking a spray of white ice into their mother's face.

"Hey," Nisa growled. She cuffed Taqqiq lightly with her massive paw, knocking him to the ground. "That's enough snowballing around. It's time to find something to eat."

"Hooray, hooray!" Kallik yipped, jumping around her mother's legs. They hadn't eaten since before the storm, two sunrises ago, and her tummy was rumbling louder than Taqqiq's walrus roar.

The sun was hidden by trails of gray clouds that grew thicker as they walked across the ice, turning into rolls of fog that shrouded the world around them. The only sound Kallik could hear was the snow crunching under their paws. Once she thought she heard a bird calling from up in the sky, but when she looked up she couldn't see anything but drifting fog.

"Why is it so cloudy?" Taqqiq complained, stopping to rub his eyes with his paws.

"The fog is good for us," Nisa said, touching her nose to the ice. "It hides us as we hunt, so our prey won't see us coming."

"I like to see where I'm going," Taqqiq insisted. "I don't like walking in clouds. Everything's all blurry and wet."

"I don't mind the fog," Kallik said, breathing in the heavy, misty air.

"You can ride on my back," Nisa said to her son, nudging him with her muzzle. Taqqiq rumbled happily and scrambled up, clutching at tufts of her snow-white fur to give himself a boost. He stretched out on her back, high above Kallik, and they started walking again.

Kallik liked finding the sharp, cool scent of the ice under the dense, watery smell of the fog. She liked the hint of oceans and fish and salt and faraway sand that drifted through the scents reminding her of what was below the ice and what it connected to. She glanced up at her mother, who had her nose lifted and was sniffing the air, too. Kallik knew that her mother wasn't just drawing in the crisp, icy smells. Nisa was studying them searching for a clue that would lead them to food.

"You should both do this, too," Nisa said. "Try to find any smell that stands out from the ice and snow."

Taqqiq just snuggled farther into her fur, but Kallik tried to imitate her mother, swinging her head back and forth as she sniffed. She had to learn everything she could from Nisa so she could take care of herself. At least she still had a long time before that day came—all of burn-sky and the next snow-sky as well.

"Some bears can follow scents for skylengths," Nisa said "All the way to the edge of the sky and then the next edge and the next."

Kallik wished her nose were that powerful. Maybe it would be one day.

Nisa lifted her head and started trotting faster. Taqqiq dug his claws in to stay on her back. Soon Kallik saw what her mother was heading for—a hole in the ice. She knew what that meant. *Seals!*

Nisa put her nose close to the ice and sniffed all around the edge of the hole. Kallik followed closely, sniffing everywhere her mother sniffed. She was sure she could smell a faint trace of seal. This must be one of the breathing holes where a seal would surface to take a breath before hiding down in the freezing water again.

"Seals are so dumb," Taqqiq observed from his perch on Nisa's back. "If they can't breathe in the water, why do they live in it? Why don't they live on land, like white bears?"

"Perhaps because then it'd be much easier for bears like us to catch them and eat them!" Kallik guessed.

"*Shhhh.* Concentrate," Nisa said. "Can you smell the seal?"

"I think so," Kallik said. It was a furry, blubbery smell, thicker than the smell of fish. It made her mouth water.

"All right," Nisa said, crouching by the hole. "Taqqiq, come down and lie next to your sister." Taqqiq obeyed, sliding off her back and padding over to Kallik. "Be very quiet," Nisa instructed them. "Don't move, and don't make a sound."

Kallik and Taqqiq did as she said. They had done this several times before, so they knew what to do. The first time, Taqqiq had gotten bored and started yawning and fidgeting. Nisa had cuffed him and scolded him, explaining that his noise would scare away the only food they'd seen in days. By now the cubs were both nearly as good at staying quiet as their mother was.

Kallik watched the breathing hole, her ears pricked and her nose keenly aware of every change in the air. A small wind blew drifts of snow across the ice, and the fog continued to roll around all three bears, making Kallik's fur feel wet and heavy.

After a while she began to get restless. She didn't know how her mother could stand to do nothing for such a long time, watching and watching in case the seal broke through the water. The chill of the ice below her was beginning to seep through Kallik's thick fur. She had to force herself not to shiver and send vibrations through the ice that might warn the seal they were there.

She stared past the tip of her nose at the ice around the breathing hole. The dark water below the surface lapped at the jagged edge. It was strange to think that that same dark water was only a muzzlelength below her, on the other side of the thick ice. The ice seemed so strong and solid, as if it went down forever. . . .

Strange shadows and shapes seemed to dance inside the ice, forming bubbles and whorls. It was odd—ice was white from far away but nearly clear up close and full of patterns. It almost seemed like things were living inside the ice. Right below her front paws, for instance, there was a large, dark bubble slowly moving from one side to the other. Kallik stared at it, wondering if it was the spirit of a white bear trapped in the ice. One that hadn't made it as far as the stars in the sky.

Taqqiq leaned over and peered at the bubble. "You know what Mother says," he whispered. "The shapes below the ice are dead bears. They're watching you . . . right . . . now."

"I'm not scared," Kallik insisted. "They're trapped inside the ice, aren't they? So they can't come out and hurt me."

"Not unless the ice melts," Taqqiq said, trying to sound menacing.

"Hush," Nisa growled, her eyes still fixed on the breathing hole. Taqqiq fell silent again, resting his head on his paws. Slowly his eyes began to droop, and soon he was asleep.

Kallik was feeling sleepy, too, but she wanted to stay awake to see the seal come out. And she didn't want to fall asleep so close to the spirit that was still moving below her feet. She flexed her paws, trying not to nod off.

Suddenly there was a splash, and Kallik saw a sleek gray head break through the surface of the water. She barely had time to notice the dark spots on its fur before Nisa was lunging headfirst into the hole. With a swift movement, she seized the seal and flipped it out of the water onto the ice. It writhed and flopped for a moment before her giant claw sliced into it, killing it with a single blow.

Kallik couldn't imagine ever being fast enough to catch a seal before it disappeared back under the ice again.

Nisa ripped open the seal and said the words of thanks to the ice spirits. Her cubs gathered around her to feed. Kallik inhaled the smell of freshly killed meat, the delicious fat and chewy skin. She dug her teeth into the prey and tore out a mouthful, realizing how hungry she had been.

Suddenly Nisa raised her head, her fur bristling. Kallik tensed and sniffed the air. A large male white bear was lumbering out of the fog toward them. His yellowish fur was matted with snow and his paws were as big as Kallik's head. He headed straight for their seal, hissing and rumbling.

Taqqiq bristled, but Nisa shoved him back with her paw. "Stay close to me," she warned. "Let's get out of here."

She turned to run, nudging her cubs ahead of her. Kallik sprinted as fast as she could, her heart pounding. What if the seal wasn't enough for the strange bear? What if he came after *her* next? As they raced up the slope, Kallik glanced back and saw that the bear wasn't chasing them. Instead, he was bent over the dead seal, tearing into it.

"It's not fair!" she wailed. "That was our seal!"

"I know," Nisa said with a sigh. Her paws seemed heavy as she slowed down to a walk.

"Why should that lazy bear get our meal, when you did all the work of catching it?" Kallik insisted.

"That bear needs to eat as much as we do," Nisa said. "When seals are scarce, you have to get used to fighting for every meal. You can't trust any other bears, my cubs. We must stick together, because we are the only ones who will look after one another."

Kallik and Taqqiq exchanged glances. Kallik knew she would do anything to take care of her mother and her brother. She hadn't seen many other bears, but when she had, they had been big and fierce and scary, just like the one that had stolen their seal. Maybe white bears weren't meant to have friends. Maybe the ice didn't allow it.

"We'll be all right if we stay together," Nisa promised. "There's food to be found if you know where to look, and if you're patient enough to catch it. So don't get your head all matted with snow about it. I'll be here to look after you until you're strong enough to hunt on your own."

She swung her head around to the left. "Can you smell that?"

Kallik sniffed. She did smell something! But it wasn't seal . . . it was something else. Something fishier, but not exactly fish. She didn't recognize it.

"What do you think it is?" she asked Taqqiq. He was crouched down as if he was stalking something, and as she spoke, he leaped forward, pinning down a snowflake that had drifted to the ground. Kallik looked up and saw that it was snowing again. Her brother was happily batting at the snowflakes. It didn't look as if he'd even tried to sniff for what her mother had scented.

"Taqqiq, pay attention," Kallik said. "You'll have to hunt for yourself one day, too."

"All right, bossy paws," Taqqiq said, twitching his nose dramatically from side to side.

"Come along, quickly," Nisa said. "Try not to make too much noise." They followed their mother across the ice, padding as quietly as possible. The scent didn't seem to be moving away.

"Is it staying still?" Kallik asked. "Does that mean it doesn't know we're coming?"

"One way to throw off your prey is to hide your scent," Nisa said. "Like this—follow me." She led them to a channel of melted water in the ice and they swam across one by one.

"Blech, now my fur's all wet," Taqqiq complained, shaking himself as they climbed out the other side.

"That should make it harder to smell us coming," Nisa said.

"And that big, old bear back there won't be able to follow our trail, either, right?" Kallik said.

"Hopefully," Nisa said, touching Kallik's muzzle with hers.

As they got closer, the fishy scent got stronger, and Kallik could smell salt and blood and faraway ocean scents mingled with it. Soon she saw a dark shape lying on the ice. At first she thought it must be a giant seal, from the way the flippers were splayed out, but then she saw that it was the carcass of a whale. Huge chunks had been torn off it, and there were large bite marks and claw slashes in its side. The snow around it was covered in blood.

"It's a gray whale," Nisa explained. "Another bear must have killed it and dragged it onto the ice."

Kallik stared at the carcass in awe. It must have been a very strong bear to overpower something so big and pull it all the way out of the water. Even with the large bites taken out of it, there was still plenty for the three of them to eat. Hungrily, she stretched out her muzzle and tugged a piece of meat free.

Nisa nudged her, making her drop the meat. "Don't forget to express gratitude to the spirits of the ice," Kallik's mother said gently. "You must always remember that you are part of a bigger world." She bowed her head and touched her nose to the ice. "We thank you, spirits of the ice, for guiding us to this meal," she murmured. Kallik imitated her mother, whispering the same words, and Taqqiq followed. Then, with happy rumbles, they began to eat.

The fog had rolled away by the time night fell, and the stars shone brightly in a clear sky. Kallik sprawled on the ice, her full belly keeping her warm. Next to her were her mother and brother. Not a hint of a breeze stirred the fur on their shoulders; for once, the wind had died down and the sea far beneath the ice was silent.

"Mother?" Kallik asked. "Please tell me again about the spirits under the ice."

Taqqiq gave a little huff of laughter, but Nisa touched her nose to her daughter's side with a serious expression.

"When a white bear dies," she said, "its spirit sinks into the ice, lower and lower, until all you can see is a shadow under the ice. But you shouldn't be frightened of them, little star. The spirits are there to guide you. If you are a good bear, they will always be there to take care of you and help you find food or shelter."

"I'd rather *you* took care of me," Kallik said with a shiver.

"I'll take care of you, too," her mother promised.

"What about the ice spots in the sky?" Kallik said, pointing her muzzle upward. "Aren't those the spirits of bears, too?"

"When the ice melts," Nisa explained, "the bear spirits escape and drift up to the sky on the snow-winds, light as snowflakes, where they become stars. Those spirits are watching you, too, only from farther away."

"What about that star over there?" Taqqiq asked. "The one that's really bright. I've even seen it in the daytime, once, and it never moves like the others do."

"That's the Pathway Star," Nisa said.

"Why is it called the Pathway Star?" Taqqiq prompted.

"Because if you follow it," Nisa said solemnly, "it will lead you to a place far, far away where the ice never melts."

"Never?" Kallik gasped. "You mean there's no burn-sky? W
could hunt all the time?"

"No burn-sky, no melting ice, no eating berries or living o
the land," Nisa said. "The bear spirits dance for joy across th
sky, all in different colors."

"Why don't we go there?" Taqqiq asked. "If it's so wonderful?
Kallik nodded. She felt a tingling in her paws, as if she coul
run all the way to this place where they would be safe forever.

"It is a long way away," Nisa rumbled. "Much too far for us t
travel." Her black eyes stared into the distance, silvery glints o
the moon swimming in their depths. "But perhaps we may hav
to make the journey . . . one day."

"Really? When?" Kallik demanded, but her mother reste
her head on her paws and fell silent. She obviously didn't wan
to answer any more questions. Kallik curled into a ball in th
curve of her mother's side and watched the ice shimmerin
under the moon until she fell asleep. In her dreams, bear spirit
rose from the ice and began to dance, their paws light as fur a
they romped and slid across the frozen landscape.

A strange creaking noise woke Kallik the next morning. I
sounded like a bear yawning loudly, or the wind howling fron
underwater, but the air was still, and the noise came from th
ice, not the sky. Her mother was already awake, padding in :
circle around them with her nose lifted.

Kallik scrambled to her paws and shook herself. Her coa
felt heavy with moisture, and the air was damp and soft instea
of crisp and clear like it had been the night before. She turne

to her brother, who was lying on the ice beside her, apparently still asleep. She nudged him with her muzzle.

"Walrus attack!" Taqqiq bellowed, suddenly leaping to his paws and knocking her over. Nisa spun around with a snarl, but stopped when she saw that her cubs were just playing.

"Quiet," she growled. "Taqqiq, stop acting like a wild goose. There is no time for playing. We have to get moving." She started across the ice without looking back. Kallik and Taqqiq scrambled to catch up. Nisa's grouchiness made Kallik nervous. Why would she scold them for playing now, when she'd let them roll around having fun the day before?

The creaking began again as they traveled across the ice. Nisa paused and swung her head around to listen. It seemed like the sound of the ice groaning and yawning underpaw was getting louder. Kallik could tell that her mother knew what this sound was—and that it meant something very bad.

Suddenly there was a loud crack and a horrible sucking noise, and Kallik felt the ground tilt below her. She was thrown off her paws and found herself sliding along ice that was no longer flat but sloped down steeply toward dark water. With a terrified squeal, Kallik scrabbled on the ice, her claws sliding helplessly on the slick surface.

A giant paw grabbed her and hauled her backward onto solid ice again. Kallik stumbled as Nisa bundled her away from the crack in the ice, where waves slapped hungrily against the new edge.

"Wow!" Taqqiq yelped. "The ice just snapped in two! Kallik, I thought you'd be swallowed up by the sea and we'd never see you again!"

Nisa hissed with frustration. Kallik peered around her mother's legs and saw that the ice in front of them had broken into two large chunks that were drifting apart on the sea.

"Already?" Nisa muttered. "But we've had no time at all on the ice! How are we supposed to survive on land if we can't hunt for long enough before?" She paced along the jagged edge of the ice, snarling at the waves that lapped at her paws.

"Mother?" Kallik whimpered. "What's happening? Is it . . . is it burn-sky?"

"It's too early for burn-sky," Nisa said. "But the ice-melt is coming earlier each season. We have less and less time to hunt." She chuffed angrily. "It can't go on like this."

"What do we do?" Kallik asked. "What's going to happen to us if the ice melts too soon?"

Nisa just growled, pawing the edge of the ice.

"Should we move to land?" Taqqiq asked. "Isn't that what we're supposed to do when the ice melts?"

"No," Nisa said, lifting her muzzle. "We must continue to hunt, or else we shall not survive the long, hungry months of burn-sky."

"But—" Kallik started, glancing at the surging water and broken ice before them. What if the ice all melted before they could get to the land?

"We must go on," Nisa insisted. "We cannot go to the land yet—or we will all die."

She moved off across the ice, and Taqqiq followed her. Kallik paused for a moment on the jagged edge, the dark water lapping at her paws. She stared at the broken chunk of ice floating across the water from her. How far was it to land? Was there enough ice left for them to get there? And if there wasn't . . . what would happen to them?

SEEKERS

Book One: The Quest Begins

Book Two: Great Bear Lake

Book Three: Smoke Mountain

Book Four: The Last Wilderness

MANGA

Toklo's Story

Also by ERIN HUNTER

WARRIORS

Book One: Into the Wild

Book Two: Fire and Ice

Book Three: Forest of Secrets

Book Four: Rising Storm

Book Five: A Dangerous Path

Book Six: The Darkest Hour

THE NEW PROPHECY

Book One: Midnight

Book Two: Moonrise

Book Three: Dawn

Book Four: Starlight

Book Five: Twilight

Book Six: Sunset

POWER OF THREE

Book One: The Sight

Book Two: Dark River

Book Three: Outcast

Book Four: Eclipse

Book Five: Long Shadows

Book Six: Sunrise

OMEN OF THE STARS

Book One: The Fourth Apprentice

EXPLORE THE WARRIORS WORLD

Warriors Super Edition: Firestar's Quest

Warriors Super Edition: Bluestar's Prophecy

Warriors Field Guide: Secrets of the Clans

Warriors: Cats of the Clans

Warriors: Code of the Clans

MANGA

The Lost Warrior

Warrior's Refuge

Warrior's Return

The Rise of Scourge

Tigerstar and Sasha #1: Into the Woods

Tigerstar and Sasha #2: Escape from the Forest

Tigerstar and Sasha #3: Return to the Clans

Ravenpaw's Path #1: Shattered Peace